KING'S INDIAN ATTACK

KEN SMITH
FIDE MASTER 2365

JOHN HALL
USCF MASTER 2484

Chess Digest, Inc.

ISBN: O-87568-174-3

Authors: Ken Smith & John Hall
Computer Typesetting: Elaine Smith
Cover: Theresa Walker
Proofreaders: David Leinbach, David Sewell & Jude Acers
Final Preparation & Diagrams: David Sewell

Publisher: Chess Digest, Inc.® , 11836 Judd Court, #338-E, Dallas, Texas 75234-4402

TABLE OF CONTENTS

INTRODUCTION

"This used to be my favorite..."
-Bobby Fischer
Quote in "The Chess Opening For You"
by Larry Evans

The King's Indian Attack is one of White's most attractive positional debuts. Basically the King's Indian Attack is founded on the thought that if the King's Indian Defense is considered sound for Black, it must be "extra sound" when White plays it a tempo ahead. Many world class Grandmasters have essayed the King's Indian Attack, including Petrosian, Ljubojevic, Fischer, Smyslov, Botvinnik, and Reshevsky to name just a few.

The King's Indian Attack formation is characterized by the moves (in various possible orders) **1 Nf3, 2 g3, 3 Bg2, 4 0-0, 5 d3, 6 Nbd2** followed soon by **e2-e4**.

One of the greatest advantages of the King's Indian Attack is its flexibility. It can be played from the starting positions of many openings. For example, after **1 e4, c5** (The Sicilian Defense) White follows **2 d3** or **2 Nf3** followed by **3 d3**--steering into the fundamental pattern outlined above. The same treatment can occur after **1 e4, e6 2 d3** (King's Indian Attack vs. the French) or **1 e4, c6 2 d3** (King's Indian Attack vs. the Caro-Kann). The only pitfalls White can fall into are (1) making unnecessary moves, and (2) opening the position too early before completing development. An example where White completely misplays is The King's Indian Attack vs The Caro-Kann in Chapter Four, Rohde-Seirawan, American Open Los Angeles, November 1987. International Master Michael Rohde is a very talented player, but he either didn't know the correct way to proceed, or was too optimistic. We are going to guide you to the right path. It will be up to you to "know" what you are playing.

In this book we give a complete discussion of various systems Black might use against the King's Indian Attack. With these lines well studied, White will have a sound, promising position out of the opening, regardless of Black's counter set-up.

You are playing a complete self contained White opening system with **1 Nf3**, followed by **2 g3** and going into the King's Indian Attack pattern.

It can also be reached by using it as a weapon against the semi-open defenses when you play **1 e4**. We start out Chapters Four through Six with **1 e4** because it is easier to learn and more complete when you approach the Black defensive set-ups from this direction. The Caro-Kann, The Sicilian and The French are treated with complete chapters. The Alekhine Defense (**1 e4, Nf6 2 d3**) transposes into one of the considered variations where the Black Knight is on **f6**. The Pirc Defense (**1 e4, d6**) pattern is considered on page 96. Even **1 e4, e5** can transpose. When you play **1 e4**, the only defense that can keep you out of the King's Indian Attack pattern is the Center Counter **1 e4, d5**.

There are two schools of thought:

(1) Best is **1 Nf3**, then **2 g3** and take on the world.
(2) Best is **1 e4** forcing a Black committment, then play the King's Indian Attack.

Either choice is correct!!

MOVE ORDER

The K.I.A. pattern is a series of moves which almost plays itself. Unless Black chooses a rare or poor move, White's moves will be virtually automatic (transpositions are rather common, though). Below we give a move-by-move account of White's strategy and tactics in the theoretically important lines against the French Defense pawn structure.

1 Nf3

This is the standard K.I.A. first move. It prevents **1...e5**, develops a Kingside piece, and leaves Black with no immediate clue as to how White will deploy his center pawns.

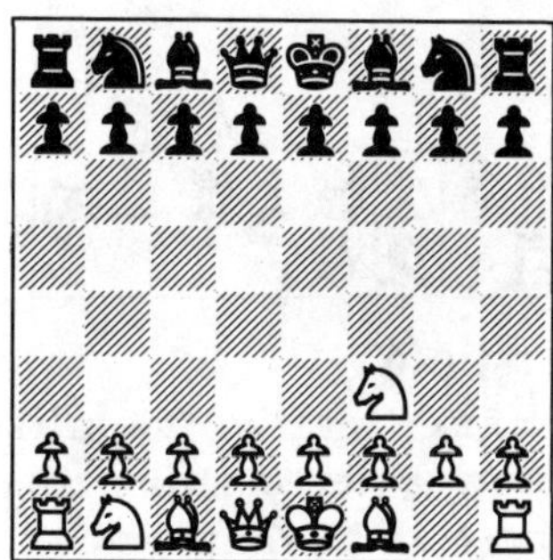

2 g3

The fianchettoed KB is the hallmark of our K.I.A.. From **g2** it strikes across the center on the fine **h1-a8** diagonal and gives extra protection to White's Kingside castled position.

(See diagram on following page)

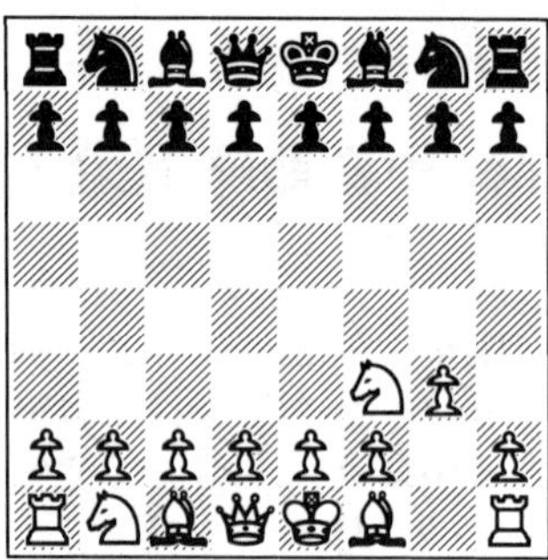

3 Bg2

Preparing to castle as quickly as possible and still not commit the center pawns.

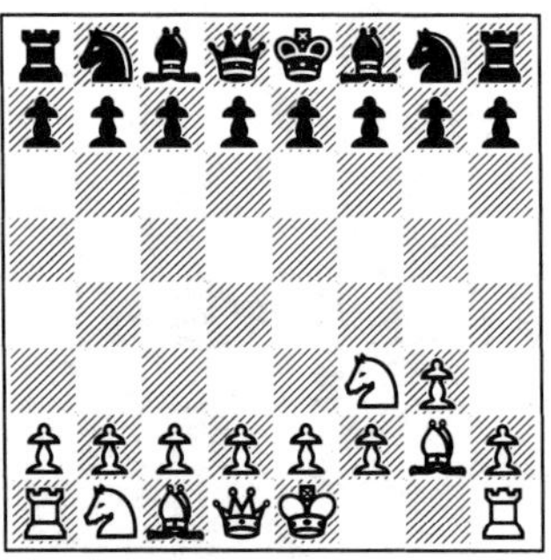

4 0-0

Now White has totally mobilized the Kingside forces. The KR is now able to move to **e1** to give support to the characteristic **e4-e5** advance.

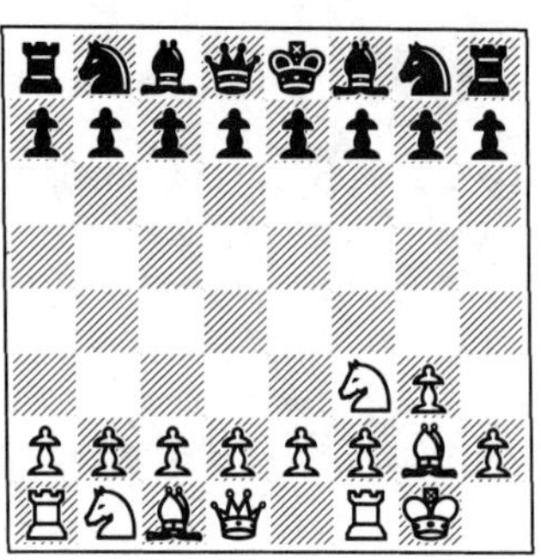

5 d3

Preparing to advance the e-pawn.

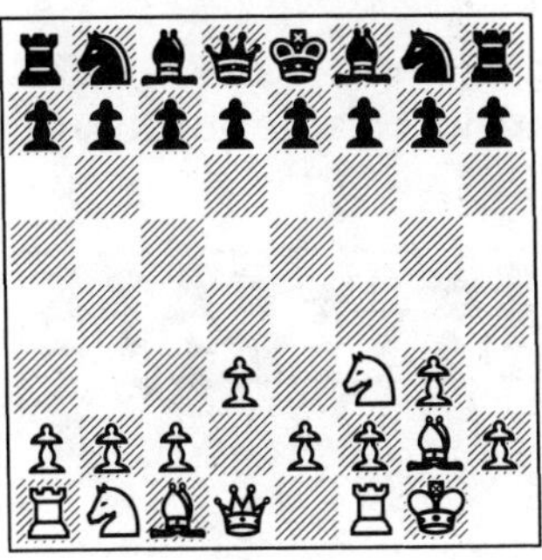

6 Nbd2

The normal square for the QN in the K.I.A. Note that we play the same moves against either the French or Sicilian, depending on Black's choice of opening moves.

7 e4

Finally occupying the center with a pawn and preparing the further push **e4-e5**.

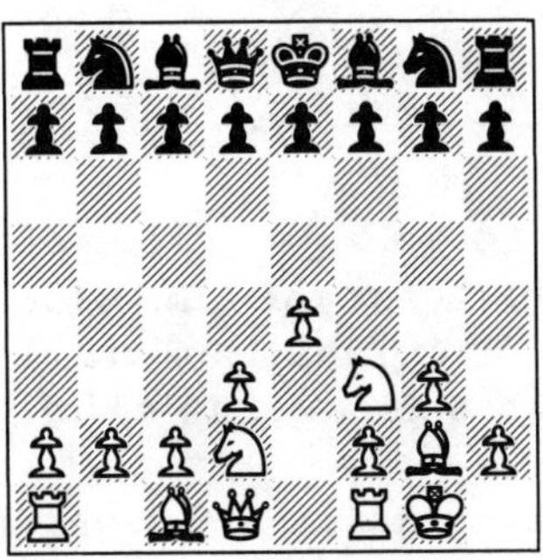

8 Re1

Centralizing the Rook while preparing to "overprotect" (Nimzovitch's terminology) the e-pawn once it reaches **e5**.

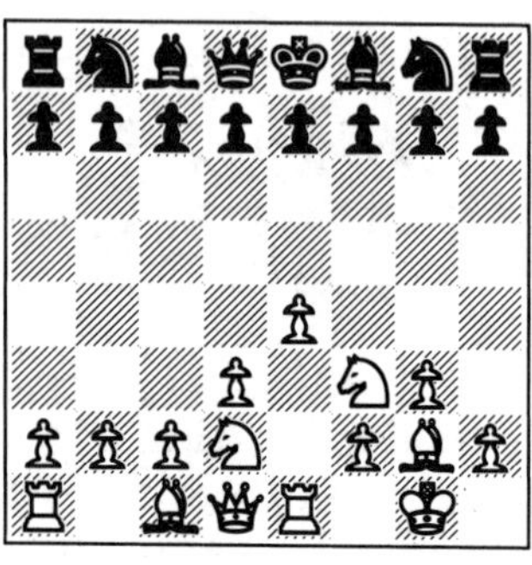

9 e5

"The die is cast". By crossing the fourth rank, White demonstrates the aggressive intentions of the K.I.A. system of moves. Now Black's Nf6 is forced back, giving White good chances to mount a vigorous attack on the Kingside.

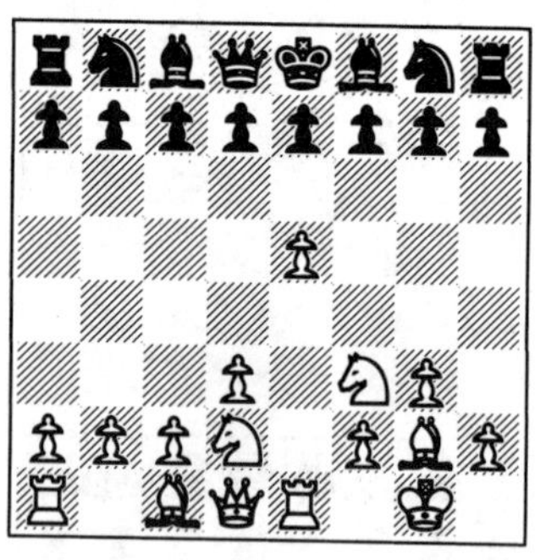

10 Nf1

Clearing a path for the QB, which usually moves to **f4** to add to the "overprotection" of the **e5** pawn. Also, from **f1** the QN can maneuver to **e3** or (after h2-h4) to **g4** via **h2**.

(See diagram on following page)

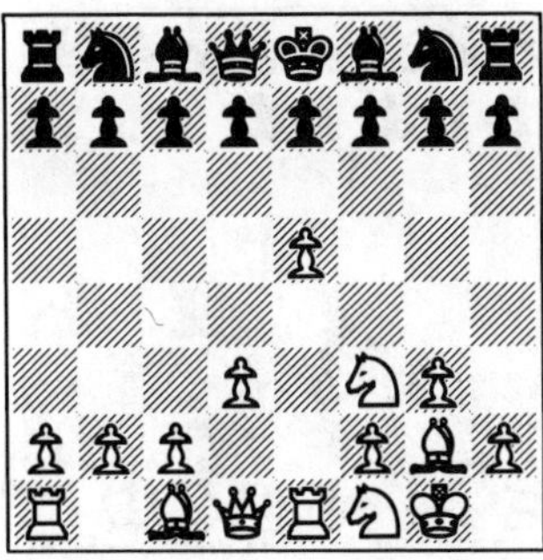

11 h4

A very important move which strikes at the dark squares in front of the Black King's fortress. The further advance **h4-h5-h6** often follows. Also the **h4** pawn helps protect **g5**, allowing White's **Nf3** to move into a menacing post (g5).

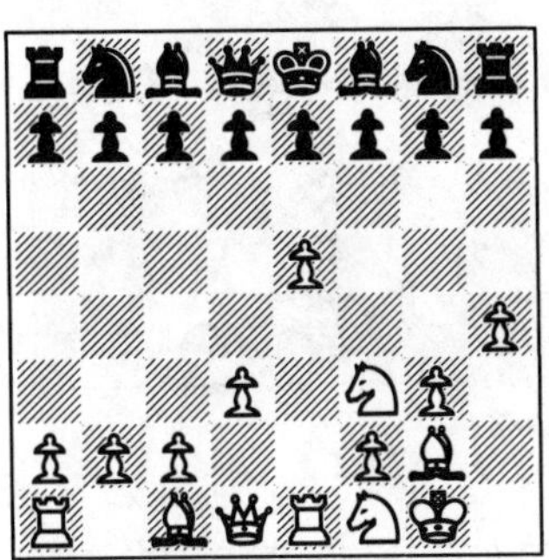

12 Bf4

More "overprotection" as mentioned. In particular, this frees the **Nf3** from guard duty (e5) so it can travel to **g5**.

(See diagram on following page)

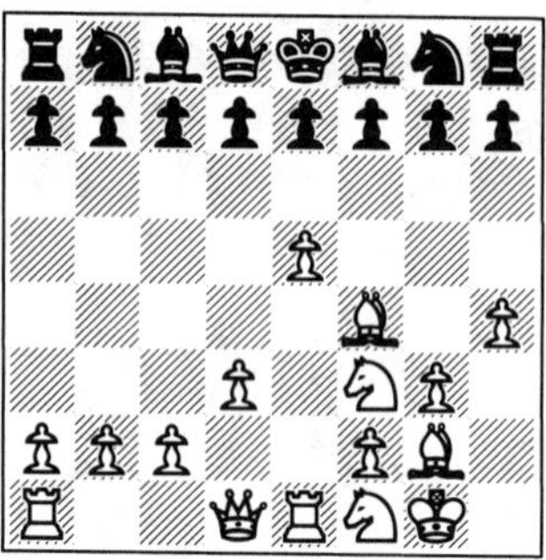

13 Ng5

White's plan is to force a weakening pawn move in the wall of pawns shielding the Black King.

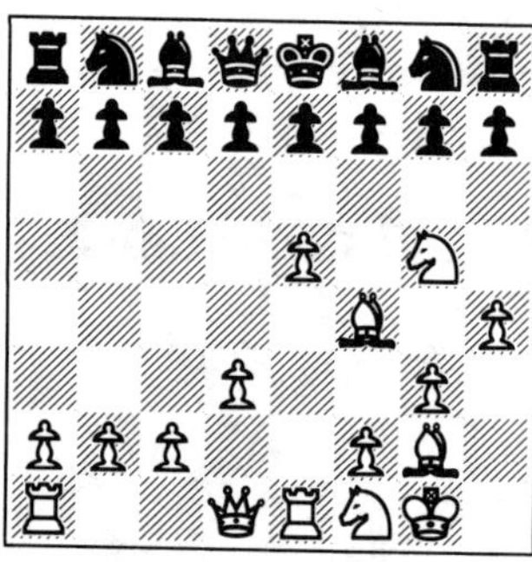

14 Qg4

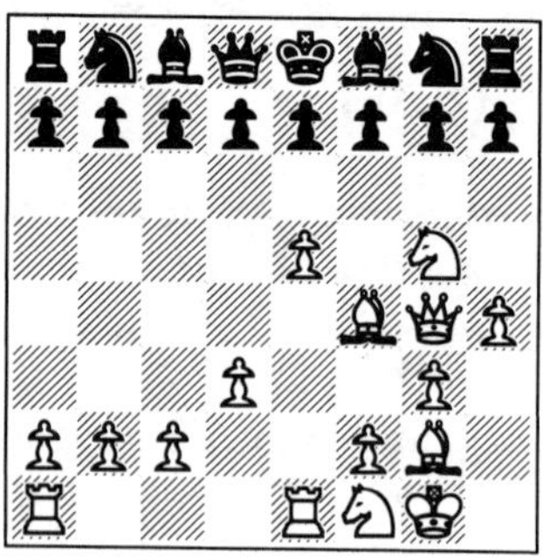

The Queen joins the fray with veiled threats against **g7** and **e6**. White has good attacking chances according to the famous Soviet GM David Bronstein.

BLACK DEFENSIVE SYSTEMS

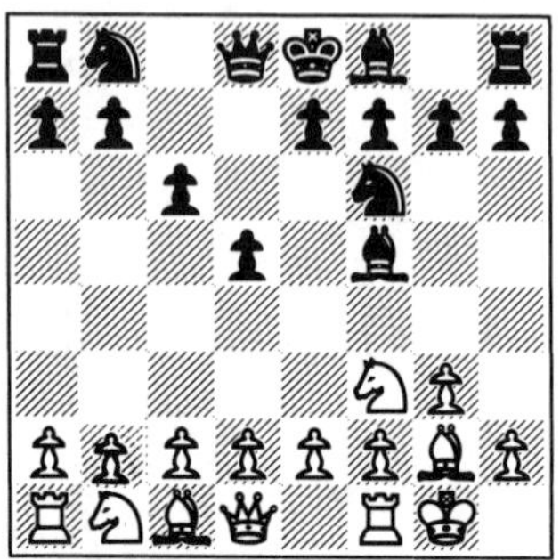

The London system is considered one of Black's most reliable defenses. Its main virtue is providing a good post for the QB on **f5**. After this is done, Black follows up by playing **e7-e6** in order to create a triangle of pawns (c6, d5, e6) which will help muffle the potentially dangerous White **Bg2**. White will play for e2-e4 (as usual) often with the threat to encroach with **e4-e5**, with consequent chances against Black's Kingside.

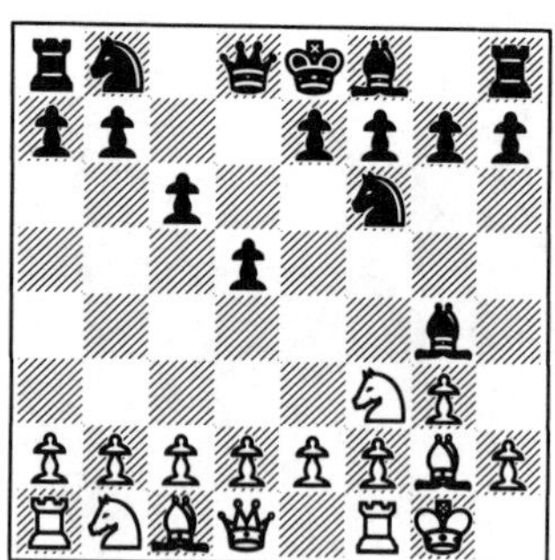

The Kere's System, named in honor of the great Estonian Grandmaster, is essentially similar to the London System. The basic difference is that the QB is developed to **g4** instead of **f5**. This is useful in two ways: when White plays the inevitable **e2-e4** the Black QB will not have to lose a tempo retreating; also, after **e2-e4** the **Bg4** exerts an unpleasant pinning effect on the **d1-h5** diagonal. White's strategy remains the same--push **e2-e4**, often followed by **e4-e5**.

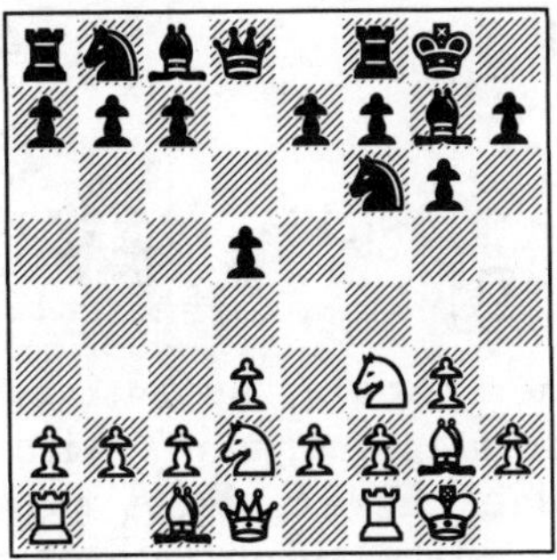

This defensive system is actually a White variation often played against the King's Indian Defense. Naturally there is the basic risk that the extra tempo White enjoys by playing the King's Indian with the White pieces, will prove valuable in later developments. White plays exactly as in the King's Indian Defense--**e2-e4** followed by an eventual **e4-xd5** if Black doesn't block the center with **d5-d4**.

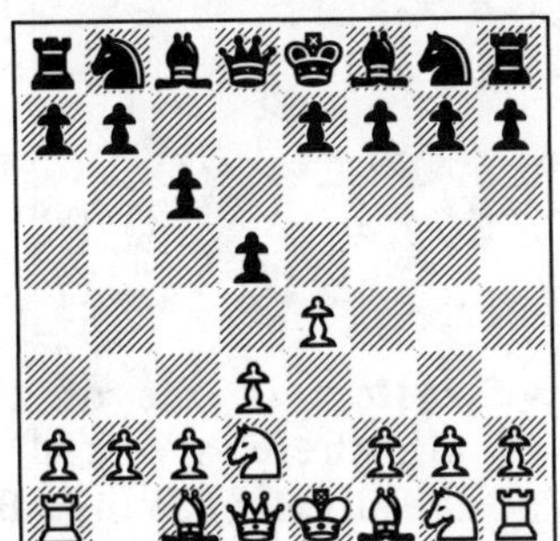

Caro-Kahn

This is a solid line of defense with considerable similarity to the London System of Chapter one. In some lines Black maintains a classical pawn center (d5 and e5), while in others Black exchanges **d5xe4** in order to stabilize the center--in particular, an early **d5-e4** exchange prevents White from having the option of opening play in the center with a timely **e4xd5**.

(See diagram on following page)

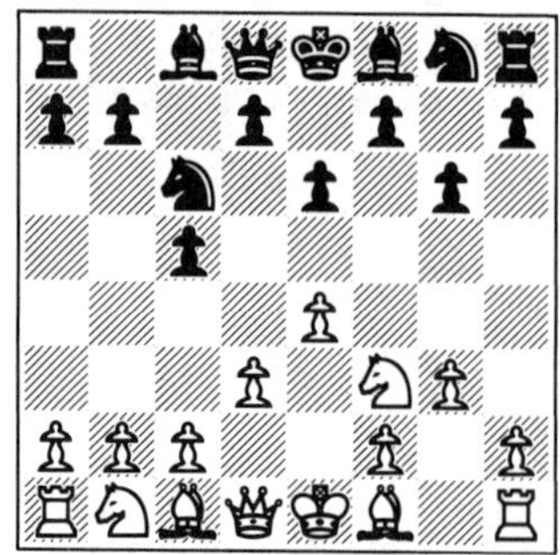

Sicilian

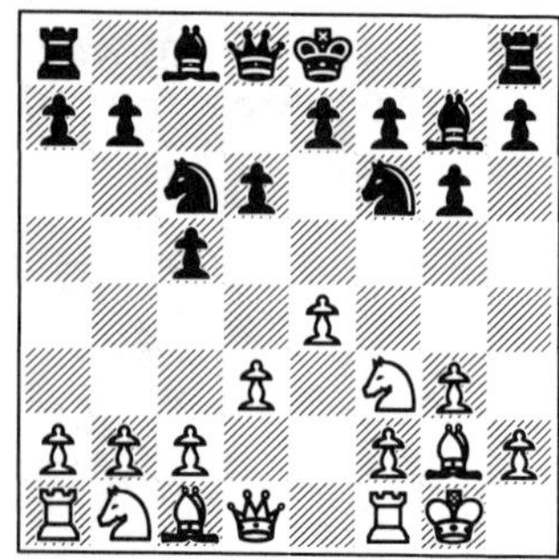

This is another popular defensive system for Black. It pleases hypermodern temperments with its characteristic fianchettoed KB. Black never places more than one pawn in the center in the early going in order to not give the White forces much in the way of a target. This is the virtual opposite strategy to that of the systems presented in Chapter Three.

French

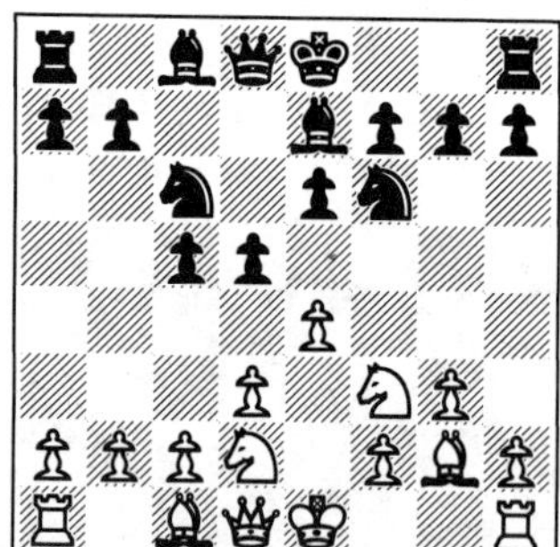

This defensive system is one of the most theoretically crucial lines of all; there are still unresolved problems for both sides. Generally speaking, Black's strategy is to push forward the Queenside pawns in order to open lines for counterplay. The **d5/e6** central pawn chain, characteristic of its French derivation, provides a solid center which is difficult to open up successfully.

(See diagram on following page)

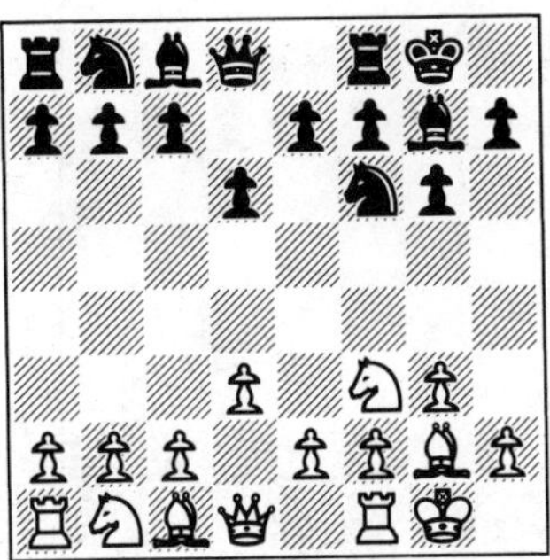

The Symmetrical Defense is rarely seen--partly because of its sterile, copy-cat approach--yet it is still open to theoretical debate. Black merely copies White's opening moves, daring White to gain anything significant from the first move.

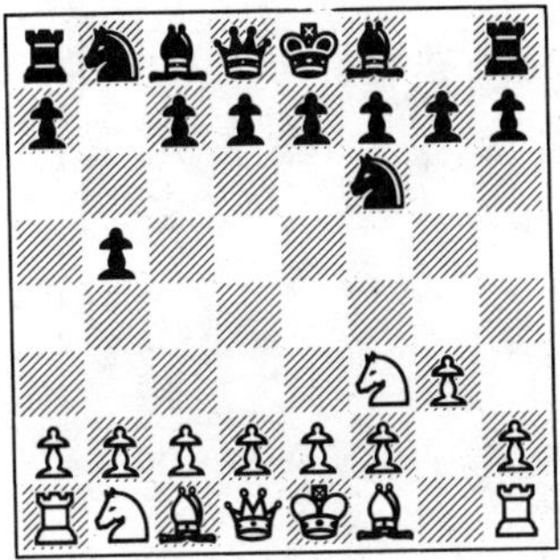

This defense is so named because it is the same pattern used as White in Sokolsky's Opening. The rather wild looking thrust of the b-pawn loosens the Queenside pawns in return for a gain of space; also Black's QB is allowed to obtain a good post on **b7** from which it helps to neutralize White's fianchettoed KB.

(See diagram on following page)

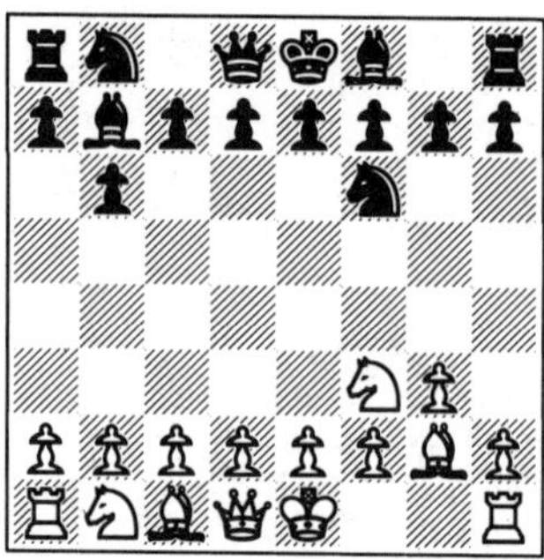

This defense is identical in structure to the Queen's Indian Defense to the d-pawn openings. It is solid, yet allows fluid play on the **a8-h1** diagonal. It is much like the Sokolsky Defense only without the weakening effect of a double b-pawn march.

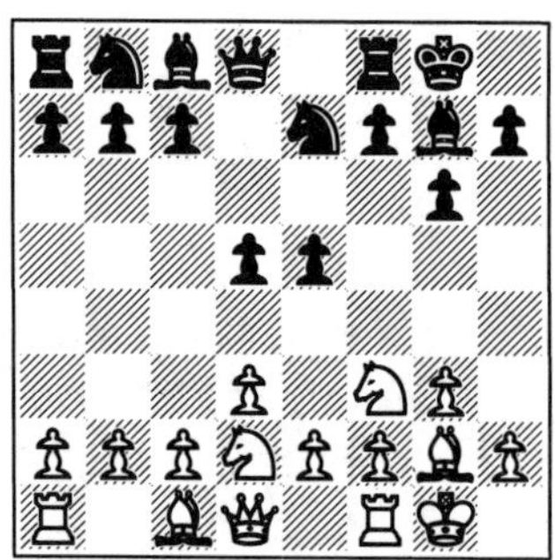

This is a very reliable line of defense combining the virtues of a classical center (pawns on d5 and e5) with the hypermodern deployment of the KB (Bg7). The great Dutch Ex-World Champion Max Euwe has championed this defense as a solid yet active way to counter the K.I.A. Often Black exchanges **d5xe4** to stabilize the center, although maintaining the tension is also theoretically feasible.

A HISTORICAL PERSPECTIVE OF THE KING'S INDIAN ATTACK

Essentially the theory and practice of the King's Indian Attack (K.I.A.) must evolve from the history of the King's Indian Defense. This is because the King's Indian Attack is a King's Indian Defense pattern with the White pieces. In the early decades of the 20th century the use of the King's Indian Defense was sporadic and only occasionally successful. In fact many players regarded it as at best, a slightly dubious attempt. In the early "40's" however, a few Soviet Grandmasters, notably David Bronstein, Yefim Geller, and Isaac Boleslavsky, developed new methods of counterplay in the K.I.D. and thus created a viable system of defense based on active counterplay.

Although it is virtually impossible to pinpoint the first game in which the K.I.A. emerged, we can safely assume that with the renewed interest in the K.I.A., due to the above mentioned Soviet theoretical work, some players realized that it would be an interesting way to deploy as White. In particular, the extra tempo with the White pieces insured its soundness even in the eyes of those who still felt the K.I.D. was a bit risky.

We shall give three games to illustrate in summary fashion the evolution of the K.I.A.

DAVID BRONSTEIN'S CONTRIBUTION

The following game, played in the 13th USSR Championship Semi-Final in Rostov-on-Don 1941, is a precursor of our K.I.A. formation. The system of moves (ironically used as Black by Bronstein) is now considered a theoretically crucial line in the K.I.A. as used against the French Defense (1 e4, e6 2 d3!, etc.) and Sicilian Defense

(1 e4, c5 2 d3!, e6). Note how powerful the King's Indian Attack is even a tempo down as Bronstein plays Black.

White: Belavenets Black: Bronstein

1 d4 Nf6
2 c4 d6
3 Nc3 e5

This is an "Old Indian" Defense, but it soon transposes into the regular King's Indian Defense with the subsequent fianchettoe of the Black KB.

4 Nf3 Nbd7
5 g3

The same system used by Black over the next several moves is also used against a formation with **5 e3** and **6 Be2**.

5... g6

Finally transposing into the K.I.D.

6 Bg2 Bg7
7 0-0 0-0

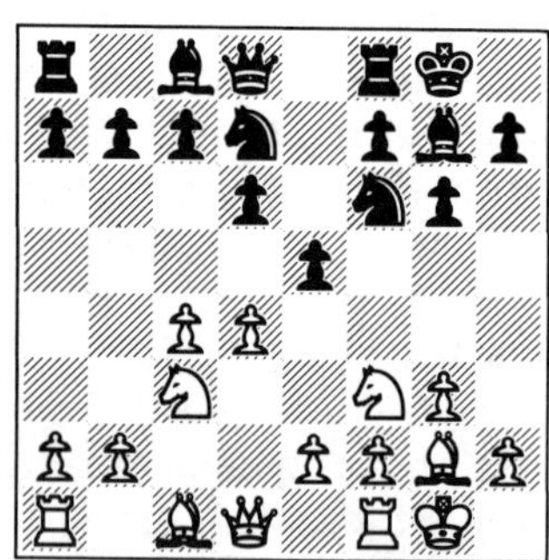

White's strategy will be to attack with pieces and pawns on the Queenside. As for Black, he must counter on the Kingside and center.

8 b3 Re8

Preparing to push the e-pawn to **e4**--exactly as we recommend (with colors reversed, of course) in our K.I.A. system vs. the French or Sicilian Defense. See Chapter Four.

9 e3 c6
10 Qc2 Qa5

This maneuver is unusual in corresponding formations (colors reversed) nowadays. This is partly because the opponent has often advanced **b2-b4** (in systems with e3 and Be2 as opposed to the present example with g3 and Bg2). Nonetheless, the basic themes illustrated in this game--the advance of the e-pawn to e4 and consequent Kingside pressure--remain the same.

11 a4

Beginning to seize more Queenside space.

11... Nf8

The typical modern regrouping of the QN. From **f8** it can go to **e6-g5**, or (after h7-h5) to **h7-g5**. In either case, Black is effectively increasing the pressure against the Kingside.

12 Ba3 Bf5

13 Qb2

White intends to hold fast in the center, and thus avoids **13 e4** which is answered by **13...Nxe4! 14 Nxe4, d5.**

13... Rad8

14 Rfd1 e4

Establishing the "beachhead" on **e4**.

15 Nd2 Ne6

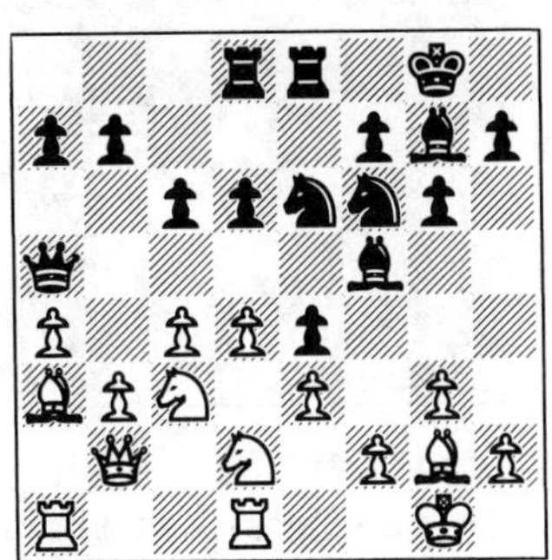

16 b4

Taking on **e4** is poor: **16 Ndxe4, Nxe4 17 Nxe4, Bxe4 18 Bxe4, Nxd4** with an excellent game for Black.

16... Qc7

White's massive pawn advance on the Queenside seems very impressive, but Black's counterattack against the Kingside will soon shift into high gear.

17 Rdb1 Qd7!

Preparing an attack on the white squares--see next two moves.

18 c5 Ng5!

Note the beautiful "overprotection" (Nimzovitch's term) of the vital e4 pawn.

19 cd

White wins a pawn, but Black's attack will overcome simple material considerations.

19... Bh3

The light squared invasion gains momentum.

20 Bh1

After **20 Bxh3, Qxh3** the threats of **Ng4** and **Nf3** are overwhelming.

20... Qf5

21 Ne2 Nd5

Mainly to trade off should White try to defend his Kingside with **Nf4.**

22 b5 Bg4

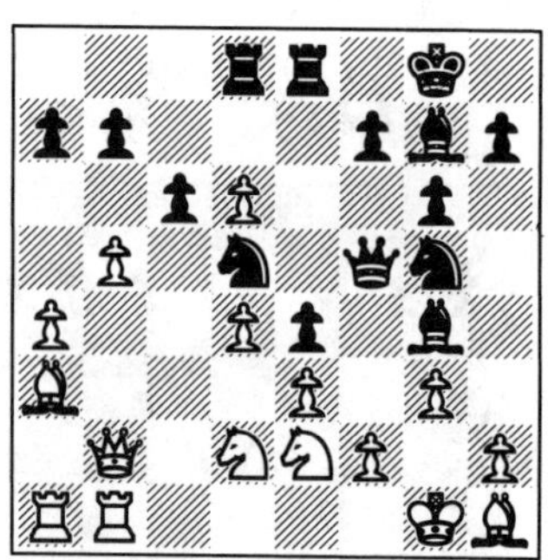

23 Kf1

This is clearly hopeless, but the more "solid" **23 Nf4** allows **23...Nxf4 24 exf4** (24 gxf4, Bh3!) **24...Nh3ch 25 Kg2** (25 Kf1, e3) **25...Bf3ch 26 Nxf3, exf3ch 27 Kf1, Qd3ch** wins.

23... Nxe3ch

Of course.

24 Ke1 Nf3ch

Now in view of **25 N(or B)xf3, exf3,** White decides to give it up.

White Resigns
The King's Indian triumphs!

This early game woke up the world to the value of this system from the Black side. We are going to teach you to play this pattern with the White pieces where you will have an extra tempo.

TIGRAN PETROSIAN'S POSITIONAL WIZARDRY

Ex-World Champion Tigran Petrosian was one of the most profound positional players of all time. Time and again, his subtle maneuvers confounded even world calibre players. He was likened to a boa constrictor slowly tightening its coils around its victim. In the following game, he combines positional play of the highest order--crowned by one of the most beautiful finishes ever seen.

BLED 1961
White: Petrosian Black: Pachman

1 Nf3 c5

Daring White to go for a Sicilian with **2 e4** and **3 d4**, but this was not in Petrosian's style.

2 g3 Nc6
3 Bg2 g6

Black fianchettoes preferring a hypermodern style of defense against an essentially hypermodern opening.

4 0-0 Bg7
5 d3 e6

Preferring to leave the KB's diagonal unblocked though **5...e5** is considered to be quite playable.

6 e4 Nge7
7 Re1

Preparing to push the e-pawn to **e5**, especially as Black's **d6** and **f6** are somewhat vulnerable.

7... 0-0

Possible is **7...d6** to restrain **8 e5**.

8 e5 d6

(See diagram on following page)

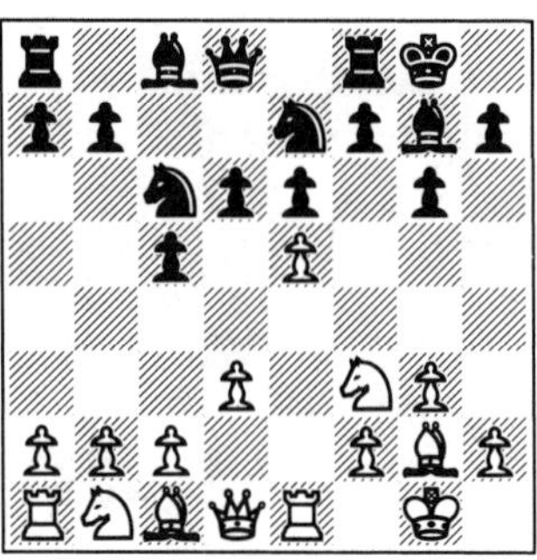

To challenge the e-pawn, but better was **8...b6** and **9...Ba6.**

9 ed Qxd6

Now Black's Queen will be exposed to White's minor pieces.

10 Nbd2

Threatening to win the c-pawn with **11 Ne4** (11...Qd5 12 c4!).

10... Qc7

Or **10...Nd4 11 Ne4, Qc7 12 Bf4, e5 13 Nxe5!, Bxe5 14 Nf6ch and 15 Bxe5, while if 12...Nxf3ch 13 Qxf3, Qb6 14 Bd6!, Re8 15 Bxc5, Qxb2 16 Nd6** is too strong.

11 Nb3! Nd4

Slightly better was **11...b6.**

12 Bf4

Gaining more time.

12... Qb6

13 Ne5!

White's forces invade with startling rapidity.

13... Nxb3

14 Nc4!

A fine interpolation.

14... Qb5

Forced, otherwise, after **14...Qd8 15 axb3** followed by **Bd6** wins the c-pawn.

15 axb3 a5

White threatened **16 Ra5!**.

(See diagram on following page)

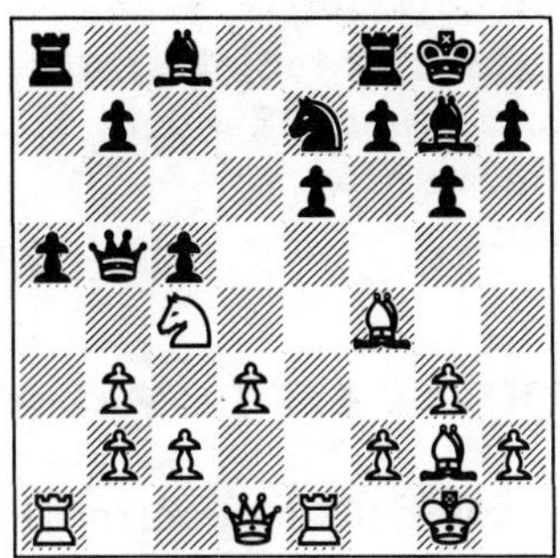

16 Bd6! **Bf6**

On **16...Re8 17 Bc7!** wins at least a pawn.

17 Qf3

The prelude to an amazing finish.

17... **Kg7**

18 Re4?!

The dubious mark is placed here only because White could immediately play the move he next chooses--a minor aesthetic flaw in a brilliant game.

18... **Rd8**

Black had to concede the Exchange with **18...Ng8** to prolong the game.

19 Qxf6ch!!

One of the most brilliant moves ever played in Grandmaster chess.

19... **Kxf6**

20 Be5ch **Kg5**

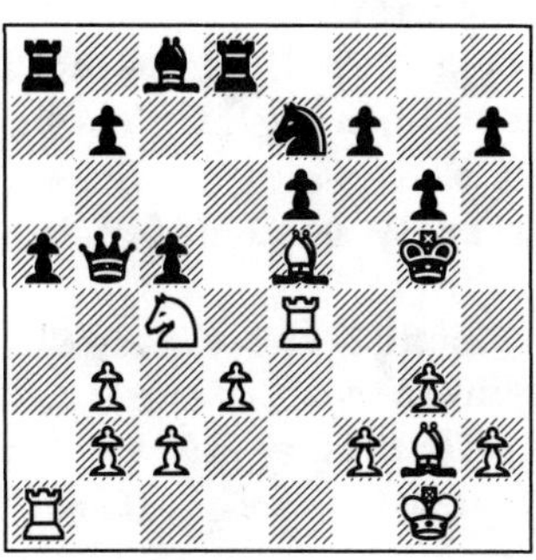

21 Bg7!!

A transcendental quiet move which seals Black's fate. Now on **21...Nf5 22 f4ch, Kg4 23 Ne5ch, Kh5 24 Bf3** is mate. Or if **21...e5**, then **22 h4ch, Kh5** (22...Kf5 23 Bh3 mate) **23 Bf3ch** is mate next.

Black Resigns.

FISCHER'S EARLY FAVORITE

In his early competitive years, the great Bobby Fischer often used the King's Indian Attack. Especially after **1 e4, c5 2 Nf3, e6** (locking in the QB), Fischer felt **3 d3(!)** gave a superior form of the K.I.A. If a player of such unsurpassed talent and aggressiveness chooses the "quiet" K.I.A., you can bet it has more bite than many would suppose.

PIATIGORSKY CUP 1966
White: Fischer Black: Ivkov

1 e4	**c5**
2 Nf3	**e6**
3 d3(!)	

As Ivkov himself said, "Tremendous, psychologically a master stroke. All prepared variations, analysis and psychological preparations for the Sicilian can be discarded after the third move."

3...	**Nc6**
4 g3	**d5**
5 Nbd2	

Of course not **5 Bg2**(?) allowing **5...de 6 de, Qxd1ch 7 Kxd1** and White has nothing left to work with.

5...	**Bd6**

This is a currently used defensive system--see Chapter Six.

6 Bg2	**Nge7**

Not **6...Nf6** which would eventually subject Black to the annoying tactical threat **e4-e5.**

7 0-0	**0-0**

(See diagram on following page)

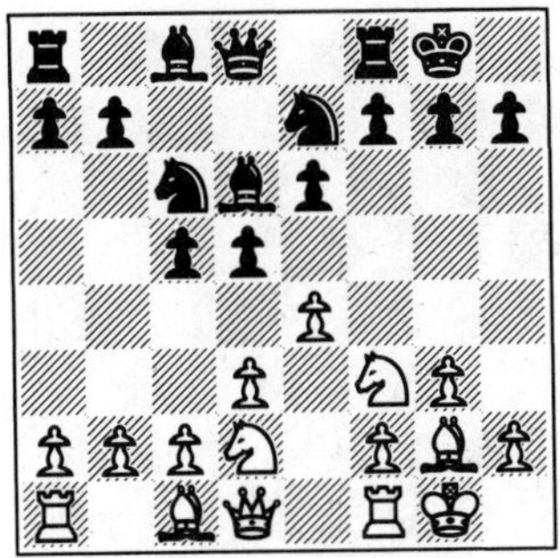

8 Nh4

Today **8 Re1** or **8 Qe2** are more frequently adopted.

8... b6

More active was **8...Be5 9 f4, Bf6 10 Nhf3, g6 11 c3, Bg7** as in **Zuckerman-Vasjukov, Polanica Zdroj 1972.**

9 f4

Beginning the Kingside advance.

9... de
10 de Ba6

This looks good but turns out to be a blow in the air.

11 Re1 c4

Ivkov recommends **11...e5** as an improvement though White would still be clearly better.

12 c3

Accurate. Black threatened the strategic pawn sacrifice **12...c3!** with prospects of pressure against the doubled, isolated c-pawns after **13 bc.**

12... Na5
13 e5

Gaining central space, in particular the **e4** square is now available as a jumping off post for White's minor pieces.

13... Bc5ch
14 Kh1 Nd5

After **14...Rc8, 15 b4!** is quite unpleasant.

15 Ne4

Now White rapidly seizes complete control.

15... Bb7

(See diagram on following page)

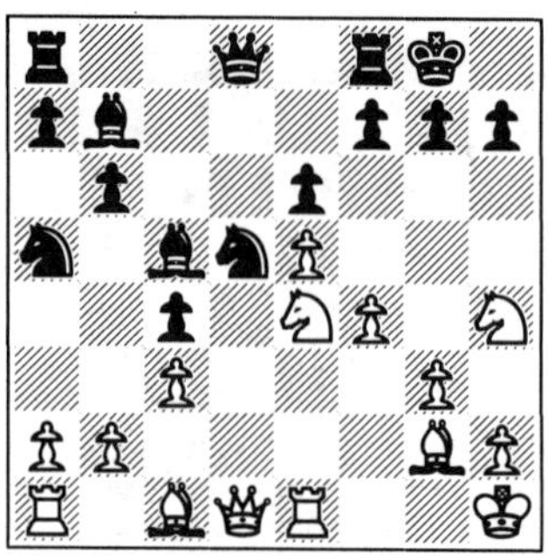

16 Qh5!

16 Nxc5 is positionally good, but White correctly goes for bigger game.

16... Ne7

Only **16...Qe8** held out any hope.

17 g4!

The Kingside pawns begin to "avalanche" on Black's Kingside.

17... Bxe4

Black desperately tries to defend by simplifying, but it is already too late.

18 Bxe4 g6
19 Qh6

Threatening **18 Nf3-g5.**

19... Nd5

Slightly better was **19...Kh8** threatening **20...Ng8**, but after **20 Nf3** White is still winning.

20 f5

Blasting through Black's porous Kingside.

20... Re8

Ivkov: "And here was the right moment for resigning. But a boxer very often is not aware of his own absurd movements, thinking that he is putting up resistance."

21 fg **fg**

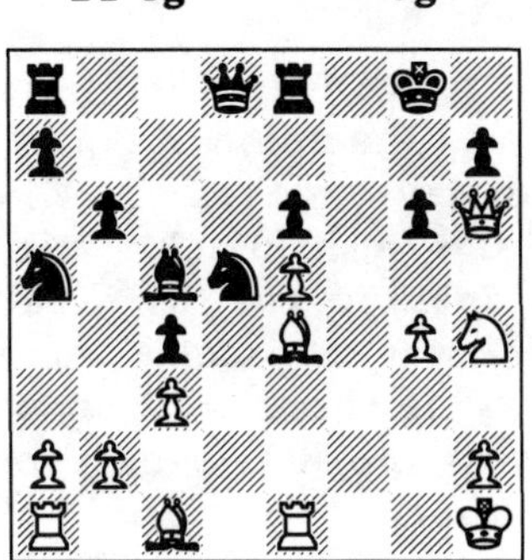

22 Nxg6!

Obvious, but none the less pleasing.

22... **Qd7**

After **22...hxg6 23 Qxg6ch, Kf8** (23...Kh8 24 Qh7 mate) **24 Rf1ch** it's over.

23 Nf4 **Rad8**
24 Nh5

Threatening **25 Bxd5** and **26 Nf6ch.**

24... **Kh8**
25 Nf6 **Nxf6**
26 exf6 **Rg8**

Sheer inertia.

27 Bf4 **Rxg4**
28 Rad1 **Rdg8**

Hoping for **29 Rxd7???, Rg1ch** and mate next. But it is difficult to catch Fischer in a simple mate in two.

29 f7

Now on **29...Qxf7 30 Be5ch** White mates by force in two moves.

Black Resigns

OVERCOMING A THEORETICAL OBSTACLE

Two of the strongest grandmasters in the world are Ljubojevic and World Champion Kasparov. When they met in Niksic 1983, Ljubojevic played the King's Indian Attack against Kasparov and lost. Black's win demoralized the proponents of this opening for three full years--until this theoretical obstacle was overcome in Dvorecki-Vulfson, USSR 1986. The play of these two games is a lesson in the evolutionary theory of the K.I.A.--one you should learn before you go any further.

NIKSIC 1983

White: Ljubojevic Black: Kasparov

1 e4

As in the previous game, this will be a transposition from an e-pawn debut into our K.I.A. setup.

1...	**c5**
2 Nf3	**e6**
3 d3	

Ljubojevic decides to avoid Kasparov's favorite Scheveningen Sicilian with our favorite system.

3...	**Nc6**
4 g3	**d5**

After an immediate **4...g6**, White can play the sharp **4 d4!?**.

5 Nbd2	**g6**

A popular Hypermodern defensive setup. Classical players prefer **5...Nf6** and **...e6** systems.

6 Bg2	**Bg7**
7 0-0	**Nge7**

(See diagram on following page)

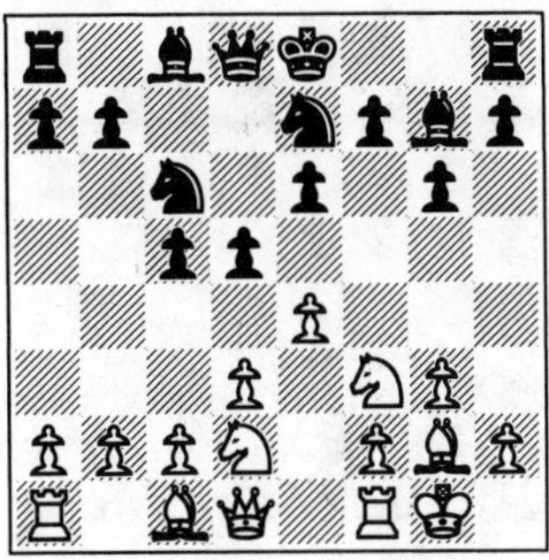

8 Re1

This is the usual and quite playable move. However **8 ed!** as played in the next game, **Dvorecki-Vulfson USSR 1986**, will be our recommendation for White.

8... b6

Black wisely avoids the natural **8...0-0** after which **9 e5** gives White an edge. Another reasonable move for Black here is **8...h6**. The game **B. Ivanovic-T. Petrosian, Niksic 1983**, continued **9 a4, b6 10 h4, a5 11 Nf1, Ra7 12 N1h2, de 13 Rxe4, 0-0 14 Re1, e5** with about even chances.

9 h4

Threatening to press on with **h4-h5.**

9... h6

Now **10 h5** allows Black to bypass with **10...g5** with a fine position.

10 c3

If **10 Nf1** then the exchange of Queen's after **10...de 11 de, Qxd1** would equalize easily.

10... a5

A good space gaining move which threatens **a5-a4** cramping White's Queenside, as well as providing for the QR's deployment via **a7.**

11 a4

To stop **11...a4**

11... Ra7!

Getting off the potentially dangerous **h1-a8** diagonal and allowing the switch to the d-file (Rd7) as needed.

(See diagram on following page)

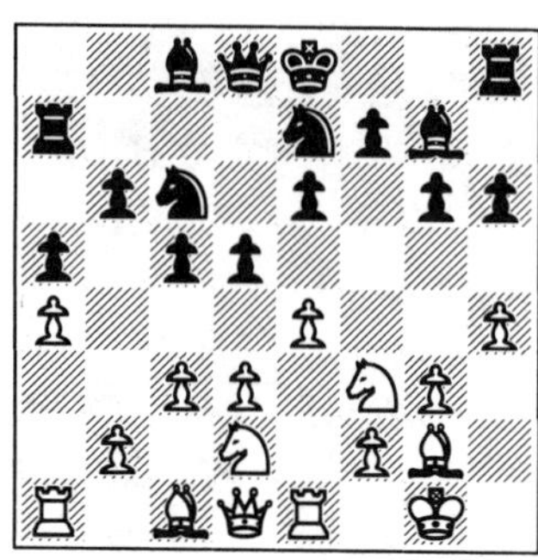

12 Nb3?!

This is dubious--the Knight has no future here. White could play the thematic **12 e5** with interesting, unclear play after **12...Ba6 13 Nf1, b5**. Also possible is the central opening **12 ed, ed 13 Nf1, d4 14 c4** again with mutual chances.

12... d4

Gaining central space.

13 cd

Sharper is **13 e5, dc 14 bc, Rd7 15 d4, Nd5** with unclear play.

13... cd

14 Bd2?

This error causes real problems. Ljubo had to play **14 e5**, and if **14...Ba6**, then **15 Re4, Rd7 16 Bf4** is complex with chances for both players.

14... e5!

Stopping **e4-e5** forever and consolidating the **d4** pawn.

15 Nc1?!

The best chance was **15 h5**, since now **15...g5** (the normal bypassing move) leaves **f5** and **g4** weakened.

15... Be6

16 Re2

Another artificial maneuver though Black stands better in any case.

16... 0-0

17 Be1 f5

Now Black rapidly takes over control.

18 Nd2 f4!

A very strong cramping move with the threat of **g5-g4** with an overwhelming position.

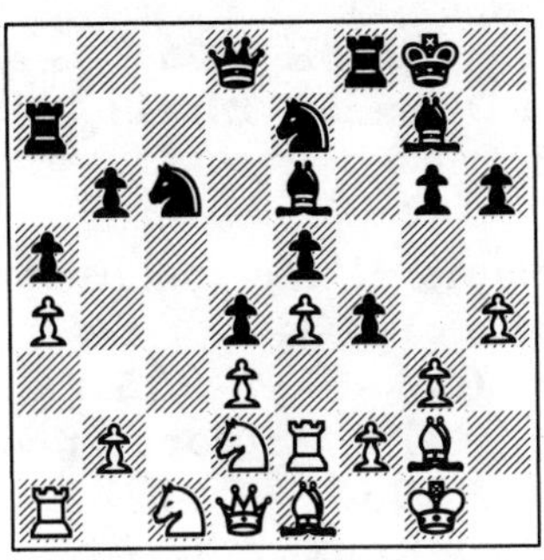

19 f3

Unpleasant, but after **19 gf, ef 20 Nf3, Ne5** White is also in dire straits.

19... fg

Now **f4** is terribly weak.

20 Bxg3 g5

Preparing **Ng6-f4.**

21 hg Ng6!

Moving in for the finish. The pawn means nothing in view of the attacking lines being opened.

22 gh

He might as well.

22.. Bxh6

Now Black's forces pour into the weakened White Kingside.

23 Nf1 Rg7

24 Rf2 Be3!

If now **25 Nxe3**, then **25...dxe3 26 Rf1, Qg5 27 Ne2, Nf4** is crushing.

25 b3

More "accurate" was Resigns.

25... Nf4

White Resigns

Note that White's game was fully viable (even without our important novelty 8 ed!) up to the 11th move. Even **13 e5** would have kept things interesting.

Now comes the game that put White's correct opening strategy forward for the whole world to see.

USSR 1986
White: Dvorecki Black: Vulfson

1 e4

Another example of the insidious flexibility of the K.I.A. which can arise even after **1 e4.**

1... c5

Black responds with the popular Sicilian Defense.

2 Nf3

Still following a "normal" Sicilian pattern.

2... e6

Black still has no idea that White is about to change course.

3 d3(!)

The exclamation is not for any objective advantage of 3 **d3**--it merely shows the pragmatic and even psychological advantage inherent in the transposition from a normal e-pawn debut into specially prepared K.I.A. system.

3... Nc6
4 g3 d5
5 Nbd2

Of course, White avoids a premature Queen trade (5 Bg2(?), de).

5... g6

Players of the classical school will prefer **5...Nf6** with no King's fianchettoe.

6 Bg2 Bg7
7 0-0 Nge7

7...Nf6 is playable but has the disadvantage of obstructing the KB.

8 ed!

An important theoretical novelty. White seizes the initiative in the center.

(See diagram on following page)

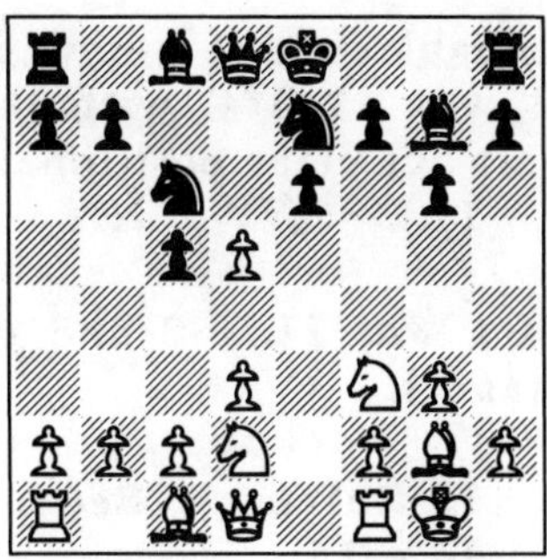

8... ed

After **8...Nxd5** White continues with **9 Nb3!**, and if **9...b6**, then **10 c4!** followed by **d3-d4** gives White a good initiative.

9 d4!

A temporary pawn sacrifice to exploit Black's laggard Kingside development.

9... cd

No good is **9...Nxd4? 10 Nxd4, Bxd4** (or 10...cxd4 11 Nb3) **11 Nb3** with a clear advantage for White. Also, on **9...c4!?** White holds a slight positional advantage.

10 Nb3

White wants to recapture on **d4**, leaving the Black d-pawn isolated and vulnerable to pressure.

10... Qb6

Grimly clinging to his **d4** pawn.

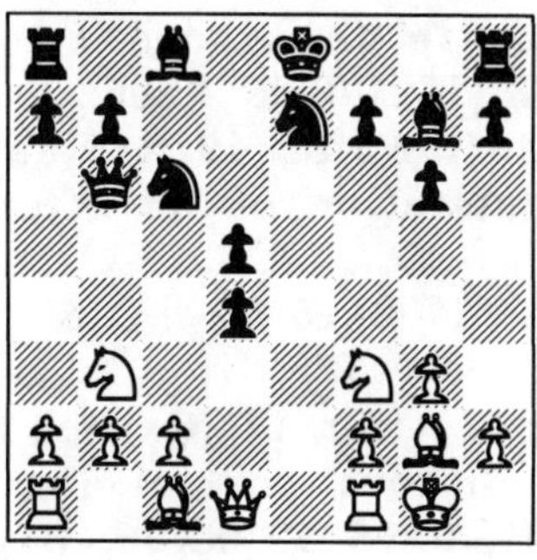

11 Bg5

This is reasonable but it allows Black a chance to hold equality. Best was **11 Bf4!** with the idea of **12 Bd6** and **Bc5** with a small but clear positional plus for White.

11... Nf5

Slightly better was **11...0-0** and on **12 Nfxd4, Nf5!** with about even chances.

12 Re1ch Be6

13 g4!

Introducing a bold tactical concept.

13... Nd6

14 Nfxd4!!

A brilliant shot, prepared by the last two moves.

14... Bxd4

On **14...Nxd4 15 Be3, Nb5** White plays **16 a4!** with a much better position.

15 Nxd4 Qxd4

Not **15...Nxd4 16 Bf6!**

16 Bxd5!

Correct. Inferior is **16 Qxd4, Nxd4 17 Bf6**, because of **17...Nxc2.**

16... 0-0

Best. If **16...Qxd1 17 Raxd1, Nb5** (after 17...Kd7 18 Bf4 is powerful) **18 Bf6!** (Also good is 18 Bxe6, but 18 Bf6! is stronger) **18...Rf8** (18...0-0 19 Rxe6!, fxe6 20 Bxe6ch, Rf7 21 Rd7 clearly favors White) **19 Re3** and Black can't prevent a decisive penetration on **d8** after **Bxc6ch** followed by **Red3!.**

17 Bxc6 Qc5!

The best line. After **17...Qxg4ch 18 Qxg4, Bxg4 19 Bg2** White's two Bishops control the board, while on **17...Qxd1 18 Raxd1, bxc6 19 Rxd6, Bxg4 20 Rxc6** White has a great advantage in the ending.

(See diagram on following page)

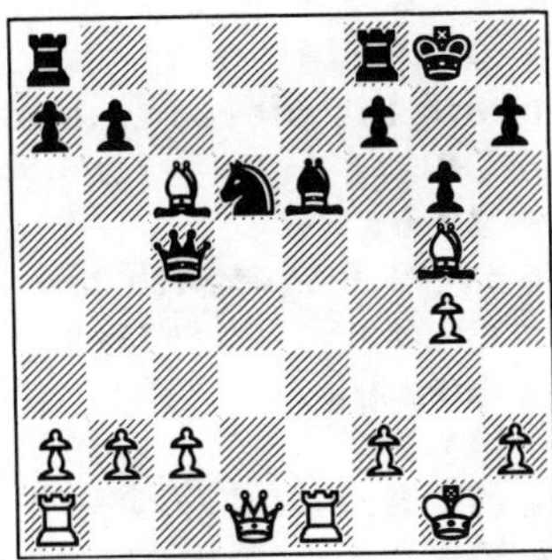

18 Bf3!

Again best. On **18 Be7, Qxc6 19 Qxd6, Qxd6 20 Bxd6, Rfd8** Black follows with **21...Bxg4** and equal chances. If **18 Bd5** then **18...Qxd5!** (Not 18...Bxd5 19 Re5!, Ne4 20 Be3 with a big plus for White) **19 Qxd5, Bxd5 20 Rad1, Bf3 21 Rxd6, Bxg4** again with equal play.

18...	**Qxg5**
19 Qxd6	**Rac8**
20 c3	**Qb5**

Black loses on **20...Bxg4 21 Qg3!** followed by **h3** and a piece goes. If **20...Rfd8**, then **21 Qe5, Qxe5 22 Rxe5** leaves White in control in the ending. Finally on **20...h5 21 h3, hg 22 hg, Bxg4 23 Qg3, Rc4** (on 23...f5 24 Re6! is very good) **24 Bxb7** with a clear advantage for White.

21 Rad1	**Bxa2**

If **21...Qxb2 22 Rxe6** wins.

22 Rd2	**Rfd8**
23 Qxd8ch	

White obtains two Rooks for the Queen which gives him the better play.

23...	**Rxd8**
24 Rxd8ch	**Kg7**
25 Rd2	

To defend **b2**.

25...	**h5**
26 h3	

Not **26 gxh5?** because of **26...Qg5ch**, spearing the **Rd2**.

26...	**Be6**
27 Re4	**a5**

28 Red4

White maneuvers his pieces to more active positions.

28...	**hg**
29 hg	

Also possible is **29 Bxg4** with similar play.

29...	**Qg5**
30 Kg2	**b6**
31 Re2	**Qc5**
32 Kg3	

Bringing the King up closer to the center.

32...	**Qb5**

Black hopes to tie down White's Rooks.

33 Rdd2	**Qg5**
34 Re3	**Qc5**

Black simply waits. The tempting **34...f5?** is strongly answered by **35 Rd4.**

35 Be2	**Qc6?**

Dubious. Probably time pressure is affecting play hereabouts.

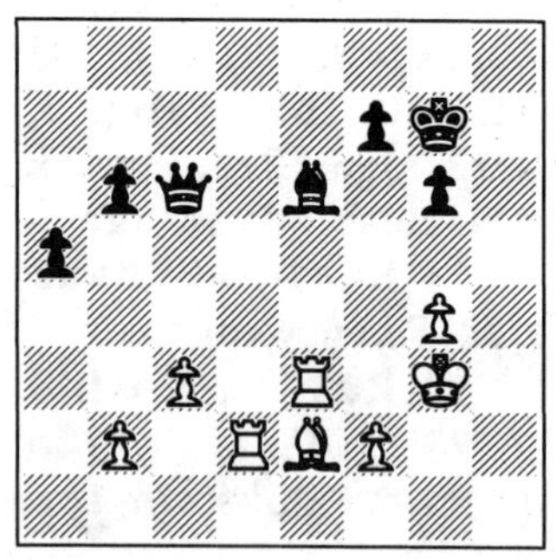

36 f3?

White misses **36 f4!** with good winning chances (36...Qh1 37 Rd1).

36...	**g5!**

Preventing **37 f4.**

37 Rd4

Now the position is a dead draw, though the players continue partly out of momentum.

37...	**Qc7ch**
38 Kg2	**Kf6**

39 Bd3 **Qc5**
40 Be4

White can only hope for a slip as Black's position is too well-knit.

40... **Qb5**
41 Rd2

The b-pawn keeps White tied down.

41... **Qe5**
42 Ree2 **Qb5**

Obviously Black can do nothing, too.

43 Bb7 **Qc5**

The "woodshifting" continues.

44 Rd4 **b5**
45 Red2

With the idea of **46 Bd5** with some prospects.

45... **Ke5!**

But Black forestalls, hence...

DRAWN

Although this game was drawn, White suggested **11 Bf4!** giving him a clear edge from the opening has revitalized this line.

CHAPTER ONE
THE LONDON SYSTEM

BLACK PLAYS Bf5
(1 Nf3, d5 2 g3, Nf6 3 Bg2)

3... c6

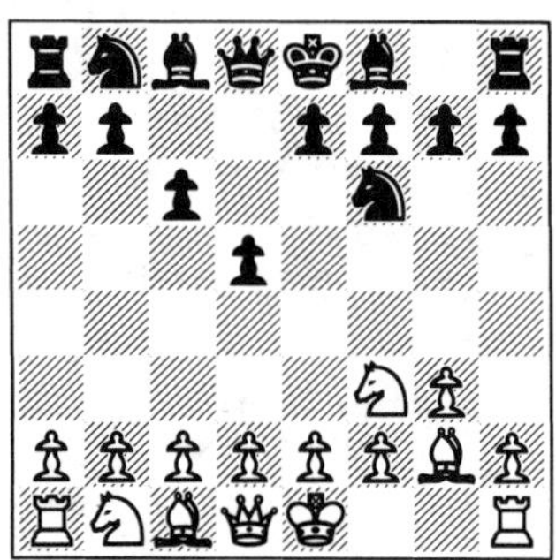

Black's idea in this variation is to establish a bulwark of pawns on **c6, d5**, and **e6** to lessen the scope of White's fianchettoed KB. But before he plays **e7-e6**, Black first deploys his QB so as to not lock it in.

White will try to gain central space with **e2-e4** (e5), usually with an aim at a Kingside buildup.

4 0-0

4 d3 will normally transpose while **4 c4** (a good move) transposes into a Reti Opening which lies beyond the scope of our discussion.

4... Bf5

This deployment of the QB initiates the so called London System, considered one of Black's most solid defenses to the K.I.A.

5 b3

The fianchetto of the QB is quite fashionable in this variation. For an excellent example of play without **5 b3**, see Illustrative Game #14.

5... e6

6 Bb2 **Be7**

Not **6...Bd6** which would give too much impetus to White's **e2-e4** as the eventual threat to play **e4-e5**, forking the **Bd6/Nf6** would be annoying to Black.

7 d3 **h6**

Providing a convenient retreat for the QB on **h7.**

8 Nbd2

This is the usual, thematic post for the QN in the K.I.A. However White might, in some cases, be interested in experimenting with **Nbc3**. For example, the game **Larsen-Polugaevsky, Le Havre 1966**, continued **8 e3** (preparing Qe2 to assist the advance e2-e4) **8...Bh7 9 Qe2, a5 10 a4, Na6 11 Nc3!?** (instead of the usual Nbd2) **11...Nc5 12 Ne5, 0-0** with interesting play.

Not recommended is **8 Nfd2?!**. The game **Quinteros-Polugaevsky, Mar del Plata 1971**, continued **8...0-0 9 e4, Bh7 10 Qe2, a5 11 a4, Na6 12 e5, Nd7 13 f4, b5 14 Nc3, Nb4 15 Nf3, Nc5** with a slight plus for Black.

8... **Bh7**

Black "sees" **e4** coming and ducks out of the way.

There are several other possibilities:

a) 8...0-0 9 Re1!, Bh7 10 e4 will transpose into our main line.

b) 8...a5 9 a4! will transpose also into the main line.

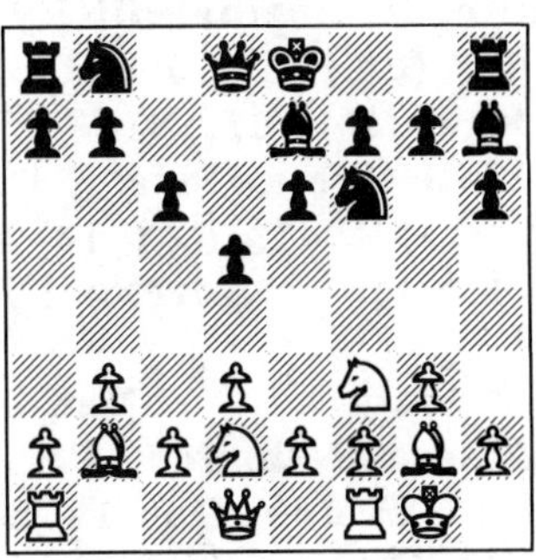

Now White has two good lines:

Ia: 9 Re1

Ib: 9 Qe1

Ia

(1 Nf3, d5 2 g3, Nf6 3 Bg2, c6 4 0-0, Bf5 5 b3, e6 6 Bb2, Be7 7 d3, h6 8 Nbd2, Bh7)

9 Re1

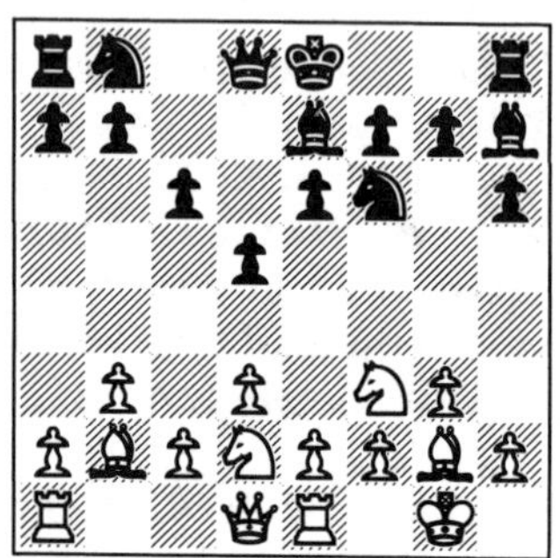

9... 0-0

After **9...Nbd7 10 e4, de 11 de, 0-0 12 Qe2, Qc7 13 e5, Nd5 14 Ne4** White's strong **Ne4** gives him an edge- **Flesch-Holmov, Pecs 1969.**

10 e4 a5

11 a4

White also has other good moves;

a) 11 e5, Nfd7 12 a3, c5 13 d4, a4 14 c4, dc 15 Nxc4 with a plus for White, **Dzindzihasvili-Rytov, USSR 1975.**

b) 11 a3, Nbd7 (or 11...Na6 12 Qe2, Nc5 13 Ne5, Qc7 14 Rc1, ed 15 de, Rad8 16 Nd3, Nfd7 17 Nxc5, Bxc5 18 e5 with an edge for White, Stein-Gufeld, USSR Championship 1965) 12 Qe2, Nc5 13 Rad1, Re8 14 h4 with the better chances for White, **Korchnoi-Bihovski, USSR Championship 1965.**

11... Na6

The game **Sturva-Dolmatov, USSR 1976**, continued **11...Nbd7 12 Qe2, Qb6 13 Bh3, Qa6 14 Nd4, Kh8 15 e5, Ne8 16 c4, c5 17 Nb5, d4 18 Ne4** with the better position for White.

12 e5 Nd7

(See diagram on following page)

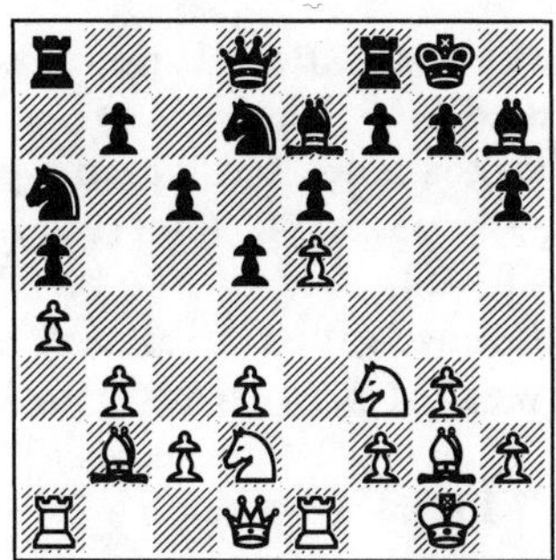

White's space advantage (e5) gives him a small plus. For example, the game **Polugaevsky-Hort, Sarajevo 1975,** continued **13 Nd4, Qb6 14 f4, Nc7 15 Qe2** and White has good chances of a Kingside attack via **g2-g4** playing for **f4-f5.**

Ib

(1 Nf3, d5 2 g3, Nf6 3 Bg2, c6 4 0-0, Bf5 5 b3, e6 6 Bb2, Be7 7 d3, h6 8 Nbd2, Bh7)

9 Qe1

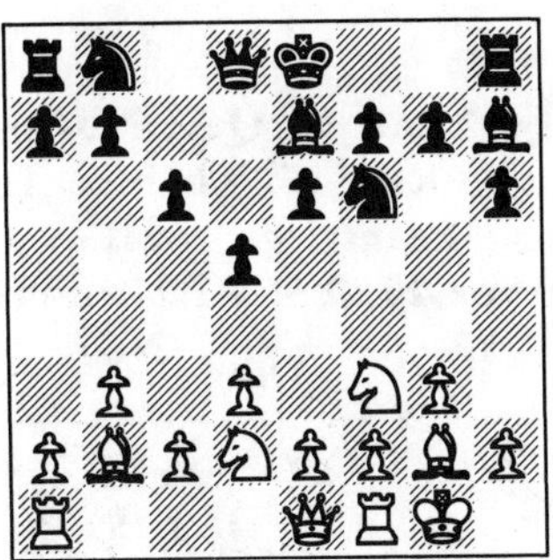

This peculiar looking maneuver intends to support **e4** while keeping the KR on the f-file for possible later Kingside action. An interesting alternative is **9 Ne5**--see Illustrative Game #22.

9...	**0-0**
10 e4	**a5**

Hoping to open up counterplay with **a4** and **axb3** or **a4-a3** cramping White's QB. The game **Polugaevsky-Planic,**

Skopje 1971, continued **10...de 11 de, Na6 12 Qe2, Nc5 13 Ne5, Qc7 14 Kh1, Rad8 15 f4, Ne8** (or if 15...Nfd7 then 16 Ng4 prevents exchanges and maintains pressure) **16 Rad1, Nd6 17 Qe3, Na6 18 a3, Bf6** (Better is 18...Nb5 though after 19 b4, c5 20 c4, Nd4 21 b5 White's excellent, centralized development gives him an advantage) **19 g4!** and White has a powerful Kingside attack in motion.

11 a4

After **11 a3, c5** (on 11...Qb6 White gained the edge in **Quinteros-Platonov, Cienfuegos 1972** after 12 Rb1, Nbd7 13 Kh1, Ne8 14 Nh4, de 15 de, Bf6 16 Nc4, Qc7 17 f4) **12 Qe2, Qb6 13 e5, Ne8** with approximately equal chances, **Nikolaevsky-Saharov, USSR 1968.**

11... Na6

After **11...Nbd7 12 Qe2, Qb6 13 e5, Ne8 14 Bh3, Nc7 15 Kh1, Rae8 16 Nh4, f6** (Black must challenge the encirclement of his Kingside by the cramping pawn at e5) **17 ef, Bxf6 18 Bxf6, Rxf6 19 f4, Qc5 20 Ndf3** with an edge for White, **Korchnoi-Reshevsky, Amsterdam (Match) 1968.**

12 e5

More effective than **12 Qe2, Nb4 13 Ne1, Nd7 14 f4, Bf6 15 e5, Be7 16 g4, Re8 17 Kh1** (so far as in the game **Polugaevsky-Addison, Palma de Mallorca Interzonal 1970**) and now Gligoric gives **17...b5!** with about even chances.

12... Nd7

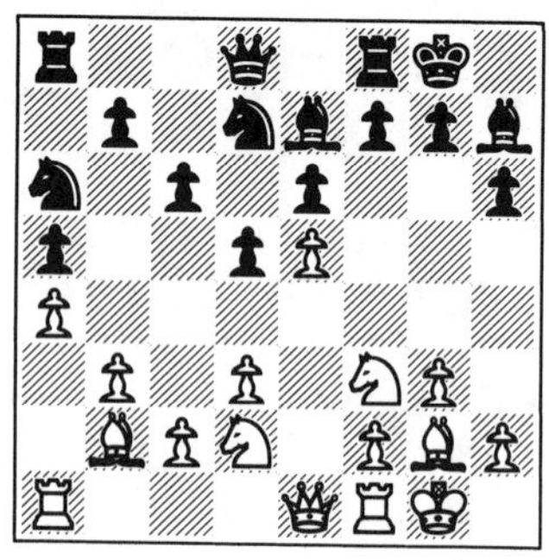

Again White's central and Kingside space advantage is due to the **e5** pawn. The game **Vladimirov-Haritonov, USSR 1977,** continued **13 Qe2, Nb4 14 Ne1, Qb6 15 Kh1, Qa6 16 f4, Rfe8 17 Rf3, c5 18 g4!** with fine attacking chances.

CHAPTER TWO

KERE'S VARIATION

(BLACK PLAYS Bg4)

Here, as in the previous section, Black develops his QB outside his pawn structure (i.e., before it is locked in by e7-e6). After a subsequent White **h3**, Black will have two basic options, **...Bxf3** or **...Bh5**. The logic behind **...Bxf3** is to simplify, thereby reducing White chances for long term pressure, while the surrender of the two Bishops by **...Bxf3** is largely offset by the strong central pawn structure (c6, d5, e6) which makes it difficult for White to activate his KB. The retreat **...Bh5** intends to retain the two Bishops and retain the tension.

We will examine two setups.

IIa Black plays Ngf6
IIb Black plays Nge7

IIa

(1 Nf3, d5 2 g3, Nf6 3 Bg2, c6 4 0-0, Bg4)

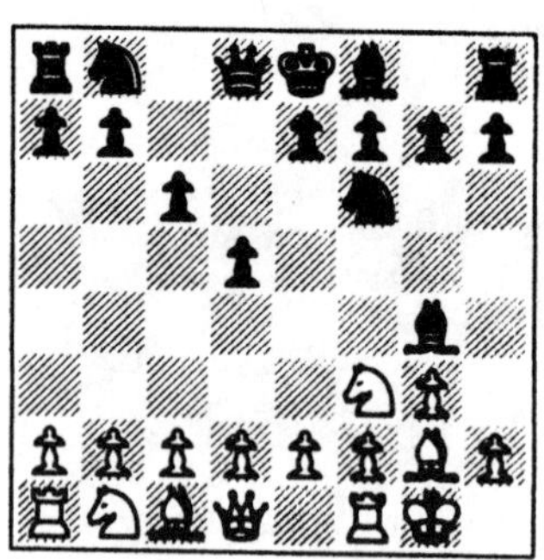

5 d3

Another possibility is **5 h3**. For example, the game **Botvinnik-Szilagyi, Amsterdam 1966**, continued **5...Bxf3 6 Bxf3** (White obtains nothing with 6 exf3, e.g., the game

Kotov-Ivkov, Sarajevo 1966, continued 6...g6 7 d3, Bg7 8 f4, 0-0 9 Nd2, e6 10 Nf3, c5 11 Ne5, Nfd7 12 Re1, Qc7 with equal chances) **6...Nbd7 7 d3, e5** (more solid is 7...e6) **8 Nd2, Bc5 9 e4, de 10 de, Qe7 11 c3, 0-0?!** (11...a5 to restrain b2-b4 is necessary) **12 b4, Bb6 13 a4, Rfd8 14 Qc2** and White has the better position.

5... Nbd7

After **5...Qc7 6 Nbd2, e5** White gained a clear positional advantage in the game **Keene-Kostra, Lugano Olympiad 1968** after **7 e4, de 8 de, h6 9 h3, Be6 10 Qe2, g5** (too ambitious) **11 Nc4, Nbd7 12 Bd2, g4 13 hg, Bxg4 14 Ne3.**

6 Nbd2

Now Black has two basic moves:

IIa1 6...e5
IIa2 6...e6

IIa1

(1 Nf3, d5 2 g3, Nf6 3 Bg2, c6 4 0-0, Bg4 5 d3, Nbd7 6 Nbd2)

6... e5

This aggressive move intends to establish a classical pawn center and prevent the typical possibility of **e2-e4-e5**. However the e-pawn is less secure on **e5** than on **e6**.

In the game **Miles-Holmov, Dubna 1976**, Black essayed **6...g6** though after this, White gains a slight positional advantage with **7 h3** winning the two Bishops (7...Be6? 8 Ng5).

7 e4

Interesting play developed in the game **Polugaevsky-Geller, USSR Championship 1969**, after **7 h3, Bxf3** (7...Bh5 is playable) **8 Nxf3, Bc5 9 Nxe5, Nxe5 10 d4, Bd6 11 dxe5, Bxe5 12 Qd3, 0-0** with about even chances.

Though our main line continues with an immediate **7 e4**, White can adopt a Queenside fianchetto in the early moves in this line. For example, the game **Szabo-Keres, Budapest 1970**, began **1 Nf3, d5 2 g3, Bg4 3 Bg2, c6 4 b3, Nf6 5 Bb2, Nbd7 6 0-0, e6 7 d3, Bc5 8 Nbd2, 0-0 9 e4, a5 10 a3** and now Keres recommends **10...de 11 de, Qc7** with equal chances.

7... de

Otherwise White could open the e-file at some point (after Re1) **exd5**, exposing the Black e-pawn to pressure.

8 de Qc7

In the game **Ivkov-Marovic, Yugoslavia 1972**, Black tried **8...Bc5** and after **9 c3, a5 10 Qc2, 0-0 11 b3, Re8 12 Bb2, Qc7 13 a3!** (White intends to gain Queenside territory with b3-b4) **13...b5 14 h3, Bxf3 15 Bxf3** White had a positional pull.

Similar play was seen in the game **Damljanovic-C. Hansen, New York Open 1987**. It began **1 g3, d5 2 Nf3, Nf6 3 Bg2, c6 4 0-0, Bg4 5 d3, Nbd7 6 Nbd2, e5** and now, instead of our main line move (7 e4), White challenged the Bg4 immediately with **7 h3**. There followed **7...Bh5 8 e4, de 9 de, Bc5 10 Qe1** (By unpinning, White places more pressure on e5 while retaining the option of the maneuver Nh4, eyeing f5.) with an edge for White. See Illustrative Game #24.

After **8...Bd6** the game **Filip-Sigurjonsson, Lugano 1968**, continued **9 b3, 0-0 10 Bb2, Re8 11 Qb1!?, a5 12 a3, Qc7 13 h3, Bh5 14 Nh4** with better play for White.

9 Qe1

Unpinning while giving the e-pawn more protection. Also of interest is **9 Qe2**. The game **Hort-Kovacs, Sombur 1968**, continued in a sharp fashion--**9...h6 10 Nc4, 0-0-0?!** (overly sharp) **11 h3, Be6 12 a4, g5 13 Nh2, Rg8 14 Be3,**

Kb8 15 Rfd1, Be7 with better chances for White in a complex struggle.

9... Nc5

10 Nc4 Nfd7

Of course, taking the e-pawn with his King on the e-file would be a losing proposition.

11 h3 Bh5

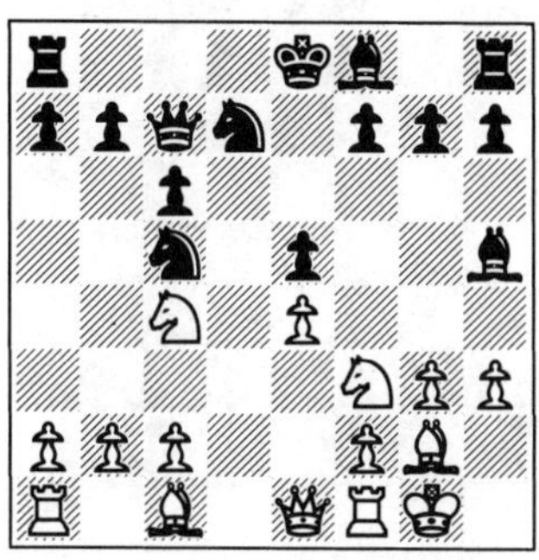

12 b4!

An important gain of space, giving White a positional initiative. The game **Panno-Korchnoi, Palma de Mallorca 1972**, continued **12...Ne6 13 a3, f6 14 c3, Nb6 15 Nfd2, Qf7 16 Na5** with better chances for White.

In the game **Gutman-Smejkal, BRD 1987**, White played **6 Qe1** (instead of our main line 6 Nbd2). This will normally transpose more or less into our main line in which White plays **Qe1** on the 9th move. For example, the game began **1 g3, d5 2 Nf3, Nf6 3 Bg2, c6 4 0-0, Bg4 5 d3, Nbd7 6 Qe1, e5 7 e4, de 8 de, Be7 9 Nbd2, 0-0 10 h3!, Bh5 11 Nc4, Qc7 12 a4, Rfe8 13 Bd2** (to be considered is 13 Nh4 with the idea of occupying f5 after g4. The drawback to this alternative scheme is the weakening of f4 after g4.) **13...Bf8 14 Bc3, Bxf3** (to reduce the pressure on the e-pawn. However this implies 10...Bh5 was a loss to tempo.) **15 Bxf3, b5 16 ab** with a positional plus for White. For the complete game, see Informant #43--Game 2.

IIa2

(1 Nf3, d5 2 g3, Nf6 3 Bg2, c6 4 0-0, Bg4 5 d3, Nbd7 6 Nbd2)

6... e6

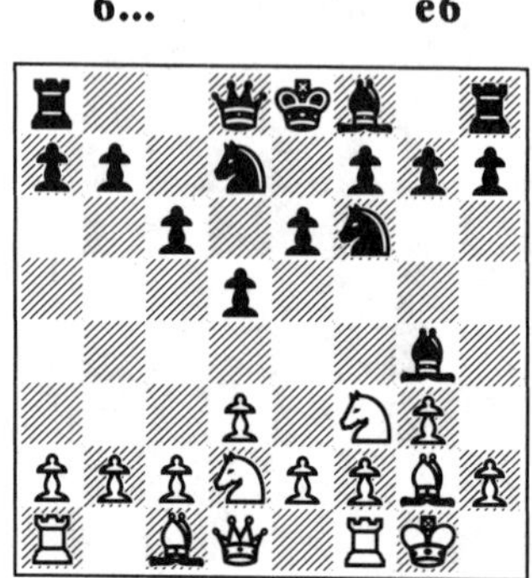

This is Black's most solid line.

7 e4

Of considerable importance is the alternative **7 h3**. For example, the game **Portisch-Hort, Lugano Olympiad 1968**, continued **7...Bxf3 8 Nxf3, Be7** (or 8...Bc5 9 Qe1, 0-0 10 e4, de 11 de, e5 12 Bg5, h6 13 Bd2, Re8 14 Rd1, Qc7 15 Nh4 with the better play for White, **Vasyukov-Trifunovic, USSR-Yugoslavia 1963**) **9 e3, 0-0 10 Qe2, a5 11 e4, a4 12 e5** (an important cramping move which, in conjunction with the two Bishops, gives White a positional advantage) **12...Ne8 13 a3** (preventing a4-a3 which would weaken White's Queenside) **13...b5 14 d4, b4** (Better was 14...Qb6 though White would still retain the edge) **15 ab, Bxb4 16 c4, Nc7 17 Qc2** and Black loses a pawn as **17...Nb6** then **18 c5** wins the a-pawn, while on **17...dc 18 Qxc4** is decisive.

7... Be7

Black can also post the KB on the seemingly more aggressive post on **c5**. However, this is not an unmixed blessing, as on **c5** the Bishop is often exposed to a timely **b2-b4** or attack by a White Knight from **b3** or **e4** (after White has played e4-e5). For example, we give the game **Korchnoi-Flear, Lugano 1986: 1 Nf3, d5 2 g3, Nf6 3 Bg2, c6 4 0-0, Bg4 5 d3, e6 6 Qe1** (To implement e2-e4) 6...Nbd7

7 e4, de 8 de, e5 (Black wants to prevent e4-e5) **9 Nbd2, Bc5 10 Nc4, Qe7 11 Ne3, h5!?** (Rather too aggressive, yet after 11...Be6 12 Nf5 White has a clear advantage, while even after the better 11...Bxe3 12 Qxe3 White's Bishop pair give him a small but definite plus) **12 a3!** with fine chances for White. See Illustrative Game #1 for the rest of the game.

8 Qe1 0-0

In some cases Black plays **...Bxf3** in response to **h2-h3**. A good illustration of this type of play comes from the game **Smejkal-Suba, Szirak 1986**, which began with a slightly different move sequence (Black plays an early Be7 instead of an early Nbd7) **1 Nf3, Nf6** (this will transpose shortly) **2 g3, d5 3 Bg2, c6 4 0-0, Bg4 5 d3, e6 6 Nbd2, Be7 7 e4, 0-0 8 h3** and now after **8...Bxf3 9 Qxf3, a5 10 Qe2, a4 11 a3, Re8 12 f4, Bf8 13 Nf3, Nfd7 14 Kh1, Qc7 15 Bd2, Na6 16 Rae1, Rab8 17 Bc1, de 18 de, Nac5 19 e5, Nb6 20 Nd4** with a clear advantage for White.

9 h3 Bh5

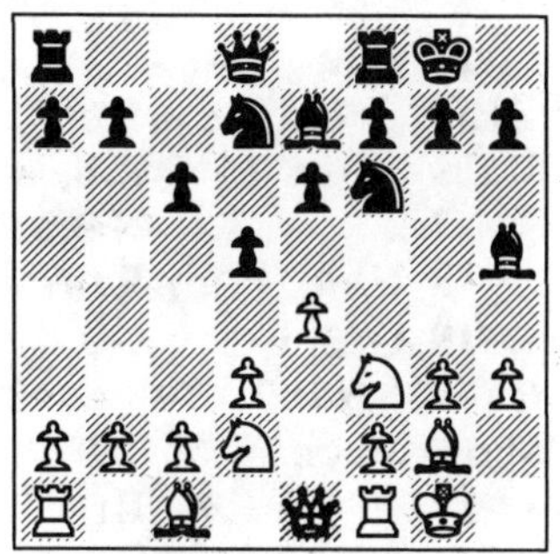

10 Kh1

Probably best. White tried **10 Nh2!?** in the game **Smejkal-Pinter, Szirak 1986**, but **10...de 11 de, e5 12 Nc4** (Not 12 f4?!, ef 13 gf, Re8!) **12...Re8 13 Nf3, Qc7 14 Nh4, b5** Black had equality. Even better than **10...de** is **10...Qb6!** according to the Hungarian GM Farago.

On **10 e5** Black can conveniently play **10...Ne8** and if **11 Nh2**, then **11...Qb6!**.

10... Ne8

The best reply. Now **10...Qb6** is weak because of **11 g4, Bg6 12 Nh2, Ne8 13 f4!.**

11 Ng1

A strategic retreat allowing White to mobilize his Kingside pawns.

11...	**Nc7**
12 Nb3	**de**
13 de	

On **13 Bxe4?!** Black gains the edge after **13...Nf6.**

13...	**e5**

To secure a foothold in the center.

14 Qa5	**Ne6**
15 f4	

White realizes he retains an edge in the ending on **15...Qxa5 16 Nxa5.**

15...	**f6**
16 Nf3	**Qb6**

Giving up the two Bishops with **16...Bxf3** is not advisable as after **17 Bxf3** the KB can reach a fine position on **g4**.

17 Bd2

But not **17 Nh4?** because after **17...Bb4!** forces the better ending for Black after **18 Qxb6, axb6!.**

17...	**Nec5**
18 Nh4	**Rfe8**
19 Qc3	

After **19 Rae1, Nxb3 20 axb3, Qxa5 21 Bxa5** chances would be about even.

19...	**Bf8**

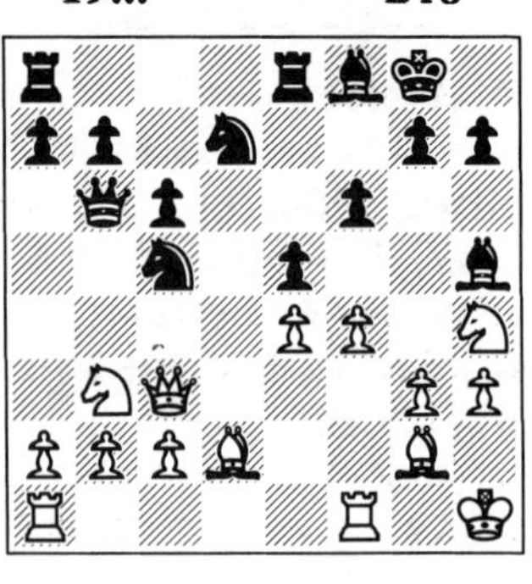

So far as in the game **Gutman-Farago, Bruxelles II 1986**, which continued **20 Rae1, Rad8 21 g4!, Bf7 22 g5!, Nxb3(!)** (The only move, on 22...ef 23 gf! followed by **Nf5** is powerful, while on 22...Na4 23 Qg3 is strong) **23 axb3, Qd4 24 gf, Nxf6 25 Qxd4, exd4** and now **26 Bf3** leaves White with a slight advantage.

IIb

(1 Nf3, d5 2 g3, c6 3 Bg2, Bg4)

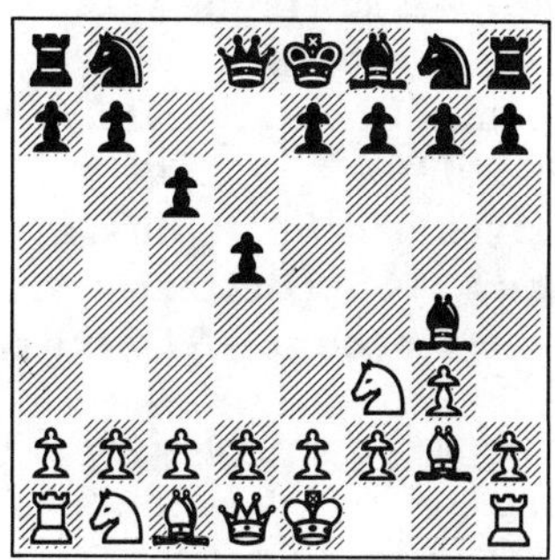

In this line we examine the defensive system with **Nge7** instead of the more usual **Ngf6** which we analyzed in IIa. Black develops his KB to **d6** followed by **Nge7**. With the KN on **f6** the **Bd6** is exposed after **e4** to the eventual tactical threat **e4-e5**; however with **Nge7** the idea is fully playable.

4 0-0

Another move of promise is the immediate **4 h3**. The game **Ermolinsky-Ehlvest, Kuibyshev 1986**, continued **4...Bxf3** (4...Bh5 seems more solid retaining the Bishop pair for at least awhile) **5 Bxf3, Nd7 6 d3, Ngf6 7 e4, de 8 de, e5** (staking out central space; 8...e6 is too passive) **9 Nd2, Bc5 10 Nc4, 0-0 11 0-0, Qe7 12 Qe2** (Another standard move here is 12 a4 to gain space and discourage ...b5) **12...Qe6 13 Kg2, b5 14 Ne3, Nb6 15 b3** (If 15 Nf5 then Black can try 15...Qc4 while 15 Bg4 is answered by 15...Nxg4 16 hxg4, Bxe3 17 Bxe3, Qc4 with reasonable counterplay) **15...a5 16 Nf5** and White's occupation of **f5** plus his two Bishops give him the advantage. For the rest of the game see *New In Chess* #6, page 430.

In the game **Kogan-Seirawan, US 1985**, Black essayed an unusual plan--**4...e6 5 d3, Bxf3** (Black gives up the Bishop pair without being provoked by h2-h3, as he wants to exchange before White plays Nbd2 in which case White could answer ...Bxf3 with Nxf3. However the idea is a bit artificial.) **6 Bxf3, Nf6 7 Nd2, Nbd7 8 e4, Bc5 9 Qe2, de** (On 9...0-0 10 e5 is good for White) and now, instead of the actually played **10 de**, White retains a slight plus with **10 Bxe4** keeping the KB's diagonal open--see Illustrative Game #18.

4... Nbd7
5 d3 e6

Here, **5...e5** gives White a plus after **6 e4, de 7 de, Bc5 8 h3, Bh5 9 Nbd2, f6?!** (Better is 9...Ngf6) 10 c3, Bf7 11 Nh4 as in the game **Korchnoi-Qi Jingxuan, Thessaloniki Olympiad 1984.**

6 Nbd2 Bd6
7 e4

Interesting is **7 h3, Bh5 8 Qe1, Ne7 9 b3, 0-0 10 Bb2, a5 11 a4, b5 12 e4, ba 13 Rxa4, c5 14 Nh4, Nb6 15 Ra1, Nc6 16 f4, Be7 17 Ndf3, Bxf3 18 Nxf3, a4** with approximate equality, from the game **Portisch-Smyslov, Hastings 1970.** Also interesting was the game **Butnoris-Keres, USSR 1972**, which continued **7 b3, Ne7 8 Bb2, 0-0 9 c4, a5 10 a3, b5 11 Qc2, e5** with equal chances.

7... Ne7
8 b3

White hopes for good activity for his QB on the **a1-h8** diagonal.

After **8 Qe2, 0-0 9 b3** (9 h3, Bh5 10 Re1, Kh8 11 d4, Rac8 12 c4, c5! with an excellent game for Black, **D. Byrne-Smyslov, Lugano Olympiad 1968**) **9...Ng6 10 Bb2, Nge5 11 Qe3, Nxf3ch 12 Nxf3, Bxf3 13 Bxf3, de 14 Bxe4, Qa5** chances are equal, **Rajkovic-Rukavina, Yugoslavia 1976.**

8... 0-0
9 h3 Bh5

(See diagram on following page)

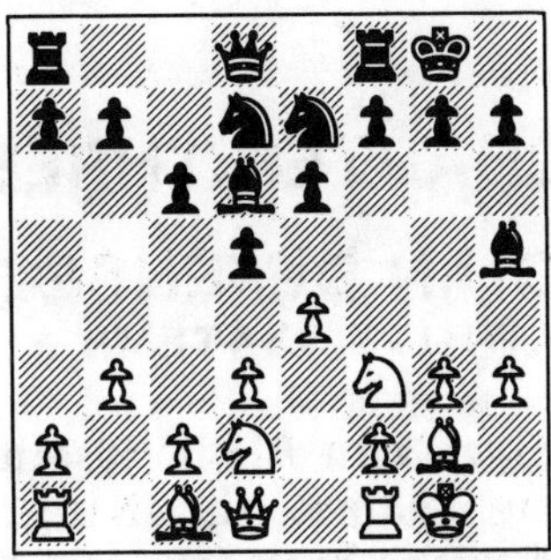

10 Bb2 **Ne5**

This is better than **10...Rc8**, which occurred in the game **Portisch-Ivkov, Amsterdam 1969**. The game continued **11 Qe1, c5 12 Nh4, Qb6 13 Qe3, Rfe8** (13...d4 is better) **14 Qg5!, Bg6 15 ed, Nxd5 16 Nxg6, hxg6 17 Bxd5, exd5 18 Qxd5, Qc7 19 Nc4, Re6 20 Rae1, Rae8 21 Nxd6** and Black Resigned.

11 g4

White begins a general advance of his Kingside pawns in order to create attacking opportunities there.

11... **Nxf3ch**
12 Qxf3 **Bg6**
13 h4 **h6**
14 h5 **Bh7**

White has good attacking possibilities based on the further advance of his Kingside pawns (e4-e5 followed by f2-f4-f5 and/or g4-g5).

CHAPTER THREE

KING'S INDIAN DEFENSE REVERSED
(BLACK PLAYS WHITE SYSTEMS A TEMPO DOWN)

We now analyze two Black systems which are basically White systems against the King's Indian Defense. Black must proceed with great care lest he fall into greater trouble due to the "missing tempo".

We now examine:

IIIa Black fianchettoes the KB
IIIb Black places pawns at c5, d5, e5

IIIa
(1 Nf3, d5 2 g3, Nf6 3 Bg2, g6 4 0-0, Bg7 5 d3, 0-0 6 Nbd2)

6... c5

Black plays just as White would play the Classical Fianchetto against the King's Indian Defense--but with that critical tempo less. See Illustrative Game #4.

7 e4 Nc6
8 c3

This seems more effective than **8 Re1**, with the following possibilities:

a) 8...h6 9 c3, de (After 9...Be6 10 ed, Nxd5 11 Nb3, b6 12 d4! White gains an initiative) 10 de, Be6 11 Qe2, Nd7

12 Nc4, b5 13 Ne3, b4 14 Bd2, bc 15 bc, Rb8 with equal chances, **Polugaevsky-Vladimirov, Sochi 1966.**

b) 8...b6 9 c3, de (Or 9...e6 10 a3, a5 11 e5, Nd7 12 d4, Bb7 (Slightly better is 12...Ba6 according to Ivanovic) 13 Nf1, b5 14 h4, cd 15 cd, Qb6 16 b3, Rac8 17 Bg5, b4 18 a4, Ncb8 19 N1h2 followed by h5 with a very strong game for White, **Quinteros-Zivkovic, Bar 1977**) 10 de, Ng4 (Or 10...Bb7 11 e5, Ne8 12 Qa4, Qc7 13 e6, f6 14 Nc4 with a definite plus for White, **Vogt-Baumbach, Leipzig 1973**) 11 Bf1, Nge5 12 Qc2, Bb7 13 Nxe5, Nxe5 14 f4, Nd7 15 Bg2 with a slight plus for White, **Botvinnik-Donner, Leiden 1970.**

c) 8...e5 (This is rather ambitious, yet playable--again the tempo difference must be kept in mind) 9 ed, Nxd5 10 Ne4, Re8 11 c3 (Not 11 a4, Ndb4! with a bind for Black) h6 with very comfortable play for White, **Wade-Browne, Hastings 1972/73**. Yet Black's position is solid if it is not "overplayed".

d) 8...d4 9 e5 (Or 9 a4, e5 10 Nc4, Ne8 11 a5, Rb8 12 Nfd2, b5 with equal play, **Jones-Sosonko, Nice Olympiad 1974**) 9...Nd5 10 a4, Rb8 11 Nc4, b6 12 Bd2, a6 13 Ng5, h6 14 Ne4, Ncb4 15 f4, Qc7 with even chances, **Planinc-Sosonko, Amsterdam 1974.**

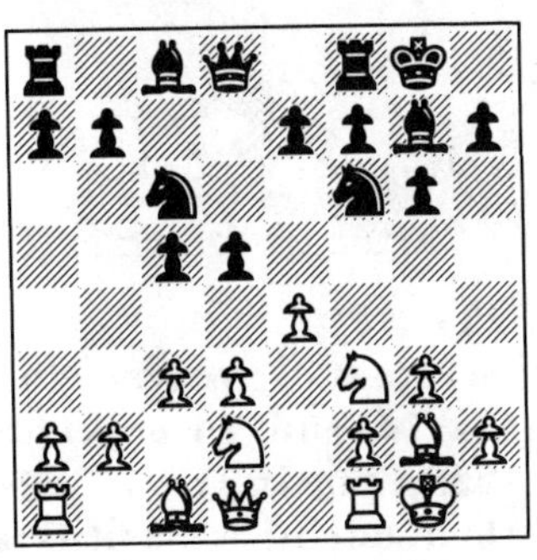

8... de

Again Black has several alternatives;

a) 8...e5 9 a3, h6 10 b4 (A thematic space gaining operation) 10...cb 11 ab, b5 12 Ba3, Re8 13 Qc2, Bg4 14

Nb3, Qc8 15 Rfc1 with a slight positional advantage to White, **Petrosian-Teschner, Stockholm Interzonal 1962.**

b) 8...Bg4 9 ed, Nxd5 10 h3, Bd7 11 Nb3, b6 12 d4 with initiative for White, **Lutikov-Bagirov, USSR Championship 1968/69.**

c) 8...d4 9 cd, cd 10 a4, e5 (Or slightly better play for White, **Balashov-Pfleger, Tallinn 1973**) 11 Nc4, Ne8 12 b4 and White seizes the initiative on the Queenside, from **Plachetka-Pribyl, Czechoslovakian Championship 1974.**

9 de h6

To play **Be6** without fear of the threat **Ng5.**

After **9...Bg4** the game **Cuderman-Suvalic, Yugoslavian Championship 1961,** continued **10 h3, Bxf3 11 Qxf3, Ne5 12 Qe3, Nfd7 13 f4** with a positional edge for White.

In the game **Knezevic-Bertok, Yugoslavian Championship 1977,** there occurred **9...b6** though after **10 Qe2, Ne8 11 Rd1, Nc7 12 Nc4, Qe8 13 Ne3** White has more play.

10 Qe2 Be6

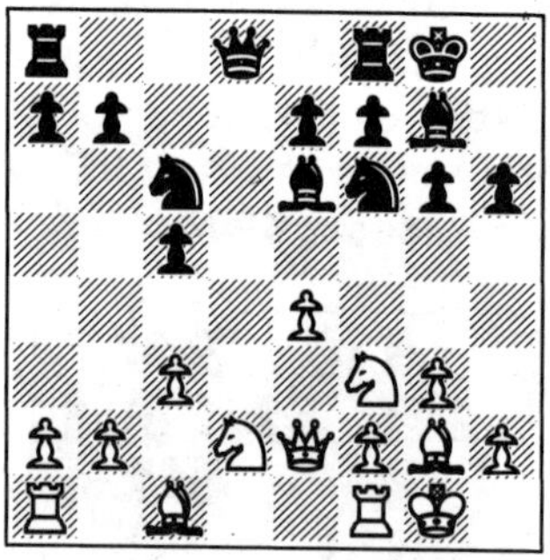

11 Ne1

White's key strategy involves gaining central and Kingside space via **f2-f4** and **e4-e5.** The game **Petrosian-Reshevsky, Zurich 1953,** continued **11...Qb6 12 h3, Rad8 13 Kh2, Nh7 14 f4** with a definite positional plus for White, though White "chickened out" when Black tactfully offered a draw a few moves later.

IIIb

(1 Nf3, d5 2 g3, c5 3 Bg2, Nc6 4 0-0, e5 5 d3)

5... Nf6

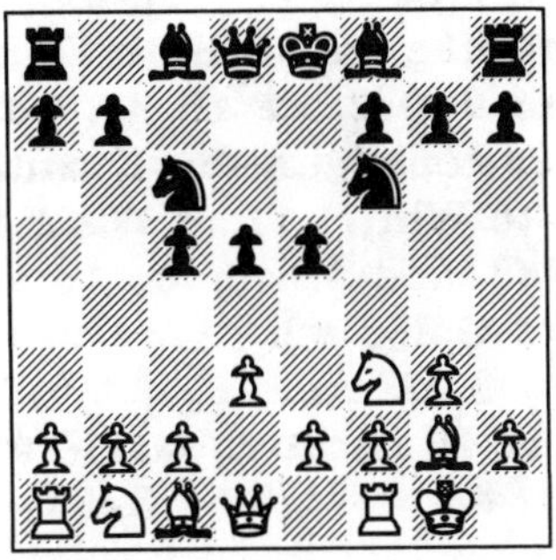

Simple, sound development while not yet committing the Black KB's deployment.

In the game **Botvinnik-Pomar, Varna Olympiad 1962**, Black tried the unusual move **5...Bd6**. The game continued **6 e4, d4 7 Nbd2, Nge7 8 c4, f6** (Black has transposed into a Samisch Variation with colors reversed) **9 Nh4, Be6 10 f4, ef 11 gf, Qc7 12 e5!** (A brilliant positional pawn sacrifice which gives White a strong outpost on e4 while simultaneously blocking the important e5 square from Black's pieces.) **12...fe 13 f5, Bf7 14 Ne4, 0-0-0 15 Qg4, Kb8 16 Qxg7** and White went on to win.

When Black plays **5...Be7**, usually play will transpose. However, in the game **Larsen-Ljubojevic, Bugojno 1978**, Ljubojevic decided on a very sharp plan involving a Samisch-like attack pattern. After **5...Be7** there followed **6 e4, d4** (since Black intends a Kingside attack, he closes the center to prevent counterplay there) **7 a4, g5 8 Nbd2, Be6 9 Nc4, f6 10 h4, h6 11 Nh2, gh 12 Qh5ch, Kd7 13 Qxh4, f5 14 Qh5, Nf6 15 Qe2, fe 16 Bxe4, Nxe4 17 Qxe4, Bxc4 18 dxc4, Qg8** with wild play in an unclear position.

In the game **Larsen-Kraidman, Manila 1974**, Black answered **6 e4** with **6...de** in order to reach an early ending. However, the weakness of the **d5** square (which cannot be controlled by a Black pawn) in this case gives White a strategic plus. The game continued **7 de, Qxd1 8 Rxd1, Bg4 9 c3, Rd8 10 Rxd8ch, Bxd8 11 Be3, b6 12 Na3, Nge7 13 Ng5, Nc8 14 h3, Be6 15 Bf1** with excellent chances for White.

6 Nbd2 Be7
7 e4 0-0

After **7...Bg4** the game **Stein-Zinn, Helsinki 1961,** continued **8 h3, Be6 9 Qe2, de 10 de, 0-0 11 c3** (Note that as in the above mentioned Larsen-Kraidman game, the d5 square is available to White) **11...Nd7 12 Nc4, b5 13 Ne3, c4 14 Rd1, Qc7 15 Nd5** and White has a definite positional plus. See Illustrative Game #3.

8 c3

For **8 Re1**, see Illustrative Game #2.

8... Re8

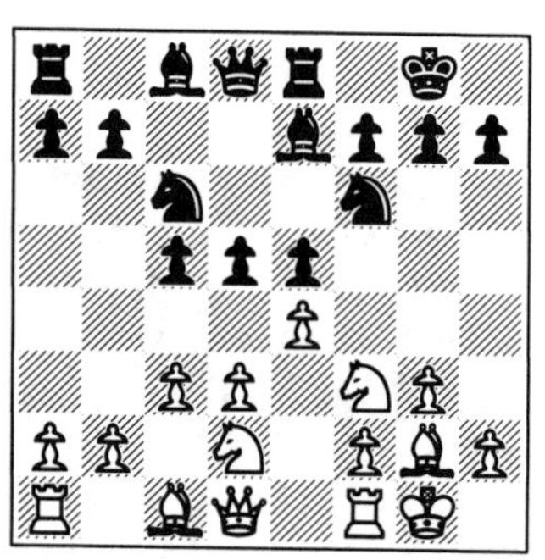

9 ed

Opening both the **h1-a8** diagonal and the e-file for pressure on Black's position.

9... Nxd5
10 Re1 Bf8
11 Nc4

White has the better chances. The game **Planinc-Rubinetti, Nice 1974,** continued **11...Qc7 12 Ng5, Rd8 13 Qe2, Nb6 14 Qe4, g6 15 Qh4** with a strong attack.

CHAPTER FOUR
THE KING'S INDIAN ATTACK
vs THE CARO-KAHN

The Caro-Kahn has long been rightly regarded as a very solid if sometimes somewhat passive, line of defense. The K.I.A. offers White good chances for an involved positional struggle quite different from the positions which arise from a "normal" Caro-Kahn (1 d4, c6 2 d4). It is important to remember that the K.I.A. can be played after **1 e4** followed by **d3, Nf3, g3, Bg2**, etc. In this section we shall assume that **1 e4**--with an eye to transposing--is played.

(1 e4, c6 2 d3, d5 3 Nd2)

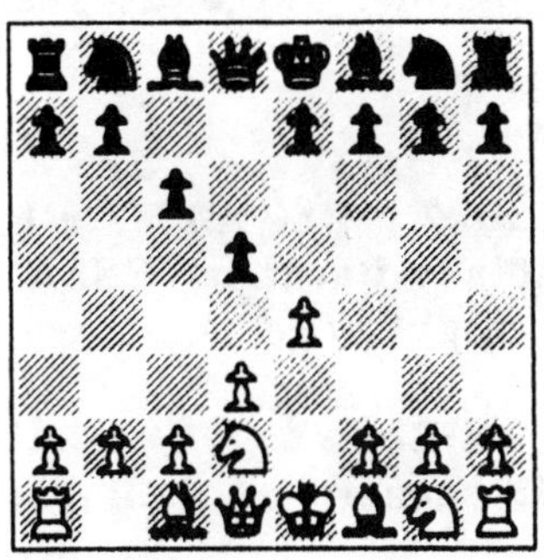

White's **3 Nd2** prevents the utterly drawn position resulting from a possible **3...de** followed by **4 de, Qxd1.**

Black now has several choices.

IVa 3...de
IVb 3...Nd7
IVc 3...Nf6
IVd 3...g6
IVe 3...e5

IVa

(1 e4, c6 2 d3, d5 3 Nd2)

3... de

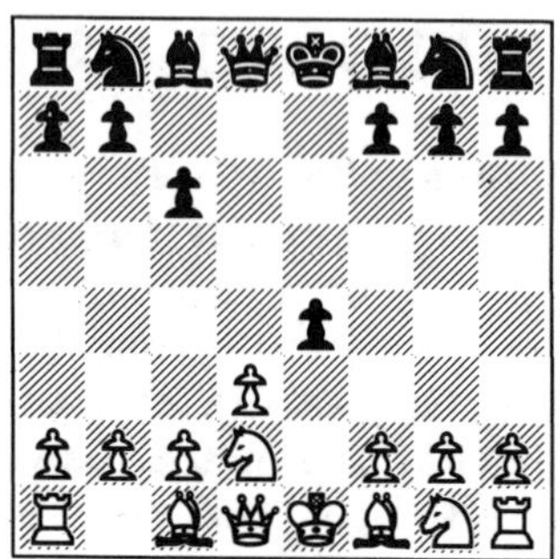

Black tries to stabilize the central situation with this exchange.

4 de

4 Nxe4 is possible, but **4 de** keeps a pawn in the center.

4... e5
5 Ngf3 Bc5

Passive is **5...Qc7 6 Bc4, Be7 7 0-0, Nf6** (so far as in the game **Nezhmetdinov-Baranov, USSR 1964**) and now **8 a4** should retain a slight edge. Also, see Illustrative Game #6.

6 Bc4

Not **6 Nxe5?** because of **6...Bxf2ch 7 Kxf2, Qd4ch** and **8...Qxe5.**

6... Nf6
7 0-0

The Czech GM Pachman gives **7 Nxe5, Bxf2ch 8 Ke2, Be6! 9 Nxf7** (not 9 Bxe6, fxe6 10 Nxc6, Nxc6 11 Kxf2, Qb6ch followed by 0-0-0) **9...Bxc4ch 10 Nxc4, Qxd1ch 11 Rxd1, Kxf7 12 Kxf2** (On 12 Nd6ch, Ke6 13 Kxf2, Rd8 14 Bf4, Black has 14...Nh5!) **12...Nxe4ch** with equality, though GM Larry Evans says **13 Kf3** gives White a slight edge, mainly because White's Bishop is a better minor piece than a Black Knight in an ending with pawns on both sides of the board.

7... Qc7

Now after **8 a4** (Restraining any possible b7-b5 and reserving a possible cramping a4-a5) followed by **c3** White's position is a hair better.

IVb

(1 e4, c6 2 d3, d5 3 Nd2)

3... Nd7

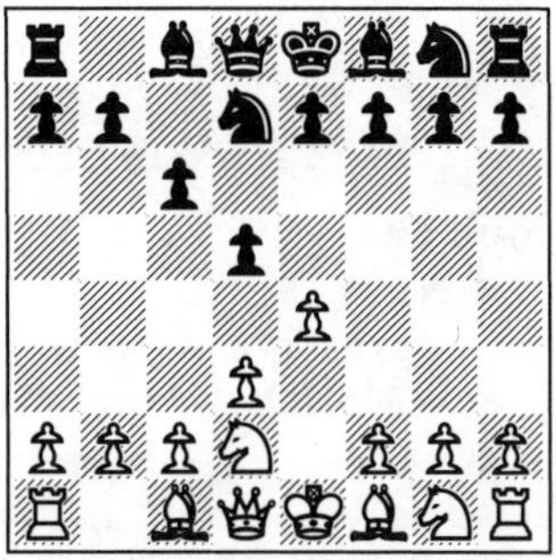

While the development of the QN is natural, Black suffers slightly from the blocking of the QB.

4 Ngf3 Qc7
5 g3 de

On advantage for delaying this trade (as opposed to IVa's 3...de) is that White's KB can no longer be developed to **c4**.

6 de e5
7 Bg2 Bc5

After **7...Ngf6 8 0-0, g6** White has **9 b3** threatening to play **Ba3** if Black fianchettoes the KB. After **7...Bc5** the game **Olaffson-Eliskases, 1960** continued **8 0-0, Ne7** (after 8...Ngf6 White seizes the initiative with 9 Nh4! taking aim at f5) **9 b3, Ng6** (A little better was 9...0-0) **10 Bb2, 0-0 11 a3, a5 12 Ne1, b6 13 Nd3, Ba6 14 Nf3, Bd6 15 h4!** with fine chances for White.

IVc

(1 e4, c6 2 d3, d5 3 Nd2)

3... Nf6

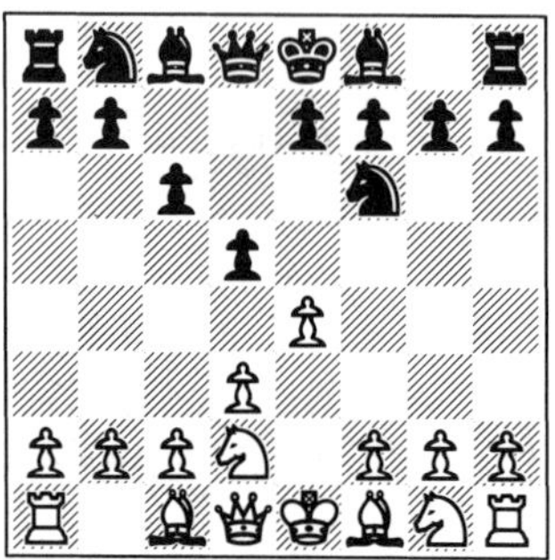

Simple development.

4 Ngf3

The seemingly aggressive **4 e5** is poor after **4...Nfd7 5 e6, fe** followed by **e6-e5** with a fine game for Black.

4... Bg4

Black does best to not lock in the QB with **4...e6, e.g., 5 g3, b6 6 Qe2, Be7 7 Bg2, 0-0 8 0-0, Bb7 9 Re1, Re8 10 e5, Nfd7 11 Nf1, c5 12 h4** with an excellent game for White, **Ignatiev-Hodos, USSR 1960.**

5 h3 Bxf3

If Black tries to retain the Bishop with **5...Bh5, then 6 g4, Bg6 7 Ne5, Nbd7 8 Nxd7, Nxd7 9 f4, e6 10 Qe2** (But not 10 f5 because of 10...ef 11 ef, Qh4ch 12 Ke2, 0-0-0! threatening 13...Re8ch) **10...Qh4ch 11 Qf2, Qxf2ch 12 Kxf2, Bc5ch 13 Kg3** gives White a better ending, from **Gufeld-Birbrager, USSR 1963.**

6 Qxf3 e6

Having given up his light-squared Bishop, Black seeks to use his center pawns to "Barricade" the weakened White squares.

7 g3 Na6
8 Bg2 Be7

After **8...Bb4** (a useless finesse) **9 c3, Be7 10 0-0, 0-0 11 e5, Nd7 12 Qe2** with an edge for White, **Smyslov-Chalibeili, USSR 1960.**

9 0-0 0-0
10 Qe2 Nc7

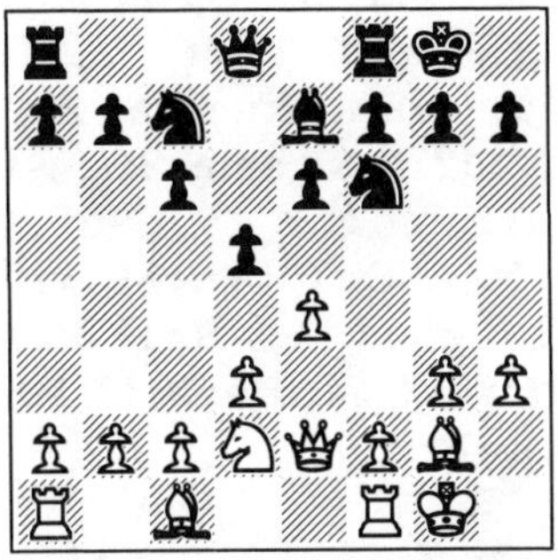

Now in the game **Shiskin-Wistanetski, USSR 1960** White essayed **11 Nf3** and after **11...a5 12 e5, Nd7** Black had equality; but better than **11 Nf3** is **11 f4** mobilizing the Kingside pawn mass, with a slight pull for White.

IVd

(1 e4, c6 2 d3, d5 3 Nd2)

3... g6

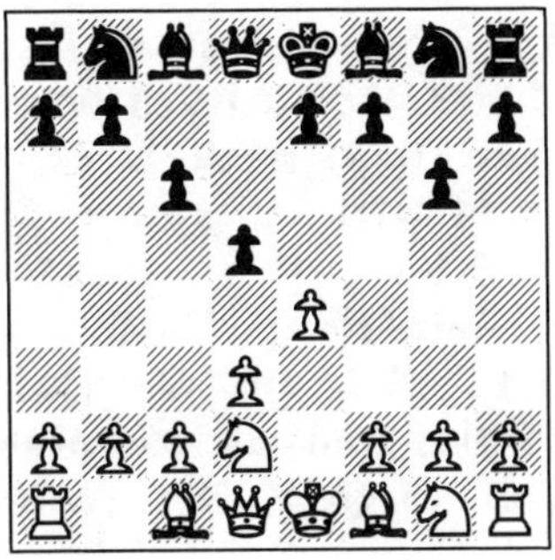

This is considered to be Black's most reliable line of defense.

4 g3

Also of interest is **4 f4** and if **4...Nf6 5 Ngf3, Bg7** then **6 Qe2** or **6 g3** leads to little explored vistas.

4... Bg7
5 Bg2

In the game **Fischer-Ibrahimoglu, Siegen 1970,** White played **5 Ngf3** and after **5...Nf6** (Better is 5...e5 transposing into our main line) **6 Bg2, 0-0 7 0-0, Bg4** (After 7...de 8 de, Nbd7 the game **Stein-Berger, Amsterdam Interzonal 1964,** continued 9 e5!, Nd5 10 e6, fe 11 Ng5, Nc5 12 Qe2, e5 13 Nc4, Qc7 14 Re1 with a big advantage for White) **8 h3** (Also good is 8 Re1) **8...Bxf3 9 Qxf3, Nbd7 10 Qe2, de 11 de, Qc7 12 a4, Rad8 13 Nb3** with advantage--see Illustrative Game #5.

5... e5
6 Ngf3 Ne7
7 0-0 0-0
8 b4

White can also try **8 Re1, e.g., 8...Nd7 9 a4** (Larsen recommends 9 ed, cd 10 c4!?) **9...a5 10 ed, cd 11 c3, Qc7 12 Nf1, b6 13 d4, e4 14 Bf4** with approximately equal chances, **Evans-Saidy, San Antonio 1972.** With **8 b4** White stakes out Queenside territory. Also possible is **8 c3** as in the game **Stein-Hort, Los Angeles 1968**-see Illustrative Game #17.

8... a5

The sharpest reply. In the game **Bronstein-Saidy, Tallinn 1973,** Black played **8...Nd7** and after **9 Bb2, b6** (On **9...Qc7 10 Re1, d4 11 c3, dc 12 Bxc3** White is on top, **Stein-Golombek, Kecskemet 1968) 10 Re1, d4 11 c3, dc 12 Bxc3, Ba6 13 Nb3, Qc7 14 d4** with advantage for White.

9 ba Qxa5

In the game **Stein-Haag, Tallinn 1969,** Black played **9...Rxa5,** but after **10 Bb2, Qc7 11 Qe2, d4 12 c3, dc 13 Bxc3, Ra4 14 Nc4** White had a clear plus--Black blundered with **14...b5** and after **15 Qc2!, Be6 16 N4xe5** White snared a pawn.

(See diagram on following page)

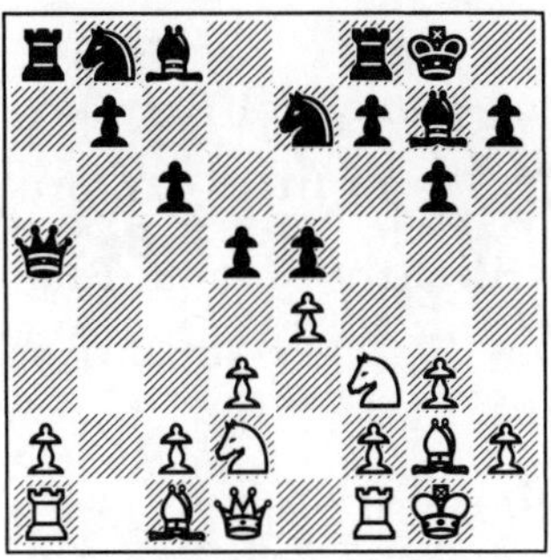

10 a4

Helping to secure **c4** as an outpost for a Knight. Also good is the immediate **10 Bb2.**

10...	**Qc7**
11 Bb2	**d4**
12 c3	**dc**

On **12...c5 13 cd, cd 14 Nc4, Nbc6 15 Ba3** White has strong pressure. Now, after **12...dc** the game **Gufeld-Sivohin, USSR 1973,** continued **13 Bxc3, Rd8 14 Nc4** with advantage for White.

IVe

(1 e4, c6 2 d3, d5 3 Nd2)

3...	**e5**

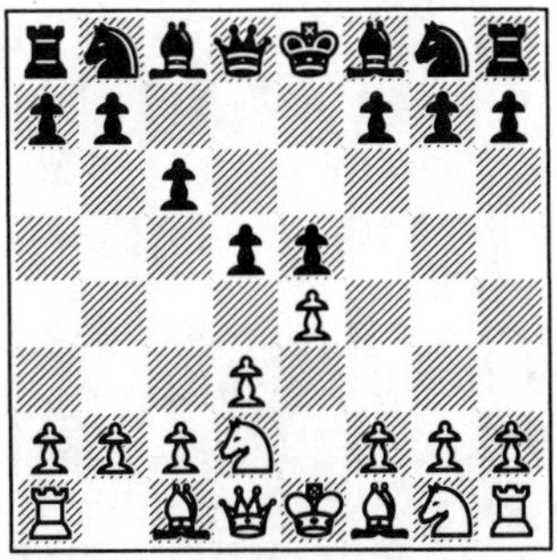

Black opts for a classical pawn center. However, since White's King's Indian formation is "made to order" against big pawn centers, White should feel comfortable.

4 Ngf3 Bd6

In the famous game **Tal-Smyslov, Candidates 1959,** Black played **4...Nd7** to which White replied **5 d4!?**. After **5...de 6 Nxe4, ed 7 Qxd4, Ngf6 8 Bg5, Be7 9 0-0-0** White went on to win brilliantly-though Black could have defended better. Hence, on **4...Nd7** the usual **5 g3** should give White a small plus.

5 g3 Ne7

Black has played the more natural move **5...Nf6.** There followed **6 Bg2, 0-0 7 0-0, Re8 8 h3.**

Here we examine **8...a5** and **8...Nbd7.**

(1) **8...a5** 9 Re1, Na6, 10 d4, de 11 Nxe5 with a positional plus for White. (**Sax-Martin, Hastings 1983-84**).

(2) **8...Nbd7** 9 Re1, Nf8 with two continuations:

(2a) The optimistic 10 d4. Without a lead in development, there is no reason to believe that opening the position will be to White's benefit. **Rohde-Seirawan, American Open Los Angeles 1987**, continued 10...Ne4 (not 10...ed because of 11 e5!) 11 Ne5, Nd2 12 Bd2, f6 13 Ng4, Re1ch 14 Be1, Be6 15 c4? Overplaying his hand. Instead of sacrificing a pawn he never regains, White should think about completing his mobilization with moves such as Qf3, Bd2 and Re1. (John Jacobs).

(2b) More in the spirit of the position would be 10 a4, a5 11 b3 intending 12 Bb2 (John Jacobs).

Instead of **8 h3**, the game **Ljubojevic-Karpov, Buenos Aires 1980**, continued **8 Re1, Nbd7 9 c3, de 10 de, Qc7** equal.

6 Bg2 0-0
7 0-0 f5

Black strives for a Kingside attack, but this is premature. In the game **Bronstein-Bagirov, USSR 1963**, White used the time-honored prescription to counter a premature Black attack. There followed **8 c4!, de 9 de, Na6 10 a3, f4 11 b4, c5 12 b5, Nc7 13 Bb2** with a significant positional plus for White.

CHAPTER FIVE
THE KING'S INDIAN ATTACK
vs THE SICILIAN

In this chapter we examine systems in which Black plays the Sicilian move **c7-c5**. As in the previous chapter, we shall assume White has played **1 e4** followed by transposing into the K.I.A. after **1...c5**.

We examine five lines. In the first four Black fianchettoes his KB, and in the last line (Ve) Black adopts the more restrained Be7.

Va Black plays 1...c5 and 2...e6 (with Bg7)
Vb Black plays e6 and d5 (Nge7)
Vc Black plays e5 and d6 (Nge7)
Vd Black plays d6 and Ngf6
Ve Black plays e6 and d6 (no fianchettoed KB)

Va

(1 e4, c5 2 Nf3, e6 3 d3, Nc6 4 g3, g6)

5 Bg2

In the game **Tal-Filipowitz, Halle 1974,** White played the sharp, unusual **5 d4!?**, trying to open the position in the center to pressure the dark squares--especially **d6**. There followed **5...cd 6 Nxd4, a6 7 Nc3** (also good is 7 Nxc6, bxc6 8 Bg2, Bg7 9 0-0, Ne7 10 Nc3, d5 11 Na4 [pressing against the weakened c5 and preparing a timely blow against Black's center with c2-c4] 11...0-0 12 Re1 with a slight plus for White, **Vasiukov-Tal, USSR 1974) 7...Bg7 8 Be3, Nge7 9 Bg2, 0-0 10 0-0, d6 11 h3, Qc7 12 Qd2, b5 13 Rad1, Rd8 14 f4, Nxd4 15 Bxd4, Bxd4 16 Qxd4, Qa7 17 Rf2, Qxd4 18 Rxd4** with a clearly better ending for White; Black's d-pawn will be a constant problem.

5...	**Bg7**
6 0-0	**Nge7**
7 c3	

Another way is **7 Re1**. For example, **7 Re1, d6** (also playable is 7...0-0 as the immediate 8 e5 is not as good as it looks. The game **Ivkov-Ree, Nice Olympiad 1974**, continued 8...b6 9 Nbd2, d6 [Black must dissolve White's e5 pawn before it can be consolidated] 10 ed, Qxd6 11 Nc4, Qd8 12 a4, Ba6 13 Nfe5, Rc8 14 h4, h6 15 Bf4, Nxe5 16 Nxe5, Nd5 17 Bd2, Qc7 18 Qe2, Bb7 with about even chances) **8 c3, 0-0 9 Na3**

The immediate 9 d4 is premature in view of 9...cd 10 cd, Qb6! (In the game **Fischer-Panno, Buenos Aires 1970,** Black played 10...d5 after which 11 e5, Bd7 12 Nc3, Rc8 13 Bf4, Na5 14 Rc1, b5 15 b3! sealing off c4 from Black's pieces 15...b4 16 Ne2 gives White a very strong attacking setup.) After **10...Qb6! 11 d5** is well answered by **11...Bxb2 12 Bxb2, Qxb2 13 dxc6** (or 13 Nbd2, Na5 14 Qa4, Qb6 15 e5, Nxd5 16 ed, Qd8 17 Ne5, b6 18 d7, Bb7 with advantage for Black) **13...Qxa1 14 Qb3** (Better than 14 cb, Bxb7 15 Qb3 (so far as in **Vasjukov-Kalinicev, USSR 1978** in which Black played 15...Rfc8 with a very murky position. However, GM Robert Huebner gives 15...Bd5! 16 exd5, Rab8 17 Qd3, Nxd5 with a big plus for Black) **14...Nxc6 15 Nc3, Nd4 16 Rxa1, Nxb3 17 axb3, Bd7** with an edge for Black, **Ljubojevic-Huebner, Buenos Aires Olympiad 1978.**

Back to our main note after **9 Na3, 9...e5** (Inferior is 9...Rb8?. The game **Torre-Taimanov, Leningrad Interzonal 1973**, continued 10 d4, cd 11 cd, b5 12 Nc2, Na5 13 Bf4, Bb7 14 b3 with a clear advantage-note the similarity to the Fischer-Panno game mentioned above) **10 Be3, b6 11 d4, ed 12 cd, Bg4 13 Nc2** with roughly even chances.

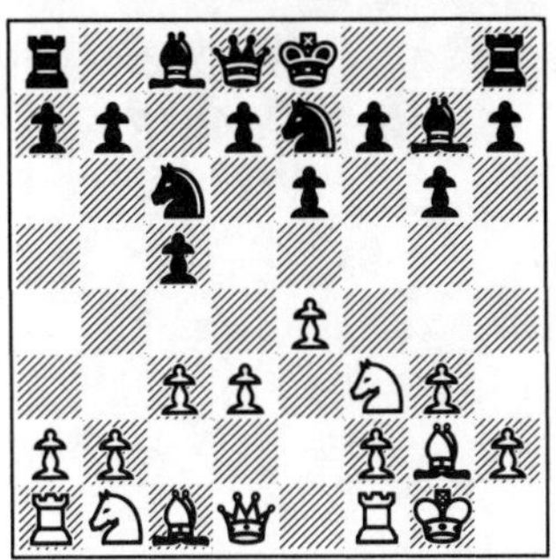

7... e5

Black plays to restrain White's intended central thrust **8 d4**. After the pedestrian **7...0-0 8 d4** is good. For example, **8 d4** (8 Be3 is tempting but not effective--the game **Radulov-Taimanov, Leningrad Interzonal 1973**, continued **8...b6 9 d4, cd 10 Nxd4** (More consistent is 10 cd) **10...Bb7 11 Nxc6, Bxc6 12 Qd6, Nc8 13 Qd2, Qc7 14 Na3, Qb7 15 Rfe1, b5!** with excellent play for Black) **8...cd** (After 8...d6 White can immediately force a favorable position with **9 dc, dc 10 Qe2, b6 11 e5, a5 12 Re1, Ba6 13 Qe4**, from the game **Fischer-Durao, Havana 1966**, see Illustrative Game #7. 9 cd, d5 (Worth consideration is 9...Qb6!?) **10 e5, f6** (after 10...Nf5 11 Nc3, f6 12 Re1, fe 13 de, Bd7 14 Bf4, h6 15 h4, Be8 16 Qd2 White has a strong positional grip. **Ljubojevis-Timman, Hilversum 1973**) **11 Re1, fe 12 de, Bd7 13 Nc3** White is better, **Ljubojevic-Tatai, Manila 1973**. If Black plays **7...d5** play will transpose into Vb. For another example of this type of position see Illustrative Game #9.

8 a3

White attempts to gain Queenside space with b4.

8... a5

9 a4

Preventing the cramping **a5-a4** as well as securing control of **c4** for a Knight outpost, since now neither Black's b or d-pawn can advance to control **c4**.

9... 0-0

10 Na3 d6

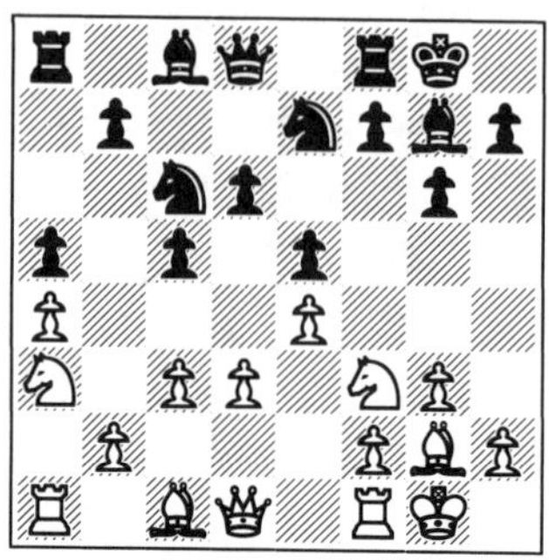

11 Nb5

White also has **b5** available for infiltration.

11... h6

Preparing **Be6** without having to be concerned by **Ng5.**

12 Nd2 Be6

So far as in the game **Hort-Knaak, Halle 1978,** which continued **13 Nc4, Nc8 14 b3, N6a7** with a slight advantage for White.

Vb

(1 e4, c5 2 Nf3, e6 3 d3, Nc6 4 g3, g6 5 Bg2, Bg7 6 0-0, Nge7 7 Nbd2, d5)

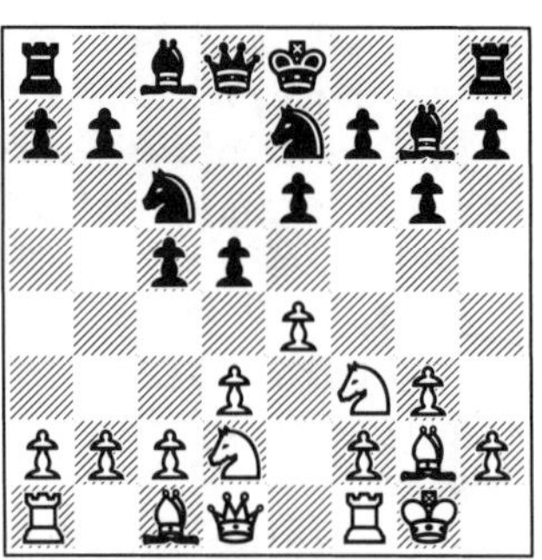

In this variation Black strives to maintain a central pawn on **d5** while completing development. A slight drawback of this line as opposed to those with a pawn on **d6** (or d7--ready to play d6) is the weakening of Black's control of **e5**. As a result, White is often able to play the e-pawn from **e4** to **e5** with good preconditions for pressure in the center and Kingside.

8 ed!

A new move here. After the older **8 Re1** Black can play **8...b6** with reasonable chances for equality. For example, **8 Re1, b6** now:

a) 9 a3, h6 10 Rb1, a5 11 h4, a4 12 ed, ed 13 Nf1, 0-0 14 Bf4, Ra7 15 c3 with equal chances, **Ljubojevic-Petrosian, Milan 1975.**

b) 9 h4, h6 10 c3 (On 10 Nf1, de equalizes immediately.) 10...a5 11 a4 (On 11 e5, a4 Black has reasonable counterchances) 11...Ra7! 12 Nb3? (Better was 12 e5, Ba6 13 Nf1, b5 with chances for both sides) 12...d4 13 cd (13 e5!?) 13...cd 14 Bd2?! (14 e5!, Ba6! 15 Re4, Rd7 16 Bf4 with unclear play and mutual chances) 14...e5! and Black was clearly better **Ljubojevic-Kasparov, Niksic 1983.** See also Illustrative Game #8.

However, an interesting possibility is the immediate 10 e5 (after 9 h4, h6). In the game **Kindermann-Short, BRD 1987,** there followed **10...Bb7** (Also possible was 10...Qc7 11 Qe2, g5!?--a pawn offer designed to undermine White's e5 outpost--12 hg, hg 13 Nxg5, Qxe5 14 Qxe5 and now 14...Bxe5 gives mutual chances in an unclear position or if 14...Nxe5?!, then 15 Nc4!? seems good for White) **11 Nf1, Qc7 12 Bf4, d4?!** (This is dubious since now e4 is accessible to the White pieces. Thematic is 12...0-0-0 with sharp play) **13 Qe2, 0-0-0 14 N1h2, Kb8 15 Ng4, Nd5 16 Bd2, Rde8 17 a3** (Preparing b4) with better chances for White. For the complete game, see Illustrative game #23.

8... ed

On **8...Nxd5** White plays **9 Nb3**, followed by **c4!** with **d3-d4** coming and a very favorable opening of the position.

9 d4! cd

On **9...Nxd4 10 Nxd4, cxd4 11 Nb3** White is better. To be considered is **9...c4**, though White has the edge here.

10 Nb3

Threatening to simply capture on **d4**, leaving Black burdened with an isolated d-pawn under fire on both the d-file and the long diagonal.

10... Qb6

After **10...Bg4 11 h3, Bxf3 12 Qxf3** White can follow up with **Rfe1, Bf4**, and Rad1 with a "full court press" and fine chances.

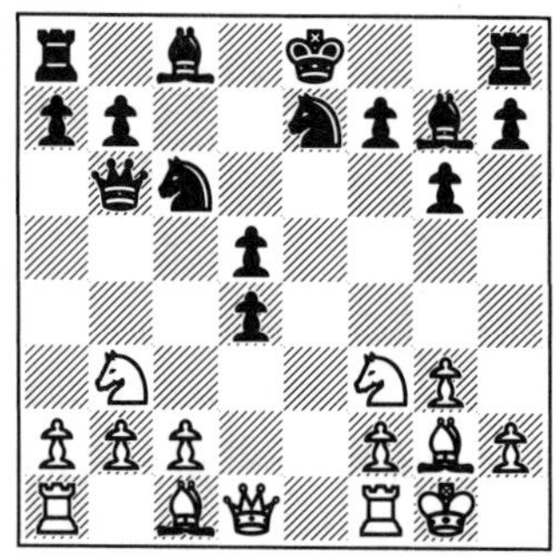

We have been following the game **Dvorecki-Vulfson, USSR 1986**. Now (instead of the actually played 11 Bg5) best is:

11 Bf4!

With the idea of **Bd6-c5** and White will eventually regain the **d4** pawn leaving Black with a weakened d-pawn on **d5**.

See the chapter "Overcoming A Theoretical Obstacle" for the continuation after the weaker **11 Bg5**.

Vc

(1 e4, c5 2 Nf3, Nc6 3 d3, g6 4 g3, Bg7 5 Bg2, e5)

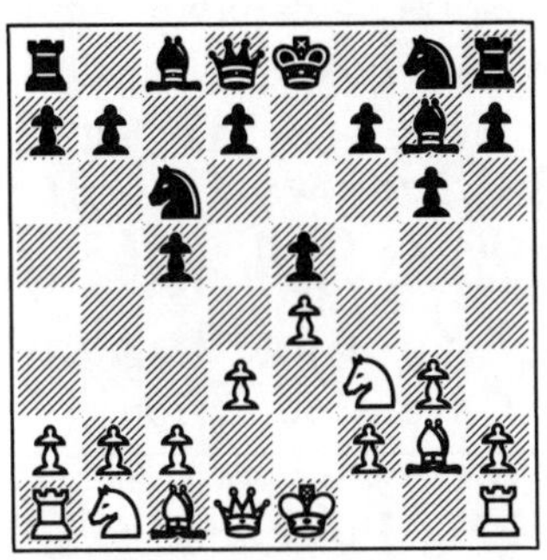

Note that in this variation Black plays **e5** in one move--in Ia Black had played an early **e7-e6** and thus lost a tempo with a later **e6-e5**.

6 0-0 **d6**

7 c3

White controls **d4**, maintaining the options of strategic pawn breaks (b2-b4 and/or d3-d4).

As is often the case, **7 Be3** is insipid. For example, after **7 Be3** the game **Tringov-Benko, Varna Olympiad 1962**, continued **7...Nge7 8 Qd2** (slightly better was 8 c3, trying for d3-d4) **8...0-0 9 Bh6, f5 10 Bxg7, Kxg7 11 Nc3, h6 12 ef, Bxf5 13 Nh4, Be6 14 f4, Qb6 15 fe, Nxe5** with advantage for Black.

7 Nbd2 will usually transpose.

7... **Nge7**

8 Nbd2

Also played is **8 a3** to threaten **b2-b4** with a space gaining operation. For example, the game **Andersson-Gheorghiu, Orense 1975**, continued **8...0-0** (Black avoids 8...a5 so as to not weaken b5 and b6--nonetheless 8...a5 is playable) **9 b4, h6** (Black wants to play Be6 without being concerned over Ng5) **10 Nbd2, Be6 11 Rb1, Qd7 12 Bb2, b5 13 Re1** and now **13...cb 14 ab, a5** gives equality

8... **0-0**

9 a4

to secure **c4** for the Knight. Also there is the possibility of a later **a4-a5** to further cramp Black's Queenside.

9... h6

Again Black wants to play **Be6** without allowing **Ng5.**

10 Nc4 Be6

10...f5 is answered by **11 b4!** as Black can't take twice on **b4** because of the weakness of the **a2-g8** diagonal--**11 b4, cb 12 cb, Nxb4 13 Qb3!.**

11 Nfd2

Unlimbering the KB's diagonal and shifting the Knight toward the Queenside action.

11... d5

Also possible is **11...Qd7** though White has "his" type of position with play similar to our main line.

12 ed Bxd5

In order to trade off White's strong KB.

13 Bxd5 Nxd5

On **13...Qxd5** White has **14 Ne4!** threatening **15 Ne3** and **16 Nxc5** as well as **15 Bxh6!--15...Bxh6 16 Nf6ch.**

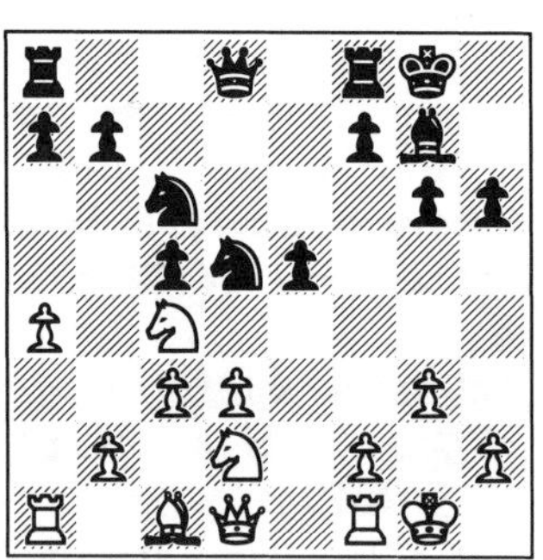

14 a5

So far as in the game **Najdorf-Ivkov, Nice Olympiad 1974**. It continued **14...Qc7 15 Qb3, Rfd8 16 Ne4**, with an edge for White.

Vd

(1 e4, c5 2 Nf3, Nc6 3 d3, g6 4 g3, Bg7 5 Bg2, d6 6 0-0, Nf6)

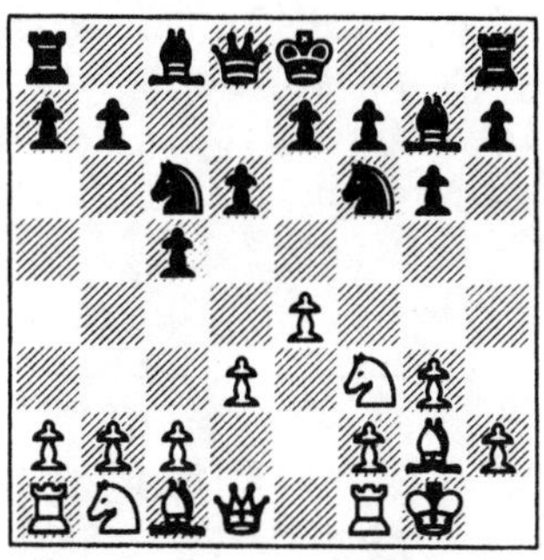

In this line Black avoids placing a pawn in the center to not create a target for a strategic attack. Sometimes Black plays **e7-e5** later in this line if White plays for **d3-d4.**

White has possibilities for play on either flank and/or in the center: on the Queenside with **c3** preparing **b2-b4**, in the center after **c3** followed by **d3-d4**, or on the Kingside via **f2-f4**. A note of caution--if White plays **c3** and then fails to achieve **b2-b4** or **d3-d4**, sometimes Black can as a result create a Queenside initiative with **a6, Rb8**, followed by **b7-b5-b4.**

7 Nbd2

As usual, **7c3** comes into consideration. For example, **7 c3, 0-0 8 Nbd2** (8 Be3 is insipid--e.g. 8...e5 9 h3, h6 10 Nbd2, b6 11 Nc4, Re8 12 Qa4, Qc7 13 b4, Be6 14 Ncd2, Qd7 with equality, **Flesch-Forintos, Budapest 1962**). **8...Bd7** the game **Petrosian-Stahlberg, Zurich 1953**, continued **9 a4, Qc8 10 Nc4, Ng4?! 11 Re1, h6 12 Qe2, Kh7 13 Nfd2, f5 14 f4, fe 15 de, Nf6 16 Nf3** with positional advantage for White. In the game **Bilek-Kavalek, Salgotarjan 1967**, Black tried **8...Bg4** but after **9 h3, Bxf3 10 Qxf3, Nd7 11 Qe2, Rb8 12 f4, Qc7 13 Nf3, b5 14 Be3, b4 15 c4, Nd4 16 Qf2** White had an edge. Probably best for Black is **8...Rb8**. For example, the game **Averbach-Keres USSR Championship 1955**, continued **9 a4, a6 10 Re1** (Interesting but unclear is 10 Qe2, b5 11 ab, ab 12 d4, Nd7 13 Nb3, c4, **Barczay-Forintos, Hungary 1968**) **10...Ng4!** (preventing 11 d4) **11 Nb3** (on 11 h3 Black has the good reply 11...Nge5!) **11...e5!** (Further restraint of d4--now on 12 d4 there follows 12...c4! 13 Nbd2, ed 14 cd, b5 15 ab, ab 16 d5, Nb4 17 Bf1, Qb6! with advantage for Black) **12 h3, Nf6 13 a5, Be6** (Threatening 14...Bxb3 and 15...Nxa5) **14 Nfd2, Ne8** with comfortable equality.

7... 0-0

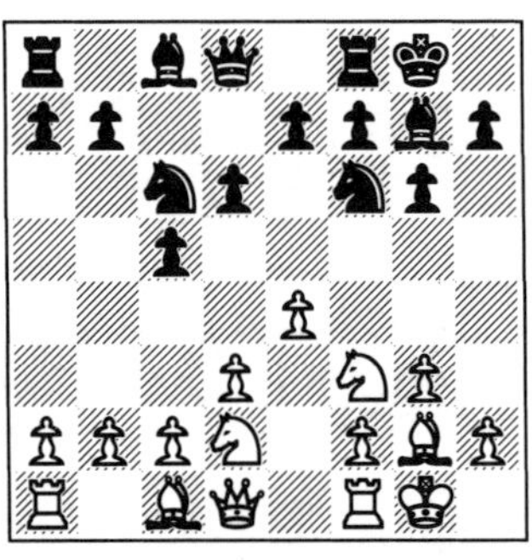

8 Re1

Or **8 a4, Rb8** (8...Bd7 is an alternative with similar play) **9 Nc4, b6** (In the game **Smyslov-Ivkov, Palma de Mallorca Interzonal 1970**, Black played **9...Nd7** which allowed White to advance favorably with **f2-f4**. The game continued **10 Nh4!, a6 11 f4, b5 12 ab, ab 13 Ne3, Nb6 14 f5, c4 15 Ng4** with a powerful attack for White.) **10 Bd2, Bd7 11 Re1, Qc7 12 Qc1, Rfe8 13 Bf4, Rbd8** so far **Botvinnik-Petrosian, USSR 1966**, and now **14 e5** gives White a slight advantage. This line is similar to our main line. See also Illustrative Game #10.

8... Rb8

Black prepares to advance on the Queenside with **b7-b5** while removing his QR from the potentially dangerous long diagonal. We are following the game **Larsen-Gligorich, Vinkovci 1970.**

9 a4 b6

The straight forward **9...a6** allows a sharp central reaction with **10 e5, e.g., 10...Ne8 11 ed, Nxd6 12 Ng5** (White begins to maneuver against the c5 pawn) **12...Bd7 13 N5e4, Nxe4 14 Nxe4, b6 15 c3** with an edge for White.

10 Nc4 Bb7

11 h4!

Ex-World Champion Tigran Petrosian called this the most strikingly original move of the tournament. Bent Larsen says about this move, "one of the ideas is **11...d5 12 ed, Nxd5 13 h5**, creating some play on the Kingside".

11... Qc7

12 Bd2 Rbd8

Black tries for **d5** but **12...a6** looks more reliable.

13 Qc1 d5

14 Bf4

"Probably correct, and the idea is worth noting: White is trying to create certain threats on the dark squares around the Black King, so the Black Queen is driven to a White square"-Larsen.

14...Qc8

15 ed Nxd5

16 Bh6

Weakening Black's Kingside defenses by trading off the important KB.

16... Rfe8

17 Bxg7 Kxg7

18 h5

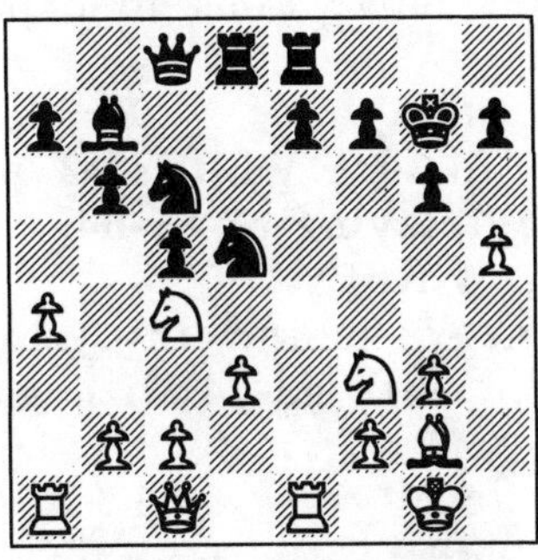

Now after **18...Nf6 19 h6ch, Kg8 20 Qf4** White has the advantage largely because of the **h6** pawn's threatening position as well as the possibility of **a4-a5** with Queenside play. (Larsen mentions that the tempting move 20...Nd4 is strongly answered by 21 Rxe7, Rxe7 22 Qxf6 and mates).

Ve

(1 e4, c5 2 Nf3, e6 3 d3, Nc6 4 g3, d6 5 Bg2, Nf6)

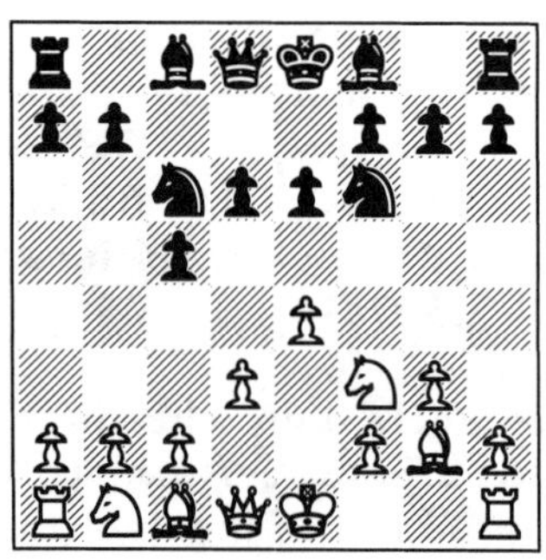

In this line Black adopts a stodgy approach, not occupying the center with a pawn but maintaining a defensive "wall" in the pawns on **e6** and **d6**. The main problem with this line is it's somewhat passive nature.

6 0-0	**Be7**
7 Nbd2	**0-0**
8 c3	

As usual this move aims to expand in the center with **d3-d4**.

8...	**Rb8**

Black hopes to turn White's **c3** pawn into a target for counteraction by playing **b7-b5-b4**.

9 Ne1!

White's strategy behind this move is to advance with **f2-f4** combined with **g3-g4** with pressure in the center and Kingside.

9...	**b5**
10 f4	**d5**

Black hopes to strike back in the center, but White is ready for this.

11 g4!

Driving the **Nf6** away from its natural defensive post.

11...	**de**
12 g5!	**Nd5**
13 Nxe4	

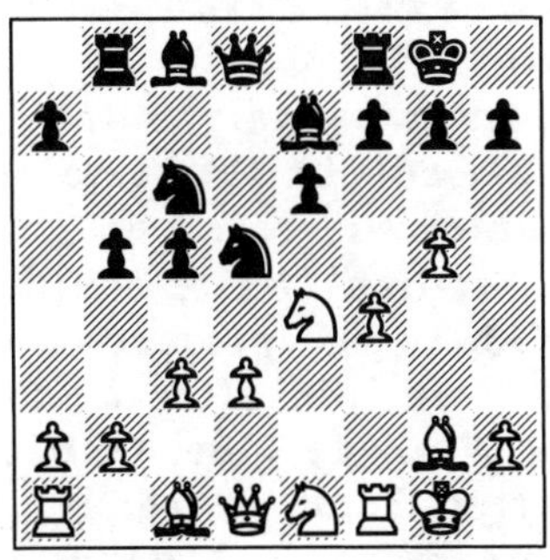

13...	**g6**

Black wishes to bring his QB into play, but the immediate **13...Bb7** allows the powerful shot **14 f5!** and if **14...ef**, then **15 Rxf5** threatening **16 Rxd5** and **17 Nf6ch**. We have been following the game **Evans-Reshevsky, U.S. Championship 1966 /67**. After the further moves **14 Qf3, Bb7 15 Qf2, c4 16 d4** White's strong grip on **e5** plus the cramping effect of the **g5** pawn give him a plus.

CHAPTER SIX
THE KING'S INDIAN ATTACK
vs THE FRENCH

In this chapter we analyze the K.I.A. versus the French Defense (1 e4, e6). In this case the correct second move for White to enter the K.I.A. is **2 d3**; in some previous lines (K.I.A. vs. Sicilian) White could enter our desired formation with **2 Nf3**. In the present case, though, after **1 e4, e6 2 Nf3** would be insipid after **2...d5** leaving White in a slight quandary as **3 d3, de 4 de, Qxd1ch** leads to a very drawish ending. After **2...d5 3 e5** is premature. Hence White's most accurate move is **2 d3** and if **2...d5**, then **3 Nd2**. Our basic position occurs after the moves **1 e4, e6 2 d3, d5 3 Nd2, c5 4 Ngf3, Nc6 5 g3, Nf6 6 Bg2, Be7** (V1a).

Another important system of defense arises after **1 e4, e6 2 d3, d5 3 Nd2, c5 4 Ngf3, Nc6 5 g3, Bd6 6 Bg2, Nge7**. We examine this line at the end of this chapter (V1b).

V1a

(1 e4, e6 2 d3, d5 3 Nd2, c5 4 Ngf3, Nc6 5 g3, Nf6 6 Bg2, Be7)

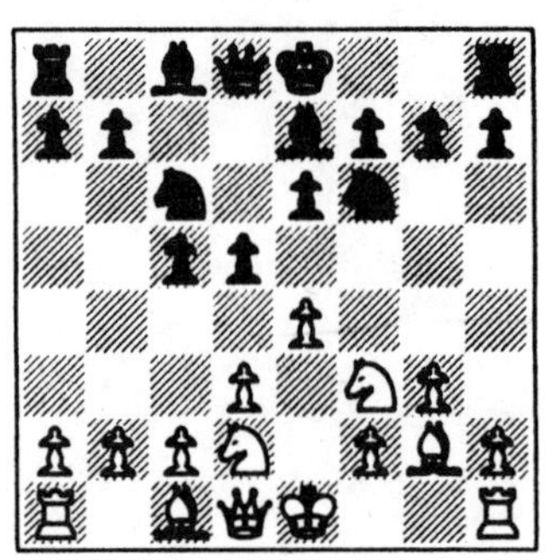

7 0-0 0-0

Black normally throws his Queenside pawns forward (b5-a5) to counterattack on the Queenside while trying to fend off White's usual Kingside buildup. However, an immediate **7...b5** is premature. The game **Schoneberg-Zinn, Germany 1972**, continued **8 ed!, ed 9 c4, bc 10 dc, 0-0 11 b3, Bf5 12 cd, Nxd5 13 Bb2** with clear advantage for White.

8 Re1

Also quite feasible is the immediate **8 e5** which will usually transpose into our main line after **8...Nd7**. In the game **Evans-Bisquier, U.S. 1954-55**, Black tried **8...Ng4** after which GM Larry Evans recommends **9 Re1** (instead of 9 Qe2 as actually played) and if **9...f6** then **10 ef, Bxf6 11 Nf1** with a slight advantage for White.

Now there are two lines.

V1a1 8...Qc7
V1a2 8...b5

V1a1

(1 e4, e6 2 d3, d5 3 Nd2, c5 4 Ngf3, Nc6 5 g3, Nf6 6 Bg2, Be7 7 0-0, 0-0 8 Re1)

8... Qc7

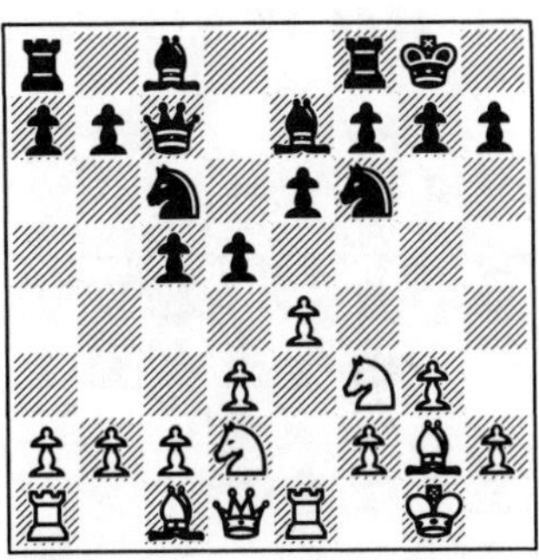

This is the older move here; now it is considered clearly better for White as often Black's **Qc7** is exposed to tactical problems.

9 e5

This thrust is the cornerstone of White's strategy. The **e5** pawn exerts a cramp on Black's center and Kingside. White's QB will usually go to **f4** or **g5**, depending on circumstances. White's QN typically maneuvers toward the Kingside via **Nbd2-f1** after which it can strike the center with **Nf1e3** or, following a later **h2-h4, Nf1-h2-g4**. Another vital link in White's Kingside plans is the advance of the h-pawn--**h4-h5-h6** to force a breach in the dark squares surrounding Black's King. If Black chooses to prevent **h5-h6** with **...h6**, then White can often sacrifice a piece on **h6** to obtain a strong attack.

Black can try to oust White's **e5** pawn by **f7-f6**, but after **e5**, the Black e-pawn become backward on the open e-file. Also characteristic of Black's strategy is the "mirror image" pawn advance **a5-a4-a3** to punch holes in White's Queenside pawn structure. However, White can block Black's **a4-a3** with **a2-a3** as Black has no dangerous sacrifice on **a3** since White's King is on the other flank.

Sharp play normally results as both sides struggle to strike first. However, in practice White usually comes first.

9... Nd7

9...Ne8 is possible but more passive. White would simply continue with his basic strategy.

10 Qe2 b5

Black's key strategical advance. Inferior is **10...Nd4** after which **11 Nxd4, cxd4 12 Nf3** leaves Black's **d4** pawn weak.

11 Nf1 a5
12 h4

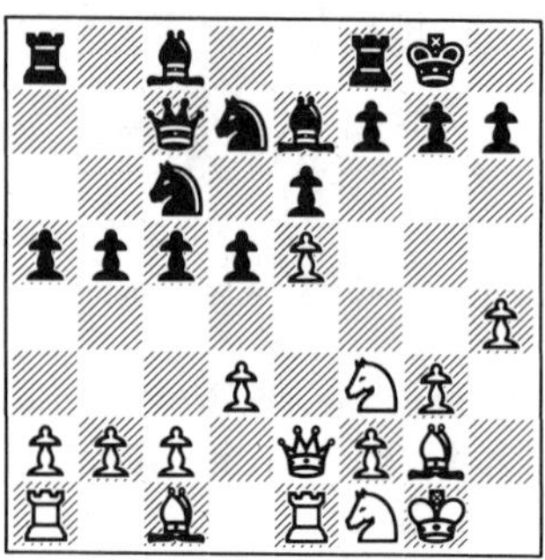

Now Black has two lines here:

V1a11 12...b4

V1a12 12...Nd4

V1a11

(1 e4, e6 2 d3, d5 3 Nd2, c5 4 Ngf3, Nc6 5 g3, Nf6 6 Bg2, Be7 7 0-0, 0-0 8 Re1, Qc7 9 e5, Nd7 10 Qe2, b5 11 Nf1, a5 12 h4)

12... b4

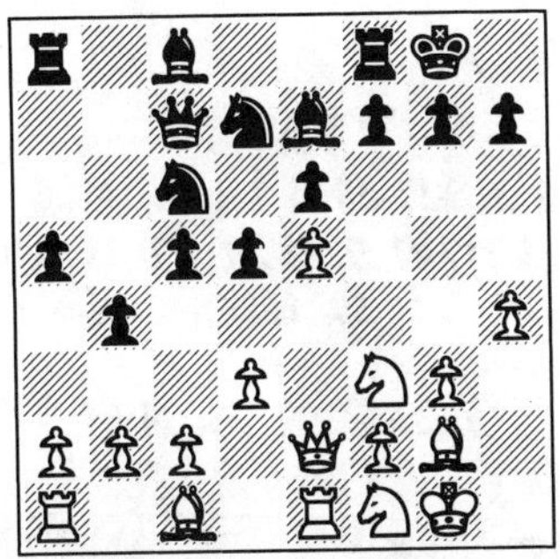

Black consistently advances his pawn to eventually create open lines for counterplay. **12...Ba6** will normally transpose.

13 Bf4

With a eye toward the Queen on **c7**, which will create tactical problems for Black.

13... Ba6

14 Ne3

With the latent threat **Nxd5** followed by **e5-e6.**

14... a4

Black can't play **14...Nd**(or c)xe5 **15 Nxe5, Nxe5 16 Nxd5!, exd5 17 Bxe5, Qc6 18 Bxg7!** winning.

15 b3

Preventing an eventual **b4-b3.**

15... Ra7

16 h5 Rfa8

Slightly better is **16...h6** to prevent **h6**.

17 h6 **g6**

So far as in the game **Vasjukov-Uhlmann, Berlin 1962** which continued with the now thematic sacrifice on **d5 18 Nxd5!** (Possible because of the exposed Queen on c7) and after **18...ed 19 e6, Qd8 20 efch!, Kh8** (after 20...Kxf7 then White wins quickly with 21 Qe6ch, Kf8 22 Ng5!, Bxg5 23 Bxd5!) **21 Ne5, Ncxe5 22 Qxe5ch, Bf6** (On 22...Nxe5 23 Bxe5ch, Bf6 24 Bxf6ch, Qxf6 25 Re8ch and mate) **23 Qe8ch, Nf8 24 Be5, Qb6 25 Bxd5, Rc8 26 Be6, Bxe5** (26...Qxe6 loses to 27 Qxe6, Nxe6 28 Bxf6ch) **27 Bxc8** and White won quickly. For those who think the K.I.A. is "too positional", we offer this game.

V1a12

(1 e4, e6 2 d3, d5 3 Nd2, c5 4 Ngf3, Nc6 5 g3, Nf6 6 Bg2, Be7 7 0-0, 0-0 8 Re1, Qc7 9 e5, Nd7 10 Qe2, b5 11 Nf1, a5 12 h4)

12... **Nd4**

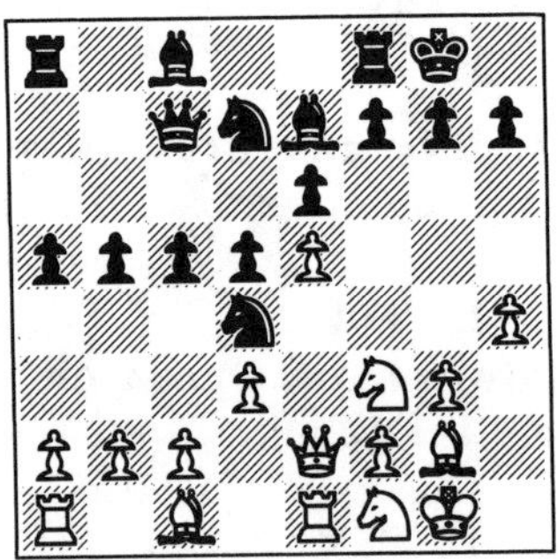

Black forces open the c-file to play against the resulting backward c-pawn.

13 Nxd4

Forced, otherwise White loses his e-pawn.

13... **cxd4**

14 Bf4

Once again this Bishop "looks" at the **Qc7**.

14... Ra6

Intending to pile up his heavy pieces on the c-file.

15 Nh2!

We are following the game **Fischer-U. Geller, Natanya 1968**. Fischer saw that the immediate sac on **d5** leads to nothing at the moment: **15 Bxd5, Bb4!** (getting the Bishop off e7 where it would be vulnerable to capture in some lines) **16 Reb1** (Poor is 16 Rfc1? because of 16...exd5 17 e6, Rxe6 18 Qxe6, Qxf4 19 Qxd7, Qxc1! and Black wins) 16...exd5 17 e6, Bd6 18 exd7, Bxd7 with equal play.)

15... Rc6
16 Rac1 Ba6?

Black had to play **16...Qb6** with only a minute plus for White.

17 Bxd5!

Now the sacrifice is "on" again.

17... exd5

Black had to try **17...Rc5** with some counterplay at the cost of a pawn, **18 Be4, Rc8** (on 18...Nxe5 19 c3! is very strong) **19 Nf3, Rxc2 20 Rxc2, Qxc2 21 Nxd4, Qxe2 22 Nxe2, Nc5**. After **17...exd5** the game continued **18 e6, Qd8** (On 18...Bd6 19 Bxd6, Rxd6 20 exd7, Qxd7 21 Nf3 winning easily) **19 exd7, Re6 20 Qg4** with a winning position for White.

V1a2

(1 e4, e6 2 d3, d5 3 Nd2, c5 4 Ngf3, Nc6 5 g3, Nf6 6 Bg2, Be7 7 0-0, 0-0 8 Re1)

8... b5

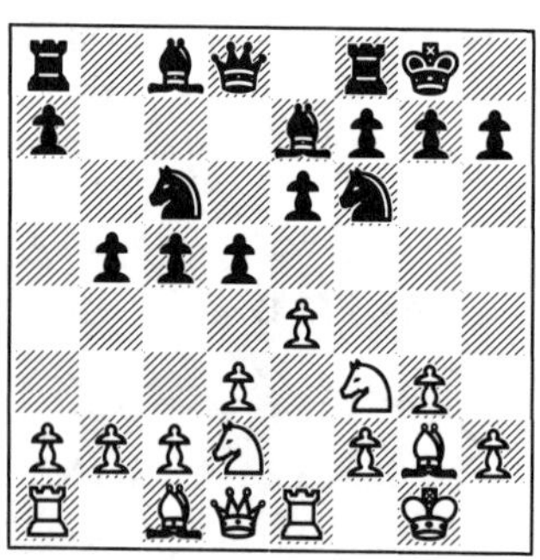

This line is now considered to be Black's best. Also played is the older **8...b6**. For example, the game **Psahis-D. Paunovic, Minsk 1986**, continued **9 a3!?** (to gain space with b4) **9...Qc7 10 c3, Bb7** (Alternative are 10...a5 or 10...0-0-0) **11 e5, Nd7 12 d4** (also feasible is 12 Qe2 followed by Nf1 and Bf4) **12...cd 13 cd, Na5 14 Nf1** (Another idea is 14 Nb1 with the idea of blocking Black's pressure down the c-file with Nc3) **14...Rfc8** with a slight pull for White. For the complete game, See Illustrative Game #25. Also see Illustrative games #12 and #15.

9 e5

White continues his standard strategy. A interesting alternative here is **9 a4!?, bxa4 10 Rxa4, a5** with unclear play, **Ljubojevic-Panno, Manila Interzonal 1976.**

9... Nd7
10 Nf1 a5
11 h4 b4

Both sides pursue their flank attacks consistently; the slightest mistake in these kinds of positions is often fatal.

12 Bf4

Now Black has two choices:

V1a21 12...Ba6
V1a22 12...a4

V1a21

(1 e4, e6 2 d3, d5 3 Nd2, c5 4 Ngf3, Nc6 5 g3, Nf6 6 Bg2, Be7 7 0-0, 0-0 8 Re1, b5 9 e5, Nd7 10 Nf1, a5 11 h4, b4 12 Bf4)

12... Ba6

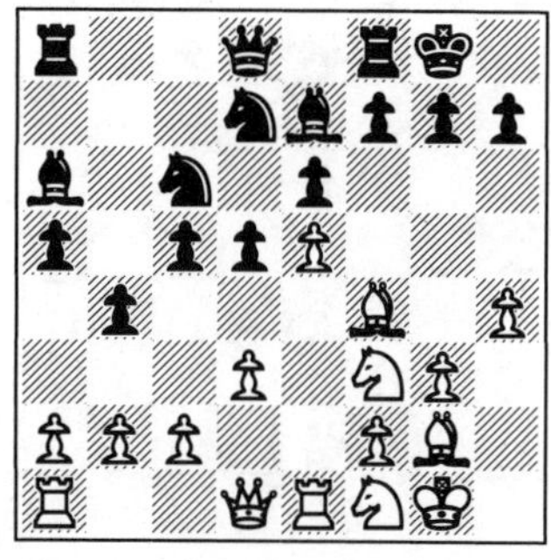

13 Ng5

This aggressive move is the invention of the Soviet GM David Bronstein.

13... Qe8

This is Black's best defense. The main idea is to be able to counter a probable White **Qh5** with **h7-h6** and on **Ng5-f3** then **f7-f5!** blocks the White attack as **e5xf6** e.p. would be answered by **Q(e8)xQh5.**

14 Qg4

As mentioned, **13...Qe8** is mainly aimed at preventing an effective White **Qh5**; if **14 Qh5** then **14...h6 15 Nf3, f5!**. We have been following the game **Bronstein-Uhlmann, Alekhine Memorial 1971**. Unfortunately, at this point Uhlmann made a horrible blunder--**14...a4??** to which White quickly replied **15 Nxe6!** winning easily after **15...fxe6 16 Qxe6ch, Kh8 17 Qxc6.** So Uhlmann had to resign immediately. However, Black's best reply **14...Kh8!** (Preventing Qxe6ch) still leaves White with the better prospects--though there is a game to play.

V1a22

(1 e4, e6 2 d3, d5 3 Nd2, c5 4 Ngf3, Nc6 5 g3, Nf6 6 Bg2, Be7 7 0-0, 0-0 8 Re1, b5 9 e5, Nd7 10 Nf1, a5 11 h4, b4 12 Bf4)

12... a4

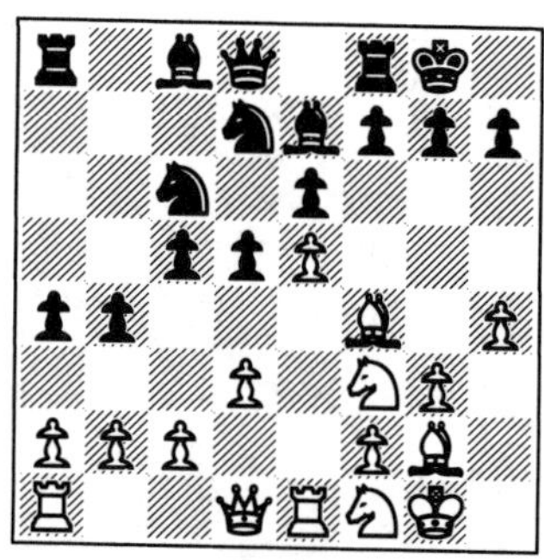

Again Black pursues his basic strategy of advancing on the Queenside.

13 a3!

Fischer's idea, designed to block the positional threat **13...a3** which would force a weakening of the dark squares.

13... ba

14 ba Na5

This decentralizes and is therefore suspect. A better try is **14...Ba6** or even **14...Nd4.**

15 Ne3 Ba6

16 Bh3!

Permanently restraining any attempt by Black to free himself with **f7-f6.**

16... d4

17 Nf1!

Much better than **17 Ng4** which would block the White Queen's access to the Kingside.

17... Nb6

18 Ng5

White begins to probe the Kingside, hoping to force a weakening move to create a target for attack.

18... Nd5

This looks good, but it leads to trouble. A better defensive try is **18...h6 19 Ne4, c4.**

19 Bd2 Bxg5

By giving up his dark squared Bishop, Black loses too much control of the dark squares around his King. However, now **19...h6** loses to **20 Nxe6, fxe6 21 Bxe6ch, Kh8 22 Bxa5, Qxa5 23 Bxd5**--White wins two pawns. **19...c4** was a last try to make a semblance of resistance.

20 Bxg5 Qd7

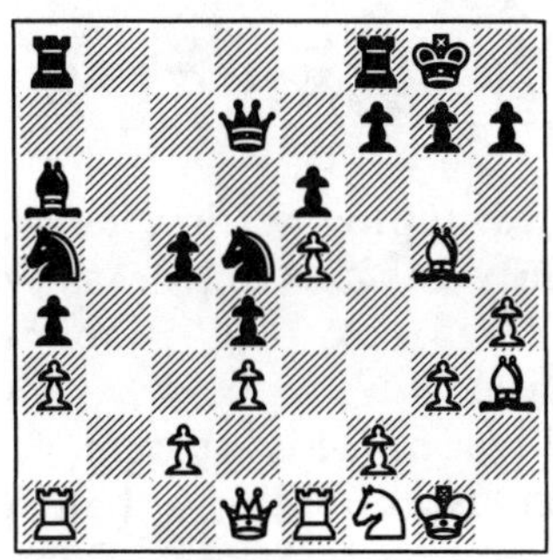

21 Qh5

White's attack is now decisive. There followed **21...Rfc8 22 Nd2, Nc3 23 Bf6!!** (Note this attack on the dark squares is made possible by the absence of Black's KB) **23...Qe8** [If 23...gxf6 White wins with 24 exf6, Kh8 25 Nf3, Nd5 (or 25...Rg8 26 Ne5!) 26 Ng5!, Nxf6 27 Qh6, Qe7 28 Bf5!, Rg8 29 Nxh7] **24 Ne4!, g6 25 Qg5, Nxe4 26 Rxe4, c4** (too late) **27 h5!, cd 28 Rh4!, Ra7** (On 28...dc 29 hg, c1=Qch 30 Rxc1, Rxc1ch 31 Kh2, fxg6 32 Rxh7! crashes through) **29 Bg2!, dc** (After 29...Qf8 White wins with 30 Be4!, dc 31 hg, fg 32 Bxg6!, hxg6 33 Rh8ch, Kf7 34 Rh7ch, Ke8 35 Rxa7) **30 Qh6, Qf8 31 Qxh7ch!** The final blow. Black resigned in view of **31...Kxh7 32 hxg6 d.ch., Kxg6 33**

Be4 is mate. Another testament to the attacking potential of the K.I.A.

V1b

(1 e4, e6 2 d3, d5 3 Nd2, c5 4 Ngf3, Nc6 5 g3)

5...	**Bd6**

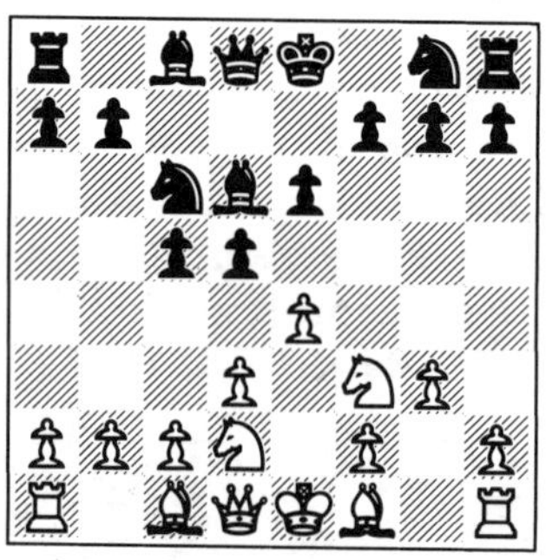

Black plans to deploy with a further **Nge7** (with the Bd6, Ngf6 would only invite trouble as White would sooner or later threaten e4-e5, causing Black to lose at least a tempo to prevent this).

The main idea of this system is to control **e5** to prevent White from establishing a beachhead on **e5** as in several of the previous variations. Towards this end, the development **Nge7** allows Black to control **e5** with a timely **f7-f6.**

It must be noted that this system can also arise after **1 e4, c5** by transposition.

6 Bg2	**Nge7**
7 0-0	**0-0**
8 Re1	**Bc7**

Getting out of the way in case **e4-e5** is played. After **8...Qc7** White does best to play **9 c3** and on **9...Bd7 10 Qe2, f6 11 a3!** (threatening Queenside expansion with b2-b4). Weak is 11 Nf1, d4! 12 Bd2, e5 with an edge for Black, **A. Zaitsev-Gufeld, Moscow 1969**. After 11 a3! the game **Fischer-DiCamillo, New Jersey 1957**, continued 11...Rae8) on **11...a5 12 a4!** secures **b5** (see our main line) **12 b4, b6 13 d4!** with an edge for White.

9 c3 a5

This weakens **b5**, which White will soon use to advantage. Best is **9...b6** with only a very slight pull for White.

10 a4 b6

11 ed ed

After **11...Nxd5** White gains another good square for his pieces on **c4.**

12 Nb1!

A fine strategic retreat--the Knight heads for **b5.**

12... Bg4

Or **12...Bf5 13 Na3, Rc8 14 Nb5, Bb8** with a slight plus for White.

13 Na3

So far as in **Vaganian-A. Sokolov, 7th Matchgame Minsk 1986**, which continued **13...d4?** (better was 13...Rc8!? though White has an edge here too) **14 Nb5, dc 15 bc** with better play for White. See Illustrative Game #13 for the complete game.

CHAPTER SEVEN
VARIOUS DEFENSES

In this final chapter we analyze four remaining defenses-the Symmetrical Defense, the Sokolsky (or Polish) Defense, Queen's Indian Defense, and Euwe's King's Indian Defense System. As the reader will see, in all these defenses we analyze, White will retain the usual K.I.A. positional game with the same strategems we have seen in previous chapters.

We present them in this order:

VIIa Symmetrical Defense
VIIb The Sokolsky (Polish) Defense
VIIc The Queen's Indian Defense
VIId Euwe's K.I. Defense System

VIIa
THE SYMMETRICAL DEFENSE
(1 Nf3, Nf6 2 g3, g6 3 Bg2, Bg7 4 0-0, 0-0 5 d3, d6)

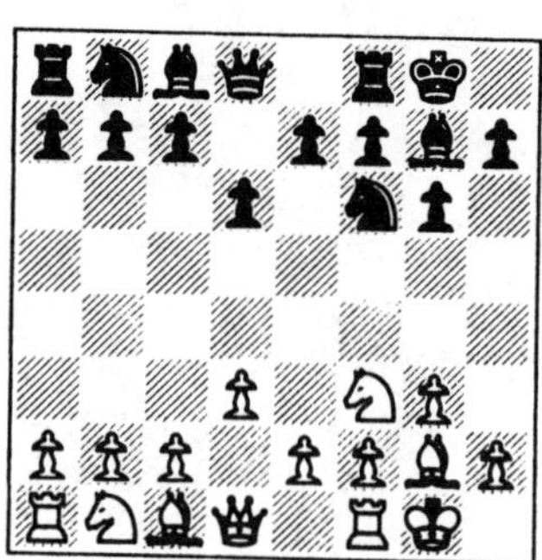

With the Symmetrical Defense, Black poses a critical theoretical challenge to the K.I.A. If Black merely copies White's opening moves, how is White to show any semblance of an edge?

Fortunately, the sterile, "chicken" attitude implied by this defense is reason enough for most players to avoid it. Yet we feel that even if theoretical equality is reached, White's first move tempo is still worth a little something.

6 e4 e5

For **6...c5** see Vd.

7 Nbd2

The logical continuation since the QB has no good square as yet (7 Be3, Ng4).

7... Nbd7

Ditto

8 a4

To secure **c4** for the QN. Weaker is **8 Ne1, Nc5 9 f4, ef 10 gf, Ng4! 11 Ndf3, f5!** with an excellent game for Black, **Fischer-Pavey, New York 1957.**

8... a5

In the game **Fischer-Fauber, Milwaukee 1957** Black decided to break the symmetry with **8...Re8**, but after **9 Nc4, h6 10 Ne1, Nf8 11 f4, d5!? 12 fe, dxc4 13 exf6, Bxf6 14 Bxh6, Bxb2 15 Rb1, Bg7 16 Bxg7, Kxg7 17 Qf3, Qe7 18 d4** White's strong pawn center gives him the advantage.

9 Nc4 Nc5

10 b3

In the game **Filip-Petrosian, Amsterdam 1956**, White played **10 Be3** (This seems a bit artificial as the Bishop might be exposed here) **10...Ne6** (not 10...Be6 11 Ncxe5!) **11 h3** (Larry Evans, in his Book "The Chess Opening for You" criticizes this move stating that 11 Nfd2 is an "obvious improvement". However, after 11...d5!--an improvement found by Senior Master John Hall--Black obtains an edge: 12 Nxe5, d4! 13 Bf4 (forced.) 13...Nxf4 14 gxf4, Nh5 White is in trouble. The lesser evil is 12 ed, Nxd5 though in view of Black's greater central control (a pawn on e5 vs. d3) and the two Bishops [after Nd5xe3] Black has a tiny plus.) **11...b6 12 Qd2, Ba6 13 b3, Nh5** and Black gained the initiative with **f7-f5**. Our main line **10 b3** is derived from Petrosian's play as Black in this game.

10... b6

11 Ba3 **Ba6**

12 Nfd2!

Preparing to break with **f2-f4.**

12... **Nfd7**

13 Rb1

Getting off the **a1-h8** diagonal before playing the f-pawn forward.

13... **Rb8**

14 f4

White is better. If **14...ef**, then **15 Rxf4** and now **15...f5** allows White to isolate the Black f-pawn, while on **14...f5** White plays **15 fe!** with clear advantage.

VIIb

THE SOKOLSKY (Polish) DEFENSE

(1 Nf3, Nf6 2 g3, b5)

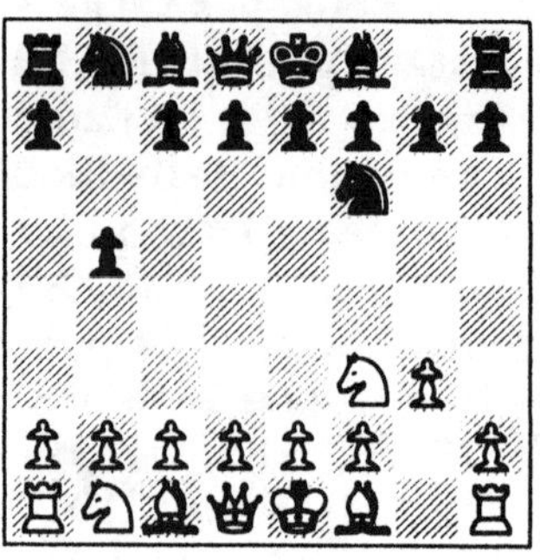

We name this the Sokolsky Defense since Black is playing the Sokolsky Opening (1 b4 or 1 Nf3 and 2 b4) with the Black pieces.

3 Bg2 **Bb7**

4 0-0

Another good line of play is **4 d3, e6 5 0-0, Be7 6 e4, 0-0 7 Nd4!?, a6 8 Nb3, Nc6,** so far as in **I. Bilek-Portisch, Magyarorszag 1985**; now best is **9 d4** followed by **Be3** with an edge for White.

4... **e6**

5 c3!

White begins an early raid on the exposed Black Queenside pawns.

5... **c5**

6 Qb3 **Bc6**

This turns out in White's favor, but the recommended **6...Qb6** still leaves White with the better chances.

7 d3 **d6**

8 Bg5 **Be7**

9 Nfd2!

A fine maneuver; by trading the white-squared Bishops the weakness of Black's Queenside is accentuated.

9... **Bxg2**

10 Kxg2 **a6**

11 Bxf6!

To weaken **d6** for tactical operations. Also the Black KN had more defensive value than the White QB.

11... **Bxf6**

12 a4 **Nd7**

As in the game **Gutman-Y. Gruenfeld, Beer-Sheva 1985**. Now White continued **13 ab, ab 14 Na3** (14 Rxa8, Qxa8ch) **14...b4 15 Nb5!, Rxa1 16 Rxa1** with much the better position. If **16...Qb8** then **17 Ne4!** (17...Qxb5 18 Nxd6ch) threatening at the same time **18 Ra8!** (18...Qxa8 19 Nc7ch).

VIIc

THE QUEEN'S INDIAN DEFENSE

(1 Nf3, Nf6 2 g3, b6 3 Bg2, Bb7)

In this line we look at a setup played by former World Champion Anatoly Karpov. Black intends to fianchetto his QB early to obstruct White's normal **d3** followed by **e4**.

4 0-0 e6

Black's layout most closely resembles the Queen's Indian Defense to the d-pawn opening.

5 d3 d5

Black's idea makes it difficult for White to get in an effective, early **e2-e4**. See Illustrative Games #11 and #12 for further examples.

6 Nfd2!

In the game **Portisch-Karpov, Moscow 1977**, White played schematically with **6 Nbd2** but after **6...Nbd7!** (Better than the routine 6...Be7 which allows White to get in 7 e4! since 7...de 8 de, Nxe4?? is answered by 9 Ne5. The game **Kochiev-Ivanov, USSR Championship 1976** continued with the astonishing blunder 8...Nxe4?? and after 9 Ne5! Black resigned in view of 9...Nd6 10 Bxb7, Nxb7 11 Qf3!.) **7 Re1, Bc5!** (pointing out the weakness of f2) Black had easy equality.

6... Nbd7

Or if **6...c5**, still **7e4** with our "usual" tiny edge.

7 e4 de

8 de Nc5

9 Qe2

White has the edge (Analysis). If **9...Ba6**, then simply **10 Nc4** since the pin is harmless, while on other moves White plays **Rd1, Nc3, Nc4, Bf4** (or Be3 in some cases) with good play.

VIId

EUWE'S K. I. DEFENSE SYSTEM

(1 Nf3, Nf6 2 g3, d5 3 Bg2, g6 4 0-0, Bg7 5 d3, 0-0 6 Nbd2)

d1

6... Nc6

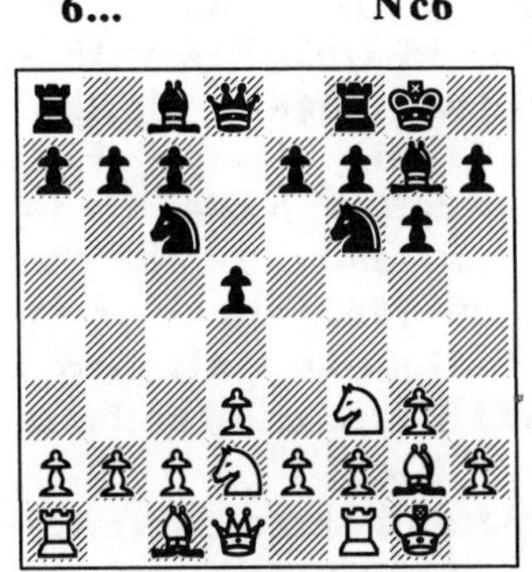

In this system, recommended by Max Euwe, Black places two pawns in the center- but not more-so as to avoid giving White extra pawns to pressure. Nonetheless, White should retain a hair of an advantage due to his first move. For the "modified" Euwe in which Black plays **Nge7** instead of **Ngf6**, see VIId2

7 e4 de

Black exchanges immediately in order to prevent any possibility of White opening the long **h1-a8** diagonal by **exd5**. A good example of what might happen if Black allows **exd5** is furnished by the game **Vasiukov-Alburt, Baku 1972**. (In this game Black played Nge7 (the "modified" Euwe) instead of Ngf6 after the subsequent exd5, N(e or f)xd5 the same position is reached by transposition) White won in 19(!) moves--see Illustrative Game

#21. However despite the result of this game, Black can maintain a reasonable position after 7...e5. For example, **7...e5 8 c3, a5** (necessary to restrain 9 b4) **9 ed, Nxd5 10 a4, h6**. (This is a more solid procedure than occurred in the Vasiukov-Alburt game--the Black QB is best developed on the c8-h3 diagonal) **11 Nc4, Re8 12 Qb3** and now the seemingly active deployment **12...Bf5?** (as in **Polugaevsky-Svesnikov, Sochi 1974**) allows White to simply grab the b-pawn: **13 Qxb7!, Nde7 14 Qb5, Qxd3 15 Re1, Bd7 16 Ncxe5** and White is winning. Best (instead of the weak 12...Bf5?) is 12...Nde7 and after 13 Re1, Be6 (After 13...Nf5 as in the game **Cvetkovic-Svesnikov, Yugoslavia-USSR 1976**, White gained the edge with 14 Be3!, Nd6. [if 14...Nxe3, then 15 Rxe3 followed by Rae1 is strong for White] 15 Nxd6, Qxd6 16 d4!) **14 Qb5, Bd7 15 Qb3, Be6** with approximately equal chances, **Nezmetdinov-Pavlenko, USSR 1965.**

8 de e5

Poor is **8...Nd4?! 9 Nxd4, Qxd4 10 c3** with White gaining an important tempo. In the game **Polugaevsky-Nei, USSR Championship 1963**, Black tried **8...h6**, but after **9 Qe2, Bg4 10 Nb3, Qc8 11 Rd1, Ne5 12 Bf4, Nxf3ch 13 Bxf3, Bxf3 14 Qxf3** White had the better game.

9 c3

Guarding **d4** and threatening to gain space with **b2-b4.**

9... b6

After **9...h6 10 Qc2, Be6 11 Rd1, Qe7 12 b4!** White retains an edge. According to Tigren Petrosian, after **9...Be6** White should play **10 Ng5, Bg4 11 f3, Bc8 12 Re1, a5 13 a4, h6 14 Nh3, Be6 15 Nf2, Nd7 16 Qc2** with the better prospects in a complex maneuvering battle. Finally, after **9...b5?! 10 Qc2, Be6 11 h3, Nd7 12 b3, f6 13 Re1, Qc8 14 Nf1, Nd8 15 Ne3** with the idea of **Nd5**, White is better, **Flesch-Barcza, Salgotarjan 1967**. For **9...Qe7**, see Illustrative Game #20.

10 Re1 a5
11 Qc2 Re8

So far as in the game **Najdorf-Unzicker, Palma de Mallorca 1969**. There followed **12 Nc4, Ba6 13 Bf1, h6 14 a4, Qc8 15 Be3** with the better game for White.

VIId

EUWE'S K.I. DEFENSE SYSTEM (Modified)

(1 Nf3, d5 2 g3, g6 3 Bg2, Bg7 4 0-0, e5 5 d3, Ne7 6 Nbd2, 0-0)

d2

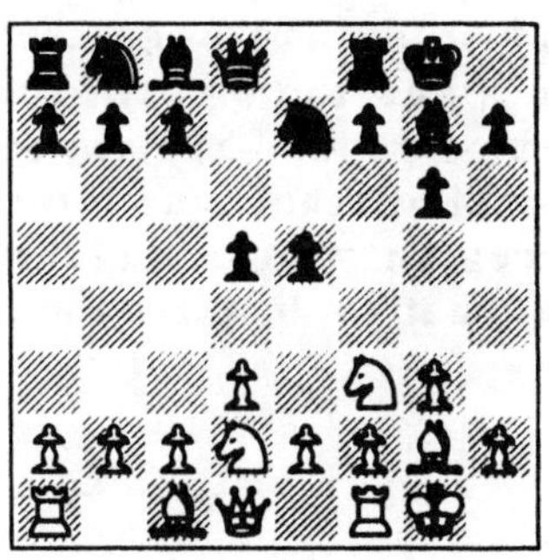

In the "modified" Euwe, Black plays the same move pattern as in d1--except that the KN goes to **e7**. Often this leads to a transposition.

7 e4 **Nbc6**

If **7...d4**, then **8 a4, f6 9 Ne1, Be6 10 f4, Nd7 11 f5!, Bf7 12 fg, hg 13 Bh3** gives White a positional advantage, **Botvinnik-Pachman, Leipzig 1960**. If Black stops for **7...h6** (preparing to play Be6 without worrying about the annoying Ng5) then **8 b4, a5 9 b5** is slightly better for White.

8 c3 **a5**

9 a4 **Re8**

9...h6 10 ed, Nxd5 transposes into d1.

10 Re1 **h6**

11 Qc2

Not **11 Qb3, Be6!** with an edge for Black since **12 Qxb7, Rb8 13 Qa6, Rb6** wins the Queen. After **11 Qc2** play is about even. Note that with **11 ed** (instead of 11 Qc2) play transposes back into d1. Also, see Illustrative Game #16.

ILLUSTRATIVE GAME SECTION

If you could study only one section of this book, these complete games and the ones in the "History" section would do you the most good. They are invaluable in learning the ideas and strategy that must be carried over to the middlegame and even into some endgames. To "know" an opening is to know what to do after the opening is over.

ILLUSTRATIVE GAME #1

LUGANO 1986
White: Korchnoi Black: Flear

1 Nf3 d5

This first move by Black more often than not indicates a classical defense (i.e. no fianchettoe of the KB).

2 g3 Nf6
3 Bg2 c6

The most solid pawn structure against a fianchettoed KB.

4 0-0 Bg4
5 d3 e6
6 Qe1!

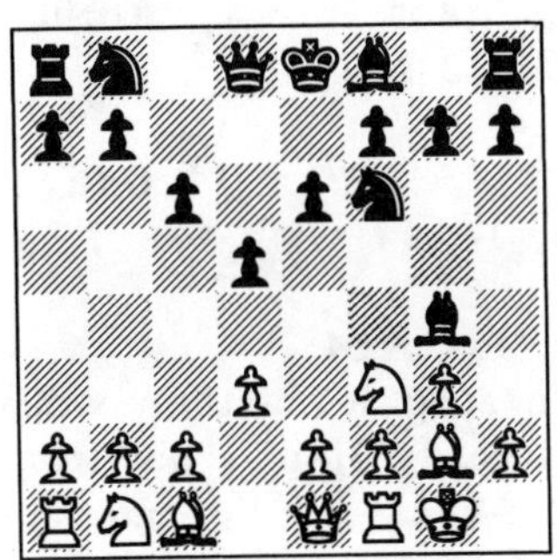

This peculiar looking maneuver is often used in this type of formation to enforce **e2-e4** immediately, while at the same time getting the Queen away from the potential pinning effect of the **Bg4** on the **d1-h5** diagonal.

6... Nbd7
7 e4 de

Usually this exchange is made in order to stabilize the center to prevent White from gaining the initiative there.

8 de e5

Now White can no longer effect the advance **e4-e5**, but this procedure has cost Black a tempo because of the double move of the e-pawn.

9 Nbd2 Bc5

The Bishop is often exposed on this square (b2-b4 or Nb3, later). More solid is **9...Be7**.

10 Nc4 Qe7

11 Ne3 h5?!

This is too optimistic. Best is **11...Bxe3** though after **12 Qxe3** White has an edge due to the Bishop pair. Also, on **11...Be6 12 Nf5** is very strong.

12 a3!

A fine move. White realizes that after **11...h5?!** Black cannot consider castling Kingside. Therefore, Black must try Queenside castling and the text move is designed to begin an advance of the Queenside pawns to attack Black's King when it arrives.

12... 0-0-0

13 b4

Onward!

13... Bd6

Or **13...Bb6, 14 a4** with the follow up **a5** is quite strong for White.

14 Nh4

Virtually forcing a further weakening (14...g6) as otherwise a Knight raids Black's position via **f5**.

14... g6

15 c4 Nh7

Hoping to press on White's slightly weakened Kingside (the "holes" on f3 and h3).

16 h3 Be6

17 Qc3 Kb8

Trying to scurry to a safer square.

18 Rd1 Bc7

19 Bb2

White continues to mobilize his reserves before striking.

19... Ng5

20 Kh2 Nf6

21 Qc2 Bc8

To be considered is simplifying with **21...Rxd1 22 Rxd1, Rd8 23 Rxd8ch, Qxd8** though after **24 c5** White has the better chances.

22 b5

To open lines for attack.

22... Ne6

Perhaps a little better is **22...cb 23 cb, Ne6** though White is slightly better in this case.

23 bc Nd4?!

A dubious attempt to complicate, though **23...bc 24 Rab1, Bb7** is hardly a comfortable situation for Black.

24 Bxd4 ed

25 cb Bxh3!?

The best chance. Black hopes White's **b7** pawn will act as a shield for his King. After **25...dxe3 26 bxc8=Qch, Kxc8 27 f4** White has a crushing position.

26 Nd5!

A nice tactical idea.

26... Nxd5

27 cxd5 Bg4

Avoiding **27...Qxh4 28 Qxc7ch!**.

28 Kg1!

An astute Exchange sacrifice to maintain the initiative.

28... Bxd1?

Black goes for a material advantage, but comes under attack; he had to try **28...g5 29 Nf3, Bxf3 30 Bxf3, g4 31 Bg2, h4** with chances to hold in a complex tactical struggle.

29 Rxd1 Qxa3

30 Nf3

The Knight returns to play with a vengeance--**Nxd4--c6** is threatened.

30... Qc3

Black hopes to defend by exchanging Queens.

31 Qb1

No thanks.

31... Bb6

Trying to stop **Nxd4-c6ch**, but now White's Knight steps in from another direction.

32 Ne5 Rd6

After **32...d3 33 Nc6ch, Kxb7 34 Rxd3, Qc5 35 Qb2!**-defending **f2** and preparing **36 Rc3!**--White has a winning position.

33 Rc1!

Preparing to mobilize his center pawns with **Nc4.**

33... Qa3

34 Nc4 Qc5

Black can only run from pillar to post.

35 e5 Rdd8

This allows a quick finish, but the alternative **34...Rxd5** is little better--simple **35 Nxb6** wins (35...Qxb6 36 Qxb6 and 37 Bxd5).

36 Nd6!

White wins by piling up on **c8.**

36... Qa3

37 Qc2

There is no defense to **38 Qc8!ch**, for example **38...a6 39 Qc8ch!, Rxc8** (or 39...Ka7 40 b8=Q mate) **40 Rxc8ch, Rxc8 41 bxc8=Q ch** and mate next.

Black Resigns.

ILLUSTRATIVE GAME #2

ROSENWALD TOURNAMENT 1966
White: Fischer Black: Seidman

1 Nf3 Nf6
2 g3 c5
3 Bg2 Nc6
4 0-0 e5
5 d3

In his early years of tournament play, Fischer adopted the K.I.A. frequently.

5... d5

By playing a White system a tempo down, Black is taking some risk in return for a double-edge game.

6 e4 Be7

Black achieves nothing with **6...de 7 de, Qxd1 8 Rxd1, Ne4 9 Nxe5!, Nxe5 10 Bxe4** with an edge for White.

7 Nbd2 0-0
8 Re1 de

This exchange is usually a weak idea as it trades the **d5** pawn (in effect) for the **d3** pawn--a clear contradiction of the strategy of establishing the pawn center.

9 de Qc7
10 c3

To guard **d4**. Note Black's **d5** cannot be guarded by his c-pawn.

10... b6
11 Qe2 a5

To play **Ba6**, but the weakening of **b5** and **c4** is a serious problem.

12 a4 Ba6
13 Nc4

Correctly realizing that the pin is not dangerous.

13... b5?

This is definitely weak, leaving both the a and c-pawns isolated.

14 ab Bxb5
15 Bf1

Shifting attention to the weak white squares on the Queenside.

15...	**Rad8**
16 Qc2	**Ng4?!**

A waste of time.

17 h3	**Nf6**

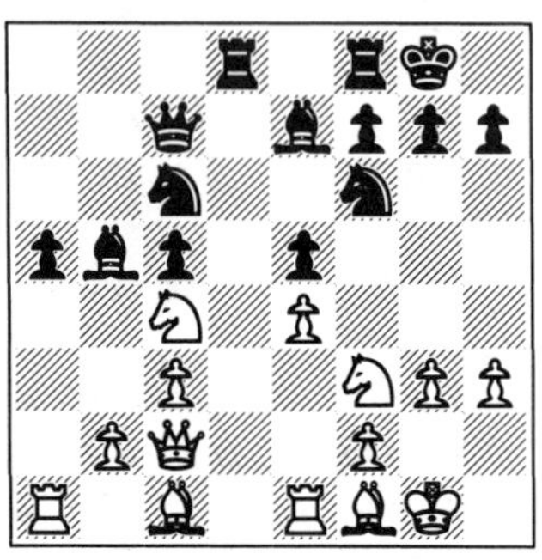

18 Nfd2!

The steeds gallop to the Queenside to attack the weakened pawns there.

18...	**Rfe8**
19 Nb3	**Qc8**
20 Kh2	

By protecting the h-pawn, White now threatens to take the a-pawn.

20...	**Qe6**
21 Nbxa5	

Now its just a matter of technique.

21...	**Nxa5**
22 Nxa5	**Bxf1**
23 Rxf1	**c4**

Another poor move--now the c-pawn will fall too.

24 Qe2	**Rd3**
25 Ra4	**Red8**
26 Nxc4	

Now Black could resign, but he apparently believes in miracles.

26...	**h6**
27 Re1	**Bc5**
28 Kg2	**g5**

Black has every justification to play "all out".

29 Nd2

To allow the QR to mobilize and return to defend the Kingside.

29...	**Qd7**
30 Ra5	**Bb6**
31 Ra6	**Qb7**

Black must play for "cheap shots".

32 Ra1	**Qd7**
33 Nc4	**Bxf2?**

An abortive "combination".

34 Qxf2	**Nh5**

Better to resign.

35 Nxe5	**Qe6**
36 Nxd3	**Rxd3**
37 Re3	

Ending any illusion of attack.

37...	**Rd1?**
38 Qf3	

Winning more material.

38...	**Qb3**
39 Qxh5	

Enough is enough.

Black Resigns

ILLUSTRATIVE GAME #3

HELSINKI 1961
White: Stein Black: Zinn

1 Nf3	**d5**
2 g3	**c5**
3 Bg2	**Nc6**
4 0-0	

Also possible is **4 d4** with transposition into a Reversed Gruenfeld (or Catalan), but this lies beyond the scope of our K.I.A.

4... e5

Black selects an aggressive line, placing many pawns in the center. However this policy has its risks since Black is playing as White does against the K.I. Defense--a tempo down.

5 d3 Be7

Or **5...Nf6** and then **Be7.**

6 Nbd2 Nf6
7 e4 Bg4

This is playable, but rather ineffective. More solid is **7...d4** closing the center.

8 h3

"Putting the question" to the Bishop.

8... Be6

After **8...Bh5** White achieves good play with **9 g4, Bg6 10 Nh4** followed by **Nf5.**

9 Qe2 de

This is strategically weak as now White can play against Blacks vulnerable **d5** square. Necessary was **9...d4** with a reasonable position.

10 de 0-0

The ambitious **10...Nd4** works in White's favor: e.g., **11 Nxd4, cxd4** (after 11...Qxd4 12 c3, Qd7 13 Nc4 White has a nice position) **12 Qb5ch, Qd7 13 Qxe5, Bxh3 14 Nb3** and Black's d-pawn is targeted. Or if **11...exd4**, then **12 f4, 0-0 13 e5, Nd5 14 Ne4** and White's mobile Kingside pawn majority gives White a very strong game.

11 c3

Covering **d4**, just in case. Note that Black's corresponding square, **d5**, is not similarly protected since the Black c-pawn has advanced too far.

11... Nd7

Preventing **Ng5** and hoping to maneuver this Knight into **d3** via **c5-c4** and **Nc5-d3.**

12 Nc4

Meanwhile White directs this Knight toward **d5** (Nc4-e3-d5).

12... b5

13 Ne3 c4

Preparing (14 Nc5, 15 d3)

14 Rd1

Intensifying the pressure against **d5.**

14... Qc7

15 Nd5

White's strategy comes first.

15... Bxd5

This lands Black into serious trouble, but even after the better **15...Qc8** White has the pleasant choice between obtaining the Bishop pair with **16 Nxe7ch** or simply leaving the powerful Knight on **d5.**

16 exd5 Na5

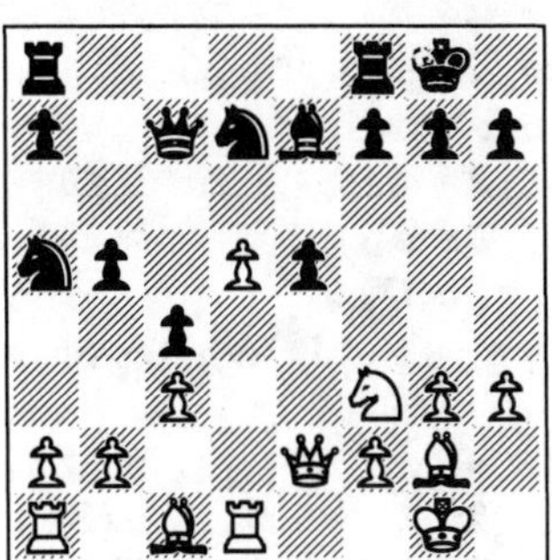

17 Nd4!

A key move which White must have envisioned several moves ago.

17... exd4

On **17...Rab8** White continues with **18 Nf5, Bd6 19 Bh6!** since **19...gxh6** allows **20 Qg4ch** and mate next. If Black defends with **18...Bf6** (instead of 18...Bd6) then **19 d6** is very strong--**19...Qd8 20 Be3, Nb6 21 b4!**, cb e.p. **22 ab, Nxb3 23 Rxa7** and White's position is overwhelming.

18 Qxe7 Rae8

This looks good, but White's reply shatters all illusions.

19 Bf4! Qxf4

After **19...Rxe7 20 Bxc7, Nb7 21 d6** White wins a piece.

20 Qxd7!

Accurate to the end. The straight forward **20 Qxf8ch, Kxf8 21 gxf4**, allows Black to build a strong fortress after **21...d3.**

20... Qf6

21 Rxd4

Now, a pawn up with the better position, White wins handily.

21...Re2

Black must counterattack.

22 Rf4

Immediately quashing the "attack".

22... Qb6

23 b4 Nb7

After **23...cb 24 ab, Nxb3 25 Rxa7** White's heavy pieces over run Black's position.

24 a4 Nd6

25 ab Nxb5

26 Qc6

Being a pawn ahead, White is happy to exchange Queens.

26... Rc2

27 Qxb6 axb6

28 Rxc4 Rxc3

29 Rc6

The most active.

29... f5

After **29...Rxc6 30 dxc6** the advanced c-pawn will decide quickly.

30 Bf1	**Rxc6**
31 dxc6	**Nd6**
32 Rd1	**Nc8**

On **32...Rd8 33 c7!** wins--**33...Rd7 34 c8=Qch, Nxc8 35 Rxd7** or **34 Rxd6.**

33 Bc4ch	**Kh8**
34 c7	

Threatening **35 Rd8.**

34...	**g6**
35 Rd8	**Kg7**
36 Be6	

Decisive. Now after the Knight moves, **c8=Q** wins.

Black Resigns.

ILLUSTRATIVE GAME #4

PIATIGORSKY 1966
White: Petrosian Black: Donner

1 Nf3	**d5**
2 g3	**g6**

Black combines some classical theory a center pawn on d5) and some hypermodern (the fianchettoed KB) hoping for a happy medium.

3 Bg2	**Bg7**
4 0-0	**e5**

With greater ambition, Black adds another pawn to the center. However, this gives White a potential target.

5 d3	**Ne7**
6 Nbd2	**0-0**

Perhaps more accurate is **6...c5** followed by **7...Nbc6.**

7 e4	**c5**

Now Black has played into an old fianchetto system (because the KN is on e7 rather than f6) White used against the King's Indian Defense decades ago.

8 ed

A recurring positional theme in this type of position. White opens the e-file and the long diagonal in order to play against Black's center and Queenside.

8...	**Nxd5**

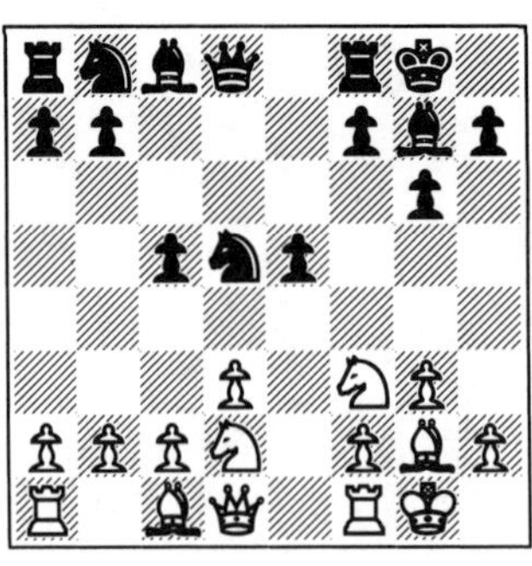

9 Nb3!

White seizes a positional initiative by attacking Black's pawns.

9... Nd7

Not an impressive square for the QN, but **9...b6?** is clearly out because of the pressure on the long diagonal.

10 Re1 Rb8

Getting off the long diagonal and hoping to unravel the Queenside with **b6** and **Bb7.**

11 Nfd2

White persists with "little" threats.

11... Nc7

Somewhat better was **11...Ne7** to protect **c6** (see White's next move).

12 Na5

An astute maneuver, now **12...b6** is not possible because of **13 Nc6.**

12... Ne6

13 N5c4

Threatening to win the two Bishops with **14 Nd6.**

13... Qc7

If **13...b6** then after **14 Nd6, Ba6 15 a4** White still has a positional grip on the Queenside--**15...Qc7 16 Nb5.**

14 Ne4

Again threatening **Nd6.**

14... Nb6

Black tries to rid himself of the marauding White Knights. If **14...b6**, then **15 Ned6, Ba6 16 a4** and **Nb5** again is good for White. After the sharper **14...b5**, there could follow **15 Ncd6, Ba6 16 a4** and if **16...f5 17 ab, fe 18 Rxa6!**. Probably best in this line would be **16...b4** though White would have a slight pull due to the weakness of **c4**

15 Nc3

Threatening **16 Nb5.**

15... Bd7

16 a4

More encroachment with the idea of **Nb5.**

16... Bc6

Possibly better is **16...Rfd8.**

17 Nb5 Bxb5

Forced; after **17...Qd7** White wins a pawn with **18 Nxe5**

18 axb5

Now White has the a-file with a ready-made target on **a7**, not to mention the two Bishops.

18... Nxc4
19 dxc4 b6

In any event, Black is in bad shape, but **19...Qb6** is a little better.

20 c3 Rfe8
21 Ra6

White's plan is simple and decisive: triple heavy pieces on the a-file.

21... Re7
22 Qa4 Rc8

Black hopes to defend the a-pawn in time by **Qb8** and **Rcc7.**

23 Bd5!

Spoiling Black's plan by threatening Bxe6 after which **...Rxe6** allows White to annex the a-pawn while **fxe6** cripples Black's e-pawns.

23... Qb8

Moving the Knight is no help--**23...Nd8 24 Bg5!, Rd7 25 Bc6.**

24 Bxe6 fxe6

Grimly holding the a-pawn, but perhaps the lesser evil was giving up the a-pawn with **24...Rxe6.**

25 Qd1

The Queen returns to the Kingside to probe the weakened pawn structure there.

25... Rd8
26 Qg4 R7e8
27 h4

Probing Black's vulnerable **g6** (h4-h5).

27... Rd7
28 h5 gh
29 Qxh5

Now Black's h-pawn is isolated on the open h-file.

29... Rf8
30 Qg4 Rf6

Better was **30...Rf5** and **h7-h5.**

31 Be3 Rg6
32 Qe4 Bf8
33 R6a1

White regroups his pieces to attack alternately Black's several weak pawns.

33... Bd6
34 Red1 Rgg7
35 Rd2 Bf8

Black must challenge the d-file.

36 Rxd7 Rxd7
37 Qg4ch Kf7
38 Qh3 Kf6

Awkward but forced to hold the h-pawn.

39 Rf1

More straightforward was **39 Qh5** with the idea of **40 Bg5ch** and **Bh6**, but the move played is also sufficient.

39... Qe8
40 Qh4ch Kg7
41 Bh6ch

Trading Bishops will leave the **e5** pawn defenseless.

41... Kg8
42 Bxf8 Kxf8

After **42...Qxf8 43 Qg4ch, Kf7 44 Qh5ch, Kf6 45 Re1** White wins.

43 Re1

Now the **e5** pawn falls.

43... Qf7
44 Rxe5 Qg6
45 Kg2

Stopping any annoying checks.

45... Qf7
46 Re4

White will win easily by combining threats to the King with pressure on the weak pawns.

46... Ke8
47 Rf4 Qe7
48 Qh5ch Kd8
49 Qe5

Threatening **50 Qb8** mate.

49... Kc8
50 Qe4

Threatening **51 Qa8ch, Kc7 52 Qxa7ch.**

50... Kb8
51 Rh4

Threatening **52 Rh6, e5 53 Rh5** winning the e-pawn.

51... Qf7
52 Rf4

Now **52 Rh6** is met by **52...Re7.**

52... Qe7
53 Qf3 Qd6
54 Rf8ch Rd8

On **54...Kc7 55 Qa8** wins.

55 Rf6

Now on **55...Rd7** there would follow **56 Qe4, Re7 57 Rf8ch, Kc7 58 Qa8.**

Black Resigns.

ILLUSTRATIVE GAME #5

SIEGEN 1970
White: Fischer Black: Ibrahimoglu

1 e4 c6
2 d3

Fischer has from time to time resorted to the K.I.A. as an alternative to more bookish main lines.

2... d5
3 Nd2

Necessary to avoid a very drawish Queen trade--e.g., **3 Nf3(?), de 4 de, Qxd1ch 5 Kxd1.**

3... g6

3...e5 can transpose into IVe.

4 Ngf3 Bg7
5 g3 Nf6

More effective is **5...e5** transposing into IVd.

6 Bg2 0-0
7 0-0 Bg4

This foray only leads to the surrender of the Bishop pair or a loss of time.

8 h3 Bxf3

Black hopes the simplifying exchange will offset the two Bishops.

9 Qxf3 Nbd7
10 Qe2

Threatening **11 e5** and **12 e6**, with a favorable opening of play on the e-file.

10... de
11 de Qc7
12 a4

Gaining Queenside space in preparation for a buildup of piece pressure against Black's Queenside.

12... Rad8
13 Nb3 b6

Anticipating the attack on his a-pawn (Be3). However, now White has a target for opening the a-file with **a5** and **axb6**.

14 Be3 c5

Restricting the White Knight and QB, but the pawn chain thereby created will soon come under pressure.

15 a5 e5

Probably fearing **f4** and **e5**, but now **d5** is permanently weakened.

16 Nd2 Ne8

To try to defend the beleaguered Queenside.

17 ab ab

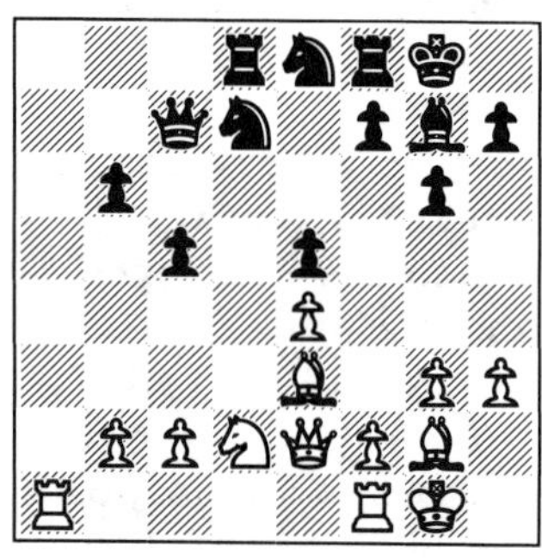

18 Nb1!

A strategic retreat--the Knight heads for the weak White squares.

18... Qb7

Hoping to be able to trade off the heavy pieces to reduce the value of the a-file.

19 Nc3 Nc7
20 Nb5 Qc6
21 Nxc7 Qxc7
22 Qb5

True, Black has achieved some trades, but the Queen is now very well placed in front of the weak b-pawn.

22... Ra8
23 c3 Rxa1
24 Rxa1 Rb8

Perhaps in hope of more simplification by **Rb7-a7.**

25 Ra6 Bf8

To bring the Bishop toward the Queenside.

26 Bf1

Ditto.

26... Kg7

27 Qa4

White continues to make progress. Now the a-file is "his".

27... Rb7

28 Bb5

With the simple threat **29 Bxd7, Qxd7 30 Qxd7, Rxd7 31 Rxb6.**

28... Nb8

29 Ra8

It's clear Black is in a real bind now.

29... Bd6

30 Qd1

The Queen redeploys to attack the Kingside and center while Black's pieces are tied down on the Queenside. This strategem was a favorite technique of Alekhine and Nimzovitch.

30... Nc6

31 Qd2

Threatening to "smoke" the King out with **32 Bh6ch** forcing **32...Kf6.**

31... h5

32 Bh6ch Kh7

33 Bg5

Threat: **34 Bf6** with crushing threats.

33... Rb8

Desperately trying to trade the dangerous Rook.

34 Rxb8 Nxb8

35 Bf6!

This is still powerful even with the Rook off.

35... Nc6

On **35...Nd7** White wins a pawn with **36 Bxd7, Qxd7 37 Bxe5.**

36 Qd5 Na7

On **36...Nd8** White wins with **37 Bxd8, Qxd8 38 Qxf7ch,** etc.

37 Be8!

A winner.

37... Kg8

There was no good defense.

38 Bxf7ch **Qxf7**
39 Qxd6

Black Resigns.

ILLUSTRATIVE GAME #6

USSR 1986
White: Azmajparasvili Black: Neverov

1 g3

In the main text of this book we analyze variations beginning with **1 Nf3** or **1 e4**, followed by our K.I.A. pattern. With **1 g3** White shows still another good way to transpose into the K.I.A. The only drawback to **1 g3** (and 1 e4 as well) is that Black can immediately play **1...e5.**

1... d5

Black intends to build a classical pawn center.

2 Bg2 Nf6
3 d3 c6

To barricade the **h1-a8** diagonal. The antithesis of this strategem would be the more aggressive **3...c5** gaining more central space (control of d4), but at the cost of loosening the long diagonal.

4 Nd2 e5

Black finally decides to accept the "invitation" to occupy **e5.**

5 e4

After the routine **5 Ngf3?** Black can play **5...e4 6 de, de 7 Ng5, e3! 8 fe, Ng4 9 Nde4, Qxd1ch 10 Kxd1, h6! 11 h3, hxg5 12 hxg4, Rxh1ch 13 Bxh1, Be7** with an edge for Black despite the extra White pawn since White's Kingside pawn structure is devastated.

5... Bc5

An aggressive looking post for the KB; however sometimes the **Bc5** is exposed to an eventual **b2-b4** or **Nb3.**

6 Ngf3 de

Forestalling any opening of the e-file via **exd5.**

7 de Bg4
8 0-0

This is O.K., but most accurate is **8 h3!** and if **8...Bxf3** then **8 Qxf3** with an edge for White (the two Bishops).

8... Nbd7

9 Nc4 **0-0**

Not **9...Nxe4? 10 Ncxe5, Nxe5 11 Qxd8ch, Rxd8 12 Nxe5** with advantage for White.

10 h3 **Bh5**

Better than giving up the two Bishops with **10...Bxf3 11 Qxf3.**

11 Qd3

The sharp variation **11 g4?** winds up in Black's favor after **11...Bg6 12 Nfxe5, Nxe5 13 Nxe5, Bxe4 14 Qxd8, Raxd8 15 Bxe4, Nxe4.**

11... **Qc7**

12 Bg5 **Rfe8**

Not best. After the accurate move **12...h6!** Black has equality--**13 Bxf6, Bxf3!** (not 13...Nxf6 14 Ncxe5) **14 Bxf3.**

13 a4

Staking out Queenside territory and discouraging **b7-b5**, which would allow White to open the a-file favorably.

13... **h6**

14 Bd2

Having provoked a slight Kingside weakness, the Bishop drops back.

14... **Rad8**

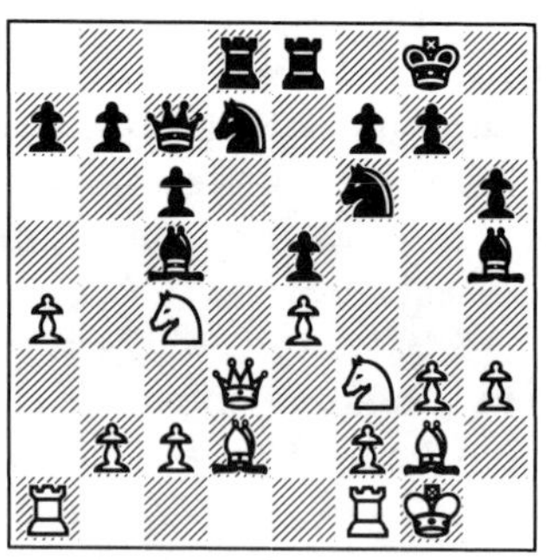

15 Qe2!

Expansion with **15 b4** while strategically desirable, is premature here: **15...Nb6! 16 bxc5, Nxc4!** (not 16...Rxd3 17 cxb6!) **17 Qxc4, Bxf3 18 Bc3, Bxg2** with an equal position.

15... **b5**

16 Ba5

Stronger than **16 ab.**

16...Nb6

On **16...Bb6** White plays **17 ab, cb 18 Nxb6, axb6 19 Bc3** with a clear positional advantage.

17 Ncd2 **b4**

White threatened **18 b4!.**

18 c3 **bc**

19 Bxc3

White must keep the c-file open to pressure Black's weak c-pawn.

19... **Bd4**

20 a5?

A serious inaccuracy. Correct was **20 Rfc1!** with a clear positional advantage.

20... **Nbd5!**

A fine resource which White obviously overlooked.

21 Bxd4

On **21 exd5, e4 22 Bxd4, exf3 23 Qc4, fxg2 24 Rfc1, Qd7 25 Kxg2, cxd5** with equality. Also, if **21 Qc4** then **21...Bxc3 22 bxc3, Ne7** gives full equality as the Black c-pawn is shielded from frontal attack.

21... **exd4**

22 Rfc1

After **22 Qc4** Black can play **22...Ne3!** gaining several pawns and attacking chances after **23 fxe3, dxe3.**

22... **Qb8**

The best line counterattacking along the b-file.

23 Qc4 **Bxf3**

24 Bxf3 **Nb4!**

Black is ready for **25 Ra4, c5! 26 Qxc5?, Rc8!** winning.

25 Qb3 **Re5**

26 Nc4 **Rb5**

27 e5 **Nd7!**

A dynamic conception. Black sacrifices the Exchange for good counterplay.

28 Nd6 **Nxe5**

29 Nxb5 **Qxb5**

30 Bg2 **d3**

31 Rc3 c5

32 Qd1!

A good maneuver to activate the Queen.

32... Rd4?!

Black falters in time pressure. Correct was **32...g6** preventing **Qh5**, with reasonable counterchances.

33 Qh5!

Now White seizes the initiative.

33... Nc2

34 Qxe5!

Returning the Exchange to maintain the attack.

34... Nxa1

35 Rxc5 Qd7

36 Bd5 Nc2

Bringing the Knight back into the fray.

37 Bb3

Not **37 Rxc2, dxc2 38 Qxd4, c1=Qch.**

37... Nb4?

Losing quickly though even after the better **37...d2** White has **38 Qb8ch, Qd8 39 Qxd8ch, Rxd8 40 Bxc2, d1=Qch 41 Bxd1, Rxd1ch 42 Kg2** with a very favorable Rook and pawn ending.

38 Rc7

The attack on **f7** is decisive.

38... Qd6

39 Bxf7ch

Now after **39...Kh7 40 Qf5ch, g6** (or 40...Kh8 41 Rc8ch) **41 Bxg6 dis. dbl. ch., Kh8 42 Rc8ch, Qd8 43 Qf6ch** White wins.

Black Resigns.

ILLUSTRATIVE GAME #7

HAVANA 1966
White: Fischer Black: Durao

1 e4	**e6**
2 d3	**c5**
3 Nf3	**Nc6**
4 g3	**g6**

See Va for this variation.

5 Bg2

Very sharp is **5 d4!?, cd 6 Nxd4** with possibilities of play against d6 (See Va).

5...	**Bg7**
6 0-0	**Nge7**

The Knight belongs on **e7** in this type of position; on **f6** it would only block the KB and allow a tempo gaining **e4-e5** advance.

7 c3

Restricting the scope of the **Bg7** but, the main idea is to play **8 d4** with a strong "two pawn" center.

7...	**0-0**

Better is **7...e5** restraining **8 d4.**

8 d4	**d6**

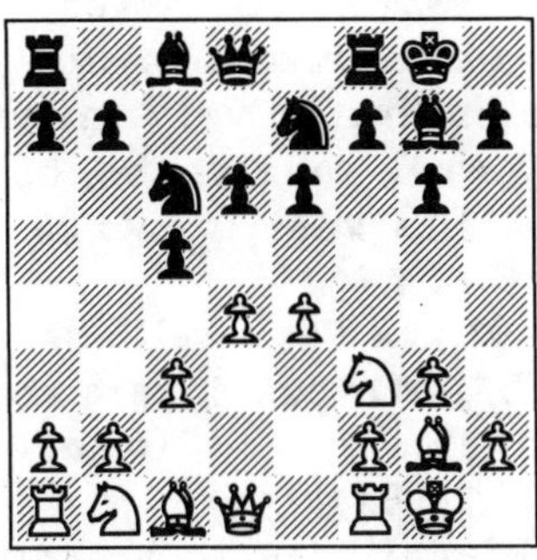

9 dc!

A fine positional move which allows White to use the d-file to target the weak **d6**; also White will play **e4-e5** establishing the typical central and Kingside cramp we have seen so often in the K.I.A. lines.

9... dc

10 Qe2 b6

If **10...e5** (to prevent e4-e5) then Black has a weakness on **d5** as well as **d6.**

11 e5 a5

This attempt to use the **a6-f1** diagonal looks good, but it is usually not a good idea in this type of pawn formation. Also **11...a5** weakens two more squares (b6 and b5) which Fischer will use to advantage.

12 Re1

Overprotecting **e5** while deftly stepping off of the **ab-f1** diagonal.

12... Ba6

13 Qe4

Note that the use of this fine central **e4** is a corollary of **11 e5.**

13... Ra7

14 Nbd2 Bd3

This looks impressive but actually is an empty gesture. A little better was **14...Rd7.**

15 Qh4

Now, give a moment, White will attack the weakened Kingside.

15... Nd5

Hurrying to trade Queens to stop the Kingside pressure. However, the ending is very much in White's favor due to Blacks many weak squares (b6, b5, c4, d6, f6).

16 Qxd8 Rxd8

17 a4

Preventing **17...a4** as well as **17...b5** and thus blockading the **b6, b5, c4** weak square complex.

17... Rad7

18 Bf1!

A good positional idea to accentuate the weakness of the white squares (b5, c4, e4).

18... Bxf1

19 Kxf1

Bringing the King up to the center.

19... Nde7
20 Nc4

Finally White is able to begin direct threats.

20... Nc8
21 Bg5 Nc6e7

If the Rook moves, then **22 Rad1** wins control of the d-file.

22 Nfd2

This Knight heads for a fine post on **e4**.

22... h6
23 Bxe7!

Seeing that the Bishop has little use, Fischer rightly trades it off.

23... Rxe7
24 Ra3!

Another fine move. White infiltrates the porous Queenside pawn structure.

24... Rc7

White threatened **25 Rb3, Rb7 26 Nxa5**. The text allows defense of **b6** by **Rc6** though the Rook is obviously in a lamentable position there.

25 Rb3 Rc6
26 Ne4 Bf8
27 Ke2

Now White shifts the pressure to the other flank to overload the Black defensive capacity.

27... Be7
28 f4 Kf8
29 g4!

Not so much to threaten **f4-f5** as to maneuver **Rf1-f3-h3** with pressure on the **h6** pawn.

29... Ke8
30 Rf1 Rd5

Black can only shift his pieces about in meaningless patterns while awaiting the inevitable.

31 Rf3 Rd8

"I pass".

32 Rh3 Bf8
33 Nxa5!

A nice combination, which quickly finishes the game.

33... Rc7

On **33...bxa5?** White forces mate in four with **34 Nf6ch, Ke7 35 Rb7ch, Rc7 36 Rxc7ch, Rd7 37 Rxd7** mate.

34 Nc4 Ra7
35 Nxb6 Nxb6
36 Rxb6 Rda8

Not **36...Rxa4?** as **37 Nf6ch** mates in two.

37 Nf6ch Kd8
38 Rc6

So that if **38...Rxa4 39 Rd3ch** mates.

38... Rc7
39 Rd3ch Kc8
40 Rxc7ch Kxc7
41 Rd7ch Kc6
42 Rxf7

With three pawns up and the better position, Black finally is "able" to see the "right move".

Black Resigns

ILLUSTRATIVE GAME #8

USSR 1984
White: Yurtaev Black: Dolmatov

1 e4

This game demonstrates the transpositional nature of the K.I.A.; White feints at an e-pawn opening, intending to transpose into "our" setup.

1... e6
2 d3

Now Black is "informed" of White's real intentions.

2... c5
3 Nf3 Nc6
4 g3 g6
5 Bg2 Bg7
6 0-0 Nge7

Black's KN is best posted here as on **f6** it would impede the KB's action on the long diagonal.

7 c3

White intends to gain central space by advancing **d3-d4.**

7... d5

Black stakes out a share of the center, but in doing so weakens his control over the important **e5** square.

8 Nbd2

Also possible is **8 Qe2**, but White prefers to avoid committing his Queen so soon.

8... b6

The only way to get the QB into decent play. **8...Bd7** is playable but, rather passive.

9 Re1

Zeroing in on **e5.**

9... h6

A subtle idea which doesn't turn out well here. Black hopes to gain counterplay with **g6-g5.**

10 e5!

Crossing the "demarcation" line.

10... Qd7

Clearing the back rank and reserving the option of Queenside castling.

11 d4 cd

12 cd

Now, with the c-file open, Black's Queenside castling option becomes dubious.

12... Ba6

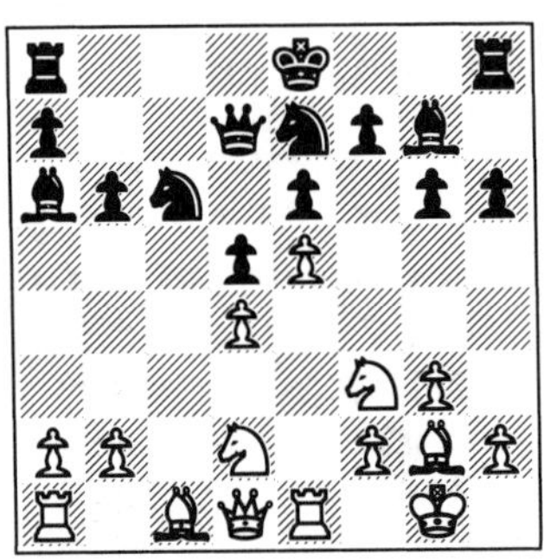

13 a3!

A fine multi-purpose move, preventing **Nb4-d3** while preparing to advance on the Queenside with **b2-b4.**

13... g5?!

Black feels nervous about castling Kingside because of White's cramping **e5** pawn, but this is too wild. He had to play **13...0-0** with only the "usual" slight edge for White.

14 Nf1

Shifting pieces toward the Kingside and defending the d-pawn against **g5-g4** followed by **Nxd4.**

14... Nf5

A natural looking move, but now White launches a driving initiative.

15 g4!

Perhaps Black hadn't expected this aggressive rejoinder.

15... Nfe7

15...Nh4? 16 Nxh4, gxh4 allows White to play for **f4-f5** not to mention the weak pawn on **h4**.

16 Ng3 0-0-0

The lesser evil.

17 b4

White wastes no time "greeting" the Black King.

17... f5

Black must try to gain counterplay against White's coming attack.

18 gf Nxf5

On **18...ef 19 Nh5, Rhg8 20 Nf6, Bxf6 21 exf6, Ng6 22 Ne5!** White's position is too strong.

19 Nxf5 exf5

20 e6?!

Plausible but ill-timed! White should have played **20 a4!** (Threatening 21 b5, winning a piece) **20...Nxb4 21 Ba3** with a very strong attack for the sacrificed pawn-**21...Nd3? fails to 22 Bf1!.**

20... Qd6

Black returns the favor. Necessary was **20...Qc7** and if **21 a4**, then **21...g4** with mutual chances.

21 a4!

White doesn't have to be asked twice.

21... g4

Grabbing the b-pawn is not much better: **21...Nxb4 22 Ba3, Bc4 23 Qb1, a5 24 e7, Rde8 25 Qxf5ch** with a tremendous attack.

22 Nh4

Now **f5** is a juicy target.

22... Nxd4

23 b5! Nf3ch

Black has nothing better.

24 Nxf3 Bxa1

25 Nd4!

Again **f5** is vulnerable.

25... Bb7

On **25...Bxd4 26 Qxd4, Bb7 27 Bf4** Black is caught in a deadly crossfire--**28 Rc1** will win easily.

26 Nxf5 Qc7

27 e7

Now on **27...Rde8 28 Qxg4, Qd7** (28...Kb8 29 Bf4) **29 Bf4** is crushing.

Black Resigns.

ILLUSTRATIVE GAME #9

ALEKHINE MEMORIAL 1971
White: Geller Black: Spassky

1 e4

Yet another example of the flexibility of transposition of the K.I.A.--White feints at an e-pawn opening.

1... c5
2 Nf3 e6
3 d3

Geller avoids the standard Sicilian move **3 d4**, going in for our K.I.A. game. This has some psychological significance as it avoids any sharp prepared line Spassky may have had up his sleeve.

3... Nc6
4 g3 d6

A rather modest but sound reply.

5 Bg2 g6

To place the KB on the long diagonal as opposed to the passive **e7**.

6 0-0 Bg7
7 c3

White threatens to occupy the center with **d4** while blunting somewhat the scope of Black's KB.

7... e5

Preventing **d4** for at least a long time.

8 a3

A typical procedure here, but perhaps more incisive is **8 Nh4** with the intention of advancing with **f2-f4**. For example, **8 Nh4, Nge7 9 f4, ef 10 gf, f5 11 ef, Nxf5 12 Re1ch, Kf8 13 Nf3** and Black's awkwardly posted King will cause problems for Black.

8... Nf6

An inaccuracy since the f-pawn is blocked. Normal and better is **8...Nge7** with a satisfactory position.

9 b4 0-0
10 b5

Gaining more space and creating a strongpoint on **c4** since now **b7-b5** is ruled out.

10... Ne7

Preferable to the decentralizing **10...Na5.**

11 a4 a6

Black attempts to challenge White's Queenside pressure.

12 Na3

White prefers to avoid exchanges on the a-file in order to maintain more pressure.

12... ab

13 Nxb5

White wants the b-file open to attack the b-pawn.

13... Nc6

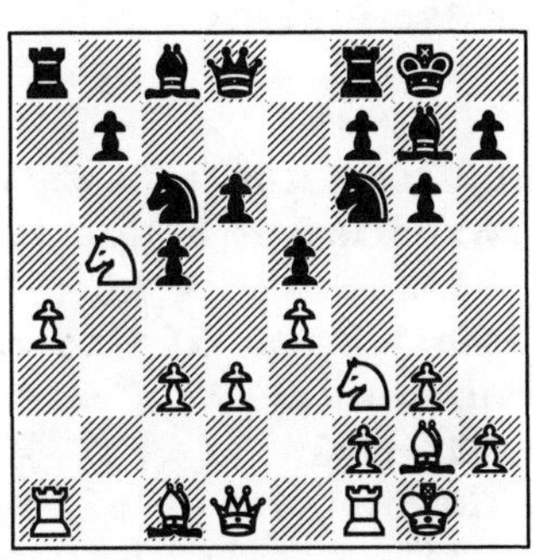

14 Bg5!

A deep strategic idea. White sees that control of the **d5** square is more important than the two Bishops.

14... h6

15 Bxf6

Removing Black's main defender of **d5.**

15... Bxf6

16 Nd2

Heading for **c4**, from which it will pressure Black's backward d-pawn.

16... Na7

Naturally, Black strives to exchange off the "visiting" Knights.

17 Na3

Which White politely declines.

17... Nc6
18 Rb1 Bg7
19 N2c4

Systematically improving the position of the Knights.

19... Ra6

Reinforcing b6 and d6.

20 Ne3 Ne7

Again Black hopes to trade off a White Knight if it reaches **d5**.

21 Nac4 Bd7

By threatening the a-pawn, at last Black is able to develop his QB.

22 a5

Nailing down the b-pawn.

22... Bc6
23 Nd5!

Now **23...Nxd5** loses the b-pawn after **24 exd5** and **25 Rxb7**, while **23...Bxd5** leaves **b7** too vulnerable.

23... h5

To activate the KB via **h6** and allowing a possible **h5-h4** to build up counterplay.

24 Qb3

Reinforcing the pressure on **b7**.

24... Bh6
25 f4

Now play becomes very sharp.

25... ef
26 gf Bxd5!

An excellent defensive resource. Black "sacrifices" his Queenside (b7) in return for Kingside counterplay based on the newly created strong square on **f5**.

27 exd5 Nf5
28 Be4

The obvious move, **28 Qxb7** allows Black to sacrifice the Exchange for good play with **28...Rxa5! 29 Nxa5, Qxa5 30 Qb3, Qd8** and Black's Queen will assume a threatening position on the Kingside.

28... Bxf4

So that if **29 Rxf4**, then **29...Qg5ch.**

29 Bxf5

To remove the strong Knight.

29... Qg5ch

Not **29...gxf5?**, leaving his pawn structure in ruins.

30 Kh1 Qxf5

31 Qxb7

A critical moment.

31... Re8

Plausible but not good enough. Best was **31...Qxd3!** with adequate counterplay, e.g. **31...Qxd3! 32 Qxa6, Qxd5ch 33 Kg1, Qg5ch** with a perpetual as **34 Kf2?** allows **34...Re8** with a terrific attack.

32 Rf2!

A very fine defensive move.

32... g5

33 Rg1

An error which could have had serious consequences (time pressure is the likely cause). Correct was **33 Qxa6, Qxd5ch 34 Kg1, Qxd3 35 Rbf1!** and if **35...Re2** then **36 Qa8ch, Kg7 37 Qf3.**

33... Rea8

Black returns the favor. After **33...h4! 34 Rgf1, Qc8** Black enters an unfavorable but not clearly lost endgame.

34 Nxd6 Rxd6

A hopeless Exchange sacrifice, but even after the better **34...Qf6** White has the winning move **35 Nc4.**

35 Qxa8ch Kg7

36 c4

Giving the vital d-pawn solid protection.

36... Rf6

37 Qb7 Qh3

On **37...Qxd3** White has **38 Qe7** with the decisive threat of **39 Rxf4** (39...Rxf4 40 Qxg5ch, etc.)

38 Qb2!

Guarding against the clever threat **38...Bxh2!** which would draw after **38 a6?, Bxh2! 39Rxh2, Qf3ch 40 Rgg2, Qf1ch** with a perpetual check.

38... Be5

39 Qe2

Now Black is totally lost and forfeits on time.

ILLUSTRATIVE GAME #10

USSR CHAMPIONSHIP 1955
White: Symslov Black: Botvinnik

1 Nf3	**Nf6**
2 g3	**g6**
3 Bg2	**Bg7**
4 0-0	**0-0**

Black copies White's moves for the time being, but, as is usual in symmetrical positions, Black cannot copy forever without risk.

5 d3 c5

In this line of defense Black avoids placing a pawn on **d5** to avoid creating a target for White's KB.

6 e4

Since Black hasn't played **d5**, White can play this without the preparatory **Nbd2**.

6... Nc6
7 Nbd2 d6

Also possible is **7...e5** immediately, which should transpose into the game.

8 a4

Securing the **c4** square for a Knight by preventing **b7-b5** (8 Nc4, b5! is fine for Black).

8... Ne8

Black plays for the initiative, intending to advance on the Kingside with **f7-f5**.

9 Nc4 e5

To prevent a possible central counterattack via **c3** and **d4**.

10 c3

As will be seen, this move has a subtle tactical point.

10... f5

This plays into White's tactics; safer was **10...h6** followed by **11...Be6**.

(See diagram on following page)

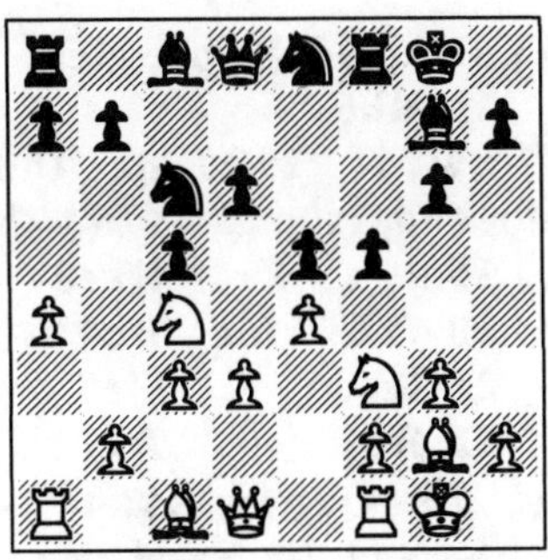

11 b4!

White counters energetically. Now on **11...f4** there would follow **12 bc, dc** (or 12...g5 13 cd, g4 14 Nh4, f3 15 Bh1, Be6 16 Nf5 with complicated play and good chances for White) **13 gf, ef 14 Ba3, b6 15 d4** and White's central activity gives him the advantage.

11... cb
12 cb fe

After **12...Nxb4** White has **13 Qb3!**. Slightly better than the text is **12...h6.**

13 de Be6

Now, with the **a2-g8** diagonal covered, Black does threaten to take the b-pawn.

14 Ne3 Nxb4
15 Rb1 a5

After **15...Na6** White should play **16 Nd5** (After the obvious 16 Rxb7, Black obtains the better of it with 16...Nc5 17 Rb4, a5 18 Rb1, Nxe4) **16...Nc5 17 Ng5, Bd7 18 Be3, Bxa4 19 Qd2, Bc6** (Not 19...Qd7 20 Bh3!) **20 Bxc5, dxc5 21 Ne6, Qd6 22 Nxf8, Bxf8 23 Qa2** threatening **Nb6** d.ch.--if **23...Bxd5** then **24 exd5, b6 25 Qa6** is good for White. Also, if **18...b6** (instead of 18...Bxa4) **19 Nc3, Bc6 20 Bxc5, Qxg5 21 Bxd6** and **21...Rd8** is in do danger in view of **22 Qb3ch**, etc.

16 Ba3 Nc7

On **16...Qb6 17 Ng5** is strong. Best was **16...Bh6 17 Bxb4, axb4 18 Nd5, Nc7 19 Rxb4, Nxd5 20 exd5, Bc8** with sufficient counterplay.

17 Bxb4 axb4
18 Rxb4 Bh6

Better was **18...Na6 19 Rxb7, Nc5.**

19 Rb6!

A finesse. Now if **19...Ra6**, then **20 Rxb7** and Black's Knight is blocked from **a6** (and then to c5).

19...	**Bxe3**
20 fxe3	**Bc4**
21 Rxd6	**Qe8**
22 Re1	**Rf7**

On **22...Qxa4 23 Qxa4, Rxa4 24 Nxe5, Nb5** (or 24...b5 25 Rc6) **25 Rb6, Nc3 26 Nxc4, Rxc4 27 e5** White has the upper hand. Or if **22...Rxa4**, then **23 Rd7** is strong-- **23...Ra1 24 Qxa1, Qxd7 25 Nxe5, Qe6 26 Rc1, b5 27 Nxc4, bxc4 28 Qd4** and Black loses a pawn.

23 Ng5	**Re7**

24 Bf1!

A fine move. By trading the white squared Bishops, the weakness of Black's Kingside is accentuated.

24...	**Bxf1**

If **24...Qxa4**, then **25 Rd8ch, Kg7 26 Rxa8** wins material. If **24...Ba2**, then **25 Re2** is good for White--**25...Qxa4 26 Qxa4, Rxa4 27 Rxa2, Rxa2 28 Bc4ch.**

25 Rxf1	**Qxa4**

On **25...h6** White responds **26 Rff6!** with a very strong attack: **26...hxg5 27 Rxg6ch, Kh8** (or 27...Rg7 28 Rxg7ch, Kxg7 29 Rd7ch) **28 Rh6ch, Kg8** (28...Kg7 29 Qg4) **29 Rdg6ch, Rg7 30 Qh5** and wins, or **26...Rg7 27 Qb3ch, Kh8 28 Nf7ch, Kh7 29 h4, Qxa4 30 Qxa4, Rxa4 31 h5, gxh5 32 Rd7** and White wins a piece. Finally, if **26...Kg7**, then **27 Rxg6ch, Qxg6 28 Rxg6ch, Kxg6 29 Qd6ch** wins.

26 Rd8ch	**Re8**

On **26...Kg7 27 Qd6** wins.

27 Qf3

Note how all of White's pieces have converged on the Black Kingside.

27...	**Qc4**

28 Rd7

Now if **28...Rf8**, then **29 Rxc7, Qxc7 30 Qxf8ch, Rxf8 31 Rxf8ch, Kxf8 32 Ne6ch** and **33 Nxc7** wins.

Black Resigns.

ILLUSTRATIVE GAME #11

MOSCOW 1985
White: Vaganian Black: Razuvaev

1 Nf3 Nf6

Black begins in Hypermodern style himself by not committing a center pawn yet.

2 g3 d5

Back to classical.

3 Bg2 e6
4 0-0 Be7

Considering that Black is intent on a Queenside fianchettoe, more accurate is the immediate **4...b6**.

Now White can get in his intended **e2-e4** more easily.

5 d3 b6

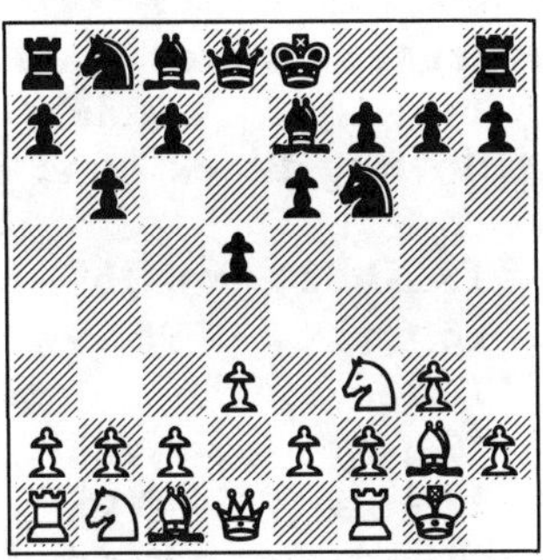

6 e4

But this inaccuracy returns the favor. Correct was **6 Nbd2!** and on **6...Bb7, 7 e4** since **7...de 8 de, Nxe4? 9 Ne5, Nd6 10 Bxb7, Nxb7 11 Qf3** wins for White.

6... de
7 Nfd2

After **7 de, Qxd1 8 Rxd1** there is little play left for either player.

7... Bb7
8 Nc3 Nbd7
9 Ndxe4

Now without a pawn on **e4** (due to the 6th move inaccuracy--6 Nbd2!) White has little to work with.

9... Qc8

White threatened **10 Nxf6ch** and **11 Bxb7.**

10 b3 0-0

11 Bb2 a6

To keep White's Knight out of **b5**--e.g., **11...c5?! 12 Nb5!** is annoying.

12 Re1 b5

The maneuver **12...Nd5**, to trade some pieces, allows White's Queen to leap into action with **13 Qg4!** and if **13...N7f6** then **14 Nxd5!** while **13...f5** allows **14 Nxd5!** again. Perhaps best is **12...c5** with about even chances.

13 a4

To provoke a weakening of the advanced Queenside pawns.

13... b4

Not **13...c6** which weakens **d6** and shuts in the QB.

14 Nb1

Hoping to maneuver onto **c4** via **d2.**

14... Bd5!

A fine idea allowing Black good play on the **h1-a8** diagonal.

15 Nbd2 Qb7

16 Qe2 Ne8

Threatening **17...f5.**

17 f4 Nd6

18 Nc4 Nf5

To reinforce **g7** and pressure **d4.**

19 h3

A good move which allows White's King to get off the drafty **g1-a7** diagonal.

19... c5

20 Kh2 Qc7?!

Razovaev recommends **20...Rfe8** followed by **Rad8, Qa7** and **Nd4** though we think White still has a tiny plus.

21 Qf2 Rad8

22 Re2 Nb8

Aiming for the central **d4** via **c6-d4.**

23 Be5 **Qa7**

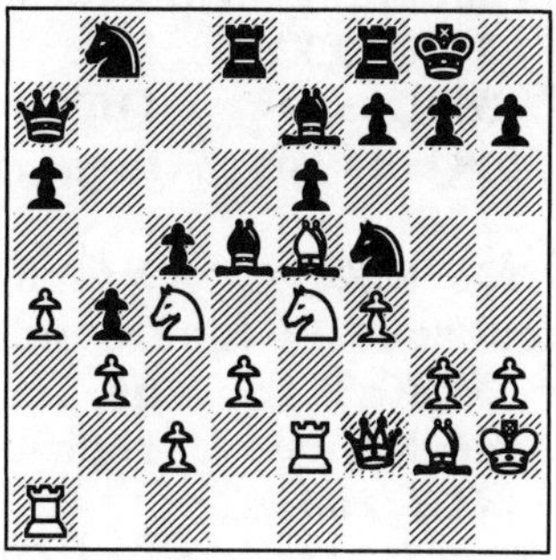

24 g4!

Seizing the initiative on the Kingside.

24... **Nd4**

Practically forced as **24...Nh6** leaves the Knight out of play, while **24...Nh4** allows **25 f5!, Nxg2 26 f6!!** with a winning attack.

25 Bxd4 **cxd4**
26 f5

Threatening to play **27 f6.**

26... **Nd7**
27 Kh1 **Nf6**
28 Ng3

To be considered is **29 Rf1**, bringing his last undeveloped piece into play.

28... **Bxg2ch**
29 Qxg2 **Nd5**
30 Rf1 **Bg5**

Black is trying to work on White's weakened dark squares, especially **e3** and **f4.**

31 fe **fe**

But not **31...Nf4?** because of **32 Rxf4!, Bxf4 33 e7** and White wins.

32 Rxf8ch **Rxf8**
33 Rf2 **Rxf2**

On **33...Nf4 34 Qe4** is good for White.

34 Qxf2 **Bh4**
35 Qf3 **Bxg3**

Due to the wholesale simplification, White has little chance to create any meaningful pressure.

36 Qxg3	**h6**
37 Qe5	**Qf7**

Preventing **38 Qxd4** since then **38...Qf3ch** is quite good for Black.

38 Kg2	**Nf4ch**

Again the weakened **f4** square aids Black's defense.

39 Kg3	**g5**
40 Nd2	**Ng6**
41 Qxd4	

There is nothing better, e.g., **41 Qb8ch, Kh7 42 Nf3, e5 43 Qxb4, e4! 44 de, Qf4ch 45 Kg2, Qxe4** leads to nothing.

41...	**Qc7ch**
42 Kf3	**Qxc2**
43 Qd8ch	

And, since there's no way to make progress...

Drawn.

A White **6 Nbd2!** would have been so much better than played.

ILLUSTRATIVE GAME #12

STOCKHOLM INTERZONAL 1962

White: Benko Black: Bisquier

1 Nf3	**Nf6**
2 g3	**d5**
3 Bg2	**e6**

Black essays a simple and sound classical defense to the K.I.A.

4 0-0	**Be7**
5 d3	**0-0**
6 Nbd2	

As usual, White prepares to place a pawn on **e4**.

6... b6

This method is playable, but somewhat passive. Best is **6...c5** allowing for a later general advance of the Queen-side pawns with **b7-b5**, **a7-a5**, etc.

7 e4	**Bb7**
8 e5	

Again a typical K.I.A. stratagem, the establishment of a cramping pawn on **e5**.

8... Nfd7

In order to keep some pressure on the **e5** pawn; **8...Ne8** is rather passive.

9 Re1 Re8

Better is **9...c5** and **10...Nc6**.

10 Nf1 Nf8

This passive move is a clear indication that Black's position is in trouble.

11 h4

This is White's typical method of encroaching on Black's cramped Kingside. Now **h5-h6** is a real threat.

11...	**Nbd7**
12 N1h2	

Heading for **g4** in order to overprotect the **e5** pawn.

12...	**c5**
13 h5	**h6**

To prevent **14 h5-h6**, but now the Black h-pawn is a potential target for a line opening operation (g4-g5) or even a piece sacrifice on **h6.**

14 Ng4 **Nh7**

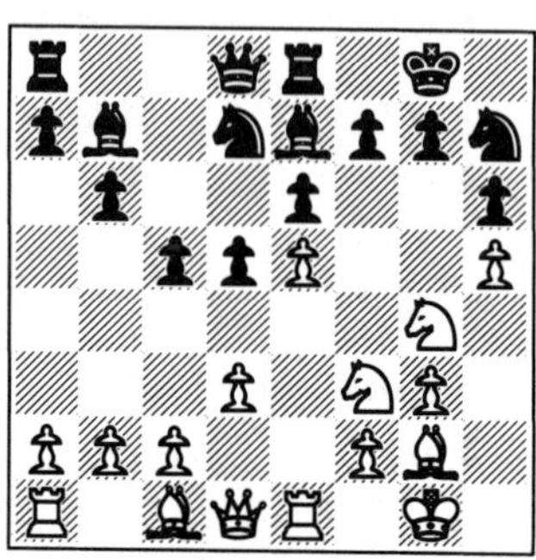

15 Nfh2!

A fine maneuver designed to allow a general King-side pawn advance after **f2-f4.**

15... **Ndf8**

16 f4

Now Black must face the possibility of a break-through via **f4-f5**, too.

16... **Rb8**

17 Bd2 **b5**

18 Nf2

Clearing the way for a timely **g3-g4.**

18... **d4**

Better was **18...a5** though in any event, White's position is much superior.

19 Bxb7 **Rxb7**

20 Qf3 **Rd7**

21 a4!

Excellent. Now if **21...a6**, then **22 ab**, ab gives White the a-file as an invasion route.

21... **b4**

Avoiding the a-file problem, but now White is able to block the Queenside, leaving Black helpless to prevent a decisive accumulation of force on the Kingside.

22 b3

Preventing **c5-c4** permanently.

22... Rd5
23 Re2 Nd7
24 Rae1 Nb6
25 Ne4

Another deficit of **18...d4** is seen, the weakening of the central **e4**.

25... Rd7
26 Qg4

The Queen takes up a menacing position in front of the Black King's position.

26... Nd5
27 Rf1

Massing on the f-file in preparation for **f4-f5**.

27... Bf8
28 Nf3 Qb6
29 Nh4

White methodically builds toward the breakthrough **f4-f5**.

29... f5

Desperation, but there was no good defense against **f4-f5** anyway.

30 ef e.p. Nhxf6
31 Nxf6ch Nxf6
32 Qg6

Taking advantage of the weak **g6**.

32... Qb8
33 Rfe1

Preventing any attempt at counterplay via **e6-e5**.

33... Rde7
34 f5!

Ironically this move still breaks through.

34... ef

On **34...e5** simply **35 Bxh6** decides.

35 Rxe7 Rxe7
36 Rxe7 Bxe7
37 Nxf5

With too many threats.

37... Bf8
38 Nxh6ch Kh8
39 Nf7ch Kg8

40 Bf4

Even the QB now enters with effect.

40... Qb7
41 Nh6ch Kh8
42 Nf7ch Kg8
43 Ng5

Black could resign here, but probably White was in time pressure.

43... Qe7
44 Be5!

A nice touch.

44... Qe8

Of course on **44...Qxe5** there would follow **45 Qf7ch, Kh8 46 Qxf8ch, Ng8 47 Nf7ch** winning the Queen.

45 Bxf6 Qe1ch

After **45...Qxg6 46 hxg6, gxf6 47 Ne6** White wins the ending with ease.

46 Kg2 Qe2ch
47 Kh3 Qf1ch
48 Kh4 Qh1ch
49 Nh3

And, with no more checks,
Black Resigns.

ILLUSTRATIVE GAME #13

MINSK 1986
White: Vaganian Black: A. Sokolov

1 Nf3 c5

Daring White to transpose into a Sicilian with **2 e4**. However, even in that case, White could continue with **d3**, **g3**, **Bg2**, etc. forcing Black to face the K.I.A.

2 g3 d5
3 Bg2 Nc6
4 0-0 e6

After **4...e5** Black is playing a 1a White--a tempo down. See IIIb.

5 d3 Bd6

Normally a **Bd6** in such formations is exposed to **e4-e5**; but, since Black plans to play **Nge7**, **e4-e5** is not nearly so effective. In some cases the **e5** pawn might come under attack by **Ng6** or **f7-f6**.

6 e4 Nge7
7 Re1

Of course **7 Nbd2** is also good.

7... 0-0
8 Nbd2 Bc7

In order to meet **9 e5**(??) with **9...Ng6**, picking off the e-pawn.

9 c3 a5

This plays into White's hands by weakening **b5**. More accurate is **9...b6**--another possibility is **9...f6**.

10 a4

Nailing down the **b5** weakness.

10... b6
11 ed

White opens some lines in order to try to seize the initiative.

11... ed

On **11...Nxd5** White can use **c4** as a good outpost for a Knight.

(See diagram on following page)

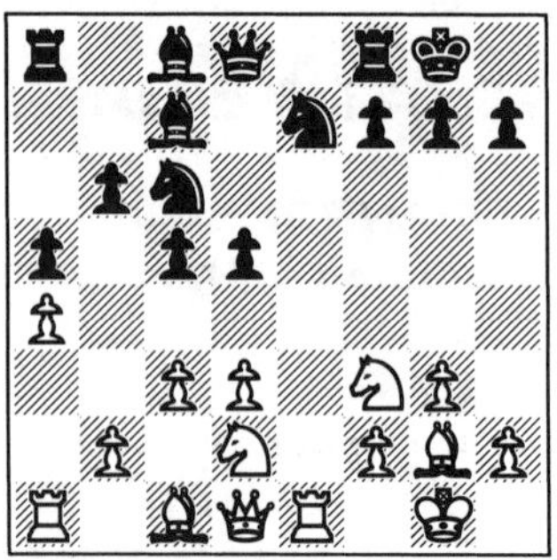

12 Nb1!

A star move, which intends to shove the QN to the **b5** square.

12... Bg4

Also after **12...Bf5** White retains the better chances with **Na3-b5.**

13 Na3 d4

Black probably fears an eventual **d3-d4**, fixing the Black d-pawn on **d5** as a target for White's KB. More cautious is **13...Rc8!?.**

14 Nb5 dc

In order to avoid a weak **d4** pawn, but now White takes advantage of the newly opened lines.

15 bc Rc8

16 Ba3 Qd7

17 d4!

The coordinated action of White's centralized pieces plus the passed d-pawn give him a very strong game.

17... cd

18 Bxe7!

Also strong is **18 h3, Bxf3 19 Qxf3, Rfd8** (not 19...dc because of 20 Rad1) **20 Na7!** and White wins.

18... Nxe7

19 Qxd4

White enters a favorable ending.

19... Qxd4

If Black tries **19...Ng6** then after **20 Rad1, Rfd8 21 Nxc7, Rxc7 22 Qxg4!, Qxg4 23 Rxd8ch, Nf8 24 Ree8** wins for White.

20 cxd4 Nd5

Trying to blockade the passed pawn.

21 Rac1! Bb8

22 Ne5 Bxe5

23 Bxd5

Removing the blockader per force.

23... Bf6

24 Bc6!

A good move which helps control **d7** while preventing Black from occupying the e-file.

24... Rfd8

25 f3?

A bad mistake which ruins the results of his previous fine play. Correct is **25 d5** and after **25...Bf3 26 Rc4!** (Threatening 27 Re3 driving back the Bishop) **26...Bg5** (On 26...Bxd5 27 Bxd5) **27 Nd4!, Bh5 28 f4, Bf6 29 Nb5** followed by **d6-d7** White should win.

25... Be6

Now Black has no problems.

26 d5

White expects **26...Bxd5 27 Bxd5, Rxc1 28 Bxf7ch, Kxf7 29 Rxc1** with only a slight pull for Black. Black decides to play it safe, however, so....

Drawn.

ILLUSTRATIVE GAME #14

NEW YORK 1955
White: Reshevsky Black: Evans

1 Nf3	**Nf6**
2 g3	**d5**
3 Bg2	**Bf5**

Initiating the London System, long considered one of Black's most solid defenses to both the K.I.A. and Reti Openings. See Chapter One.

4 0-0 **c6**

Buttressing the **h1-a8** diagonal, one of the main points of this solid line of defense.

5 d3 **e6**
6 Nbd2

White simply plays our standard K.I.A. pattern, virtually ignoring Black's setup.

6... **Na6**

An older move which has been superceded. Nonetheless the game is very instructive.

7 a3!

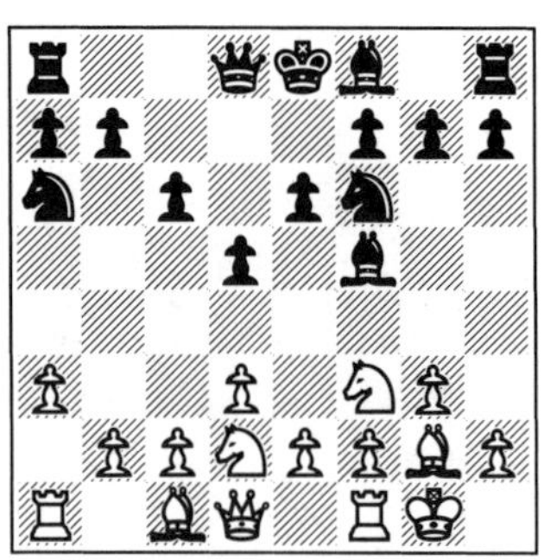

The idea of **6...Na6** was to answer **7 Qe1** with **7...Nb4**. The simple text nullifies this idea while preparing to gain Queenside space with **b2-b4.**

7... **Be7**

The consistent **7...Nc5**, to restrain **e2-e4**, runs into **8 b4!, Na4 9 c4**, and if **Nc3 10 Qe1** with clear advantage for White.

8 b4

Keeping the **Na6** restricted and allowing the QB to assume the fine **a1-h8** diagonal.

8... 0-0

9 Bb2 h6

To allow the **Bf5** a convenient retreat square on **h7.**

10 Re1 Nd7

Hoping to challenge the **Bb2** with **Bf6.** A better idea was **10...Nc7** returning the errant QN.

11 e4 Bh7

11...de 12 de is weak since it gives up Black's bastion on **d5.**

12 c4!

Gaining more space.

12... dc?

A definite strategic mistake (see note to Black's 11th).

13 Nxc4

Even better than **13dc.**

13... c5

Otherwise White obtains a big pawn center with **d3-d4.**

14 b5 Nc7

15 a4

Now it is clear that Black forces have been misplayed--none of Black's minor pieces are beyond the 2nd rank.

15... Bf6

16 d4 cd

17 Bxd4 Bxd4

Black hopes to reduce the pressure somewhat by exchanging.

18 Qxd4

Note the Queen's powerfully centralized location.

18... b6

Although this weakens **c6**, it is practically unavoidable since on **b7** the b-pawn would be too exposed on the **h1-a8** diagonal.

19 Red1 Nc5
20 Qe3 Qe7
21 Nfe5

Heading for **c6**.

21... Rfd8
22 Nc6

Forcing Black to concede the d-file.

22... Rxd1ch
23 Rxd1 Qf8
24 Qf4!

White's forces now quickly overrun the Black center and Queenside.

24... Ne8

Forced, **24...Qc8** allows **25 Ne7ch.**

25 a5!

A clever breakthrough.

25... ba
26 b6!

The point.

26... ab
27 Nxb6 g5

Black struggles on with "coffee-house" inertia.

28 Qe5 Ra6

If **28...f6**, then **29 Qb2, Ra6 30 Bf1** wins the exchange.

29 Qb8!

Threatening **30 Bf1** and **30 Rd8.**

29... Bg6

Not **29...Bxe4** because of **30 Bxe4, Nxe4 31 Nd7!** winning immediately.

30 Rd8

Note that four (!) of White's pieces have invaded Black's first three ranks.

30... f6
31 Bf1

Winning material. The rest is simply a matter of technique.

31... Rxb6
32 Qxb6 Nxe4
33 Qxa5

Black's weakened Kingside makes the win easy.

33... N4d6
34 Qa7 Bf7

Black doesn't believe in "early" resigning.

35 Rb8 e5
36 Qd7 Kg7
37 Ne7

Heading for **f5**.

37... Qh8
38 Bd3 h5

Hoping for "counterplay".

39 Nf5ch

Forcing favorable simplification.

39... Nxf5
40 Bxf5 Kf8

White threatened **41 Be6, Qf8 42 Bxf7, Qxf7 43 Qxe8.**

41 Rb7

Seizing the 7th rank with decisive tactical threats.

41... Qg7

On **41...Qg8 42 Be6** wins as **42...Bxe6 43 Qe7** mate.

42 Qe7ch Kg8
43 Be6

Now on **43...Bxe6 44 Qxe6ch** wins handily.

Black Resigns.

ILLUSTRATIVE GAME #15

BUDAPEST 1952
White: Petrosian Black: Barcza

1 Nf3 Nf6
2 g3 d5
3 Bg2 c5

This precludes the solidifying **c7-c6**, thus giving more possibilities for White's fianchettoed KB.

4 d3 Nc6
5 0-0 e6

Black opts for the "French Defense" setup which can be obtained after **1 e4, e6 2 d3, d5 3 Nd2, Nf6 4 Ngf3, c5 5 g3, Nc6,** etc.

6 Nbd2 Be7
7 e4

The standard K.I.A. central pawn push. Unless a favorable chance for **exd5** occurs, White's main plan is usually the further advance of the e-pawn, **e4-e5.**

7... 0-0
8 Re1 b6

This move has been superceded nowadays by the more aggressive **8...b5.**

9 e5 Nd7
10 Nf1

Shifting the Knight towards the Kingside action and preparing to "over protect" the **e5** pawn with **Bf4.**

10... Ba6

A further inaccuracy. Since White has not played **c3**, the Bishop is "biting on granite". Better was **10...Bb7** or **10...a5.**

11 h4

The standard thrust aimed at exploiting the dark squares on the Kingside.

11... Qe8

Black hopes to play **Bd8-c7** to pressure White's e-pawn, but as we shall see, this is easily handled.

(See diagram on following page)

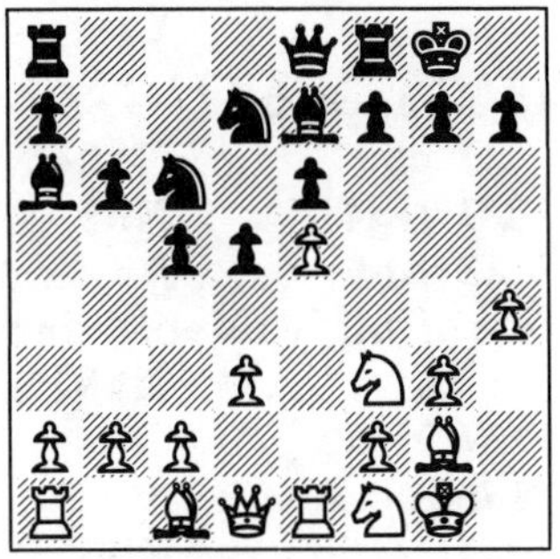

12 Bh3!

A fine strategical finesse which ties down Black's Kingside by restraining **f7-f6**.

12... Bd8
13 Bf4 Bc7

Black's strategy of pressuring the **e5** pawn will come to naught, as White's plan involves "over protection", as mentioned.

14 N1h2

Heading for **g4** (more overprotection).

14... Nd8

Protecting **e6** and with the hope of playing **f7-f6.**

15 Qd2 d4

Black decides against **15...f5** as after **16 exf6 e.p., Bxf4 17 Qxf4, Rxf6** Black's e-pawn is very weak, while **17...gf** (to control e5) loses to **18 Bxe6ch!, Nxe6 19 Qg4ch** and White wins material.

16 Bg2 Bb7
17 Re2

White calmly builds up in the center with more (!) overprotection of **e5**, while reserving options of further Kingside progress.

17... Nc6
18 Rae1 b5

Black hopes for Queenside counterplay with the incidental threat of **Ba5**.

19 c3

Neutralizing the threat while opening up more lines in the center.

19... dc

20 bc **b4**

Black plays to weaken **d4**.

21 cb **Nxb4**
22 Ng4 **Nd5**
23 Bg5

White must retain his valuable dark squared Bishop.

23... **Kh8**
24 Nfh2

Pinning the **Nd5**.

24... **Rb8**
25 h5

Preparing to further his dark squared attack with **h5-h6**.

25... **f6?**

This only creates more targets for attack. Black had to try **25...Bd8**, though after **26 h6, g6** White is still clearly better.

26 ef **gf**
27 Rxe6 **Qxh5**

This indirect trade of pawns leaves all of Black's pawns isolated.

28 Bh4

Keeping the pressure on **f6**.

28... **Bd8**
29 Rd6 **N5b6**
30 Bxb7 **Rxb7**
31 Qb2

White attacks **f6** from every angle.

31... **Qf5**
32 Ree6

Sealing the fate of the **f6** pawn.

32... **Rb8**
33 Qe2 **Bc7**
34 Bxf6ch **Nxf6**
35 Rxf6

The rest is a matter of technique, one of Petrosian's strongest points.

35... **Qg5**
36 Rxf8ch **Rxf8**
37 Rc6 **Qg7**

38 Rxc5

Another isolated pawn has fallen.

38... Na4

Or resigns.

39 Rc4 Nc3?

40 Qb2

Winning more material.

40... Ba5

On Knight-moves timely **41 Qxg7çh, Kxg7 42 Rxc7ch** decides.

41 Rc5!

Now Black must lose still more material.

41... Bb6

42 Qxc3

Not **42 Rxc3. Bd4!.**

42... Bxc5

43 Qxc5 Rd8

44 Ne5

White's cavalry rides in to finish Black's desperate resistance.

44... Qb7

45 Nhf3 Rc8

46 Qd4

Black Resigns.

ILLUSTRATIVE GAME #16

MOSCOW 1963
White: Polugaevsky Black: Maslov

1 Nf3 d5
2 g3 g6

Again a combination of classical and hypermodern motifs.

3 Bg2 Bg7
4 0-0 e5

More popular nowadays is the system with **c5, Nc6, e6**, and **Nge7.**

5 d3 Ne7

5...Nc6 and **6...Nf6** transposes into the Ivkov-Golombek (Illustrative Game #20).

6 Nbd2 0-0
7 e4 de

This gives up the **d5** central pawn. More solid is **7...Nc6.**

8 de b6

As in Ivkov-Golombek, Black wishes to develop his QB at **a6.**

9 b3

White intends to play his QB to **b2** from where it can pressure important center squares.

9... a5

Intending to open the a-file with **a4** and **axb3** or cramp White's QB with **a4-a3.**

10 Bb2

Not best. Routine and good is **10 a4**, preventing **a5-a4**. Also reasonable is **10 a3** to bypass **a4** with **b3-b4.**

10... Nbc6
11 Qe2

Still **11 a4** or **11 a3** is best here.

11... a4

Now Black is guaranteed counterplay.

12 Nc4 Ba6

13 h4!

White correctly tries to stir up play on the Kingside.

13... Qc8

14 Rad1

Also reasonable was **14 h5** immediately.

14... Bb5

Unblocking the a-file, but Black fails to follow up consistently.

15 h5 Qa6?

A tempting but artificial maneuver which allows White to build a strong Kingside attack. Necessary was **15...ab 16 ab, Ra2** with quite satisfactory play for Black.

16 hg hg

16...fg weakens **e6** too much (Ng5).

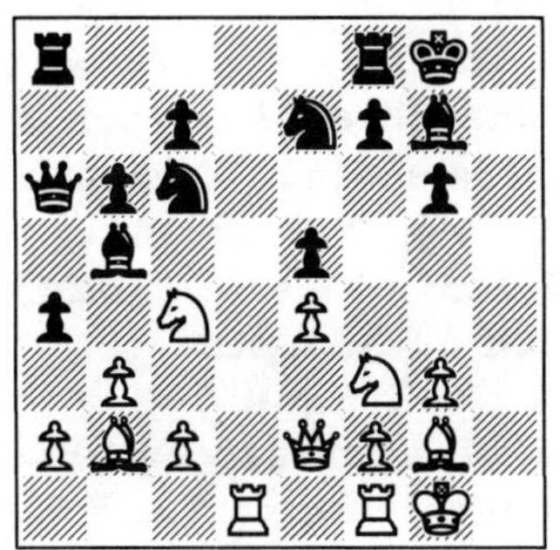

17 Ng5!

This move is still very strong. White intends **18 Qg4-h4** with very strong threats.

17... Na5

Slightly better was **17...Rfd8** though White is still much better after **18 Qg4** and a following **f2-f4**, zeroing in on the **f7** square.

18 Qg4!

Moving into attacking position.

18... Nxc4

19 bxc4 Bxc4

20 Qh4 Rfe8

Trying to protect **e6**, but it is already too late.

21 f4!

White steps up the attack, focusing on **f7** and **e6**.

21... Qb5

White would be happy indeed after **21...Bxf1 22 Bxf1** followed by **Bc4** with an overwhelming position.

22 Bxe5 f6

23 Qh7ch Kf8

24 Bh3!

Threatening to invade **e6** with decisive threats.

24... Rad8

The best chance. **24...Qc6** allows **25 Bd7!**

25 Rd5!!?

Brilliant but not best. White should precede **25 Rd5** with **25 Bxf6, Bxf6** and then **26 Rd5!!** really works in all lines--e.g. **26...Bxd5 27 exd5, Bd4ch** (If 27...Bxg5 then 28 Be6 mates) **28 Kh2!, Qe2ch 29 Kh1** and Black has no good defense.

25... Nxd5

After **25...Bxd5 26 exd5, Qc5ch 27 Rf2** White wins due to the dual threats of **28 Ne6ch** and **28 Bxf6** since **27...Nxd5** allows **28 Be6, Ne7** (28...fxe5 29 Qg8ch, Ke7 30 Qxg7ch, Kd6 31 Qxe5ch, Ke7 32 Bxd5 dis.ch) **29 Bxf6, Rd1ch 30 Kg2, Qc6ch 31 Nf3**, etc.

26 Be6

This looks like a winner but Black could now defend with the amazing resource **26...Rd7!!** and the position is unclear.

26... Rxe6

27 Nxe6ch

Now White wins quickly.

27... Ke7

28 Nd4!

An important gain of time which seals Black's fate.

28... Qc5

Due to the **Nd4!**, this is no longer with a check.

29 Qxg7ch Ke8

30 Qxg6ch

The rest is easy.

30... Ke7

31 Rf2

Also quite sufficient is **31 exd5.**

31... **fxe5**
32 Qe6ch **Kf8**
33 fe dis.ch.

Now it is mate in three--**33...Kg7 34 Rf7ch, Kg8 35 Qg6ch, Kh8 36 Qh7** mate.

Black Resigns.

ILLUSTRATIVE GAME #17

LOS ANGELES 1968
White: Stein Black: Hort

1 e4

Still another case of **1 e4** being transposed into our K.I.A.

1... c6

The Caro-Kahn, one of Black's most solid defenses, has long been a favorite of the Czech GM Hort.

2 d3 d5
3 Nd2 g6

See IVd for this line.

4 g3 Bg7
5 Bg2 e5

This is not so much to occupy the center, per se, as to block the forward progress of the K.I.A. e-pawn thrust **e4-e5.**

6 Ngf3 Ne7
7 0-0 0-0
8 c3

To protect **d4** and gain Queenside space with **b2-b4.**

8... Nd7

Possibly best is **8...a5** restraining **b2-b4.**

9 b4!

Now White has the better of it on the Queen's flank.

9... b6

The only way to get the QB into play.

10 Bb2 Bb7
11 Re1 Re8

Both sides quietly develop, but with everything on the board the tension is bound to increase.

12 Bh3

With threats against the Black e-pawn.

12... Qc7

Hort responds with an interesting pawn offer.

13 ed cd!?

So that if **14 Bxd7, Qxd7 15 Nxe5, Bxe5 16 Rxe5, Nc6 17 Rxe8ch, Rxe8** and Black would have dangerous counterplay on the weak white squares.

14 c4

Stein, being an attacking player of the highest order, prefers to refuse the tainted pawn.

14... d4

After **14...dc? 15 Nxc4** Black e-pawn is under too much pressure.

15 Rc1 f5

Now both players strive to advance their respective pawn majorities--White's on the Queenside, Black's in the center. As we shall see, White's will be more effective.

16 Bg2 Bf6

To prevent the annoying **Ng5**, e.g. **16...Qd6? 17 Qb3, Qe6 18 Ng5!**.

17 c5!

Threatening to win material with **18 c6** (18...Bxc6 19 b5).

17... b5

Not **17...bc 18 bc, Nxc5 19 Nb3**. Also, on **17...bc 18 bc, Bd5 19 Nc4** Black would have to give up the two Bishops in view of the threat of Nd6 (19...Nc8 20 Nxd4).

18 Nb3

To reach the fine outpost square on **a5**.

18... Bd5

19 a4!

Opening the a-file and weakening Black's b-pawn.

19... a6

After **19...ba?** White would recover the pawn quickly with a fine target on **a7**.

20 Na5 Nc6

Black is already "under the gun" but is blissfully unaware of that. Better was **20...Kg7** though then White could push the c-pawn to **b6** with obvious advantage.

(See diagram on following page)

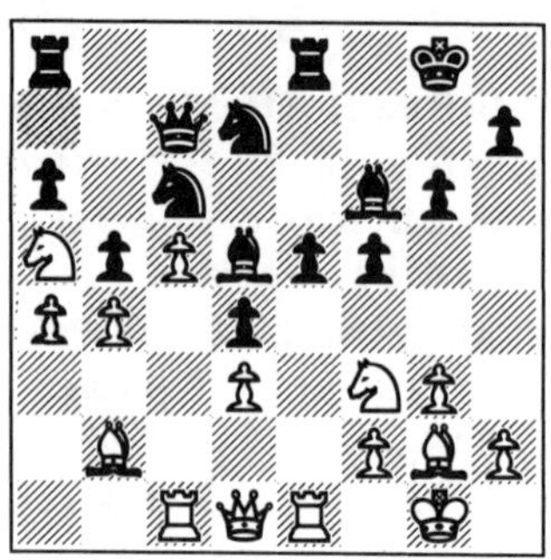

21 ab

Also good is **21 Nxe5!, Rxe5 22 Bxd5ch, Rxd5 23 Qb3, Nxb4 24 Ba3!**, but Stein's "other" combination is much more attractive.

21... ab

22 Nxe5!!

A stunning blow out of a clear sky.

22... Nxb4

The main line runs **22...Rxe5 23 Bxd5ch, Rxd5 24 Qb3, Nxb4 25 Ba3!** with excellent chances for White. Also strong is **24 Qf3!?** with fine chances.

23 Nxd7 Qxd7

24 c6!

White's Queenside majority strikes first.

24... Qf7

25 Rxe8ch Rxe8

26 Nb7!

Threatening **27 Nd6.**

26... Be5

27 Bxd5 Qxd5

28 Rc5

White now wins by combining the advance of the c-pawn with tactical threats.

28... Qf7

Not **28...Qe6** because of **29 c7, Rc8 30 Qe2** winning immediately.

29 Qf3 g5

This only accelerates defeat, but even after the better **29...Na6** White is winning easily.

30 c7!

Excellent. Now Black goes down after a flurry of clever tactical blows.

30... g4

Not **30...Bxc7** because of **31 Rxf5.**

31 Qd1 Bxc7

32 Qd2

Black loses largely because of his ventilated King-side.

32... Bb6

A better try was **32...Be5.**

33 Rxb5 Nxd3

On **33...Qxb7** White replies **34 Rxb4!** (not 34 Qxb4? because of the clever recourse 34...Qf3! with a draw).

34 Nd6 Qd7

35 Qg5ch Kh8

Forced, on **35...Kf8 36 Rxf5ch** wins.

36 Qf6ch Kg8

37 Qg5ch Kh8

In time pressure, White repeats moves to make the time control.

38 Nxe8 Qxe8

39 Qxf5

Defending **f2** against the threatened **39...Qe1ch.**

39... Ne5

40 Rxb6 Nf3ch

41 Kg2

Of course not **41 Kf1??, Qe1ch 42 Kg2, Qg1** mate.

41... Qa8

42 Qf6ch Kg8

43 Qe6ch Kh8

On **43...Kf8 44 Ba3ch!, Qxa3 45 Rb8ch, Kg7 46 Rg8** is mate.

44 Qc6

Neutralizing all threats.

Black Resigns.

ILLUSTRATIVE GAME #18

U.S. 1985
White: Kogan Black: Seirawan

1 Nf3 d5
2 g3 c6

Perhaps the most solid reaction to White's King's fianchettoe--Black builds a barrier on the **h1-a8** diagonal.

3 Bg2 Bg4
4 0-0

White calmly mobilizes with the usual K.I.A. moves.

4... e6

More usual is **4...Nd7** or **4...Nf6**--see II.

5 d3 Bxf3?!

Although this is playable, it seems gratuitous for Black to voluntarily give up the two Bishops.

6 Bxf3 Nf6
7 Nd2 Nbd7
8 e4 Bc5

More solid is simply **8...Be7.**

9 Qe2 de

If **9...0-0,** then **10 e5** is good for White.

10 de

More effective is **10 Nxe4** in order to keep the KB's diagonal open, e.g., **10...Nxe4 11 Bxe4, Nf6 12 Bg5, Be7** with a slight but persistent positional advantage for White.

10... Qc7

Again Black must prevent **e4-e5**; after **10...0-0 11 e5** White's greater central space (e4) would be a useful advantage.

11 Nc4

More usual and better would be **11 a4** to discourage Black from dislodging the **Nc4** via **b7-b5.**

11... b5

Of course.

12 Ne3 0-0
13 Bd2

Interesting is **13 a4!, a6 14 Bd2.**

13... Nb6
14 Bg2 Rfd8
15 Ba5 Qe5

Black must unpin before further tactical inconvenience results.

16 Bc3 Bd4

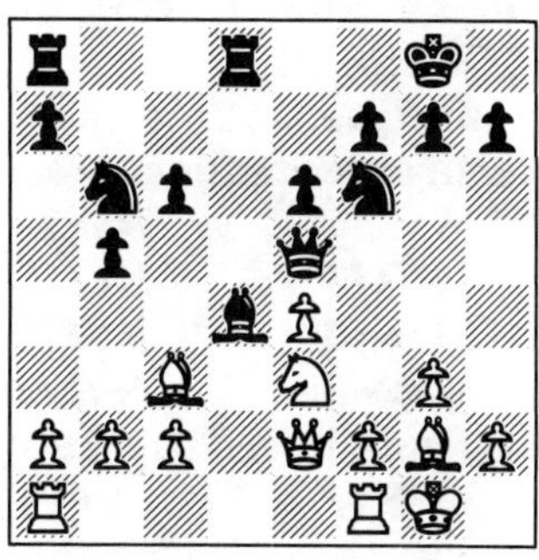

17 f4!

Best. Poor would be **17 Bxd4?, Qxd4 18 c3, Qd2** with positional advantage for Black.

17... Qc5
18 Bxd4 Rxd4

After **18...Qxd4 19 c3, Qd2 20 Rf2!** White retains the edge (Note 20 Rf2 is made possible by 17 f4!).

19 c3 Rd7
20 Kh1 Rad8

Black hurries to force some trades on the d-file to lessen the pressure inherent in White's spatial advantage.

21 Rad1 h6
22 Rxd7 Rxd7
23 e5!?

Unlimbering the KB's long diagonal.

23... Nfd5
24 Nxd5 cxd5
25 f5!

A fine move giving White attacking chances.

25... Nc4

After **25...ef 26 e6!, Re7 27 efch, Rxf7 28 Qe8ch, Qf8 29 Qxb5** White has a clear advantage.

26 fe fe

27 Bh3

Focusing on Black's vulnerable **e6.**

27... Re7

28 b3!

Ousting the Knight from its outpost.

28... Qe3

After **28...Nb6 29 Qh5!** is very strong (the threat is 30 Bxe6ch, Rxe6 31 Qf7ch).

29 Qxe3

Entering a favorable endgame.

29... Nxe3

30 Rf3 Nc2

31 Kg1 Ne1

32 Re3 Nc2

Black Knight finds itself driven out of play.

33 Rf3

White acquiesces to a draw, though after **33 Re2, Na3 34 Kf2, Kf7 35 Ke3, Rc7 36 Kd4, a5 37 Rf2ch, Ke7 38 Bf1** White's centralized King and "better" Bishop give him excellent chances with precise play.

33... Ne1

34 Re3 Nc2

The players agreed to a draw though it is clear that from the 10th move on, White enjoyed a positional plus.

ILLUSTRATIVE GAME #19

AMSTERDAM 1966
White: Botvinnik Black: Szilagyi

1 g3 d5
2 Nf3 c6
3 Bg2 Bg4

A favorite defense of the late Paul Keres--see II.

4 d3 Nd7
5 h3

Immediately determining the Bishop's intentions.

5... Bxf3

This seems premature. A better idea is **5...Bh5** reserving options.

6 Bxf3 e5?

An instructive positional error, weakening **d5**. Correct was **6...e6** to limit the White KB's diagonal.

7 Nd2 Ngf6
8 e4 de

Black trades to avoid the possibility of White playing **exd5**, with pressure on the **h1-a8** diagonal.

9 de Bc5
10 0-0 Qe7
11 c3

To gain space with **b2-b4**, again a routine K.I.A. strategem in this kind of position.

11... 0-0?

Black had to prevent **b2-b4** with **11...a5**, though White would still be better, of course.

12 b4! Bb6
13 a4

White has rapidly seized a big positional advantage on the Queenside due to Black's omission on move 11.

13... Rfd8
14 Qc2 Rac8

Pointless.

15 Be2!

Another fine concept. Botvinnik sees a future for the KB on the **a2-g8** diagonal.

15... c5?

This is the last straw, positionally. Now Black has almost no good moves. Necessary was **18...Nf8.**

16 b5

More space.

16... Ne8

17 Nc4 Nd6

Hoping to trade off the dominating **Nc4.**

18 Bg5!

A clever tactical blow, setting off White's advantage.

18... f6

Practically forced, since **18...Qxg5 19 Nxd6** followed by **Bc4** is crushing. Also, if **18...Nf6** then simply **19 Ne3** with the idea of **Nd5** is tremendous for White.

19 Be3 Nxc4

20 Bxc4ch

Now the **a2-g8** diagonal will be instrumental in White's winning plan.

20... Kh8

21 a5 Bc7

22 Rfd1 Nf8

Black desperately tries to reduce some of the pressure by simplifying, but it is far too late.

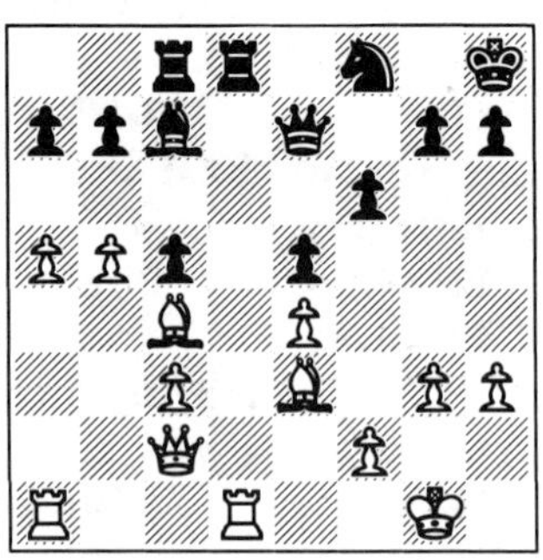

23 Qa2!

Preventing **23...Ne6.**

23... Rxd1ch

24 Rxd1 Rd8

As will be seen, even with all the Rooks off, White's advantage is overwhelming.

25 Rxd8 Bxd8

26 a6 b6

27 Kg2

Botvinnik calmly puts his house in order before further aggressive attempts.

27... Qd7

28 Qe2

Preventing **28...Qd1** and preparing a winning line-up on the **a2-g8** diagonal

28... Ng6

29 Bb3 Ne7

30 Qc4

Now if the **Ne7** moves, **Qg8** is mate.

30... h6

31 Qf7

Black is virtually in Zugswang.

31... Kh7

32 Bc4 Qd6

Black can only shift his pieces about aimlessly.

33 h4 Qd1

34 Qe8

Now White threatens **h5**, **Bf7** and Bg6ch followed by mate.

34... f5

A truly desperate move.

35 ef Nxf5

36 Bg8ch Kh8

Better was **36...**Resigns.

37 Bf7ch

It is mate next by **38 Qg8**.

Black Resigns.

ILLUSTRATIVE GAME #20

VENICE 1966
White: Ivkov Black: Golombek

1 Nf3	**Nf6**
2 g3	**d5**
3 Bg2	**g6**

Black prefers a blend of classical (center pawn on d5) and hypermodern (fianchettoed KB) strategems.

40-0	**Bg7**
5 d3	**0-0**
6 Nbd2	**Nc6**

Black avoids **c7-c5** in order to avoid creating a potential target for White's pieces; also a tempo is saved for other operations.

7 e4	**de**

More natural is **7...e5**. Note that without a supporting pawn at **c5**, the space gaining thrust **7...d4** is strategically risky as White could undermine **d4** by **Nb3** and **c2-c3** in the near future.

8 de

8 Nxe4, while playable allows Black to achieve a dead drawn position by **8...Nxe4** and **9...Qxd1.**

8...	**e5**

Otherwise White could soon play **e4-e5.**

9 c3

To control **d4** while threatening to gain space with a timely space gaining **b2-b4.**

9...	**Qe7**
10 Re1	

Giving the e-pawn extra protection.

10...	**b6**

To deploy the QB via **a6.**

11 a4

Threatening **12 b4** and if **12...a5**, then **13 b5** followed by **14 Ba3** winning the Exchange.

11...	**a5**
12 Nc4	

White maneuvers to seize control of **d5** (Nc4-e3-d5).

12... Rd8
13 Qb3 Ba6
14 Qa2

Preparing **15 Ne3**. If **14 Ne3**, then **14...Nxe4 15 Nh4, Nc5** is fine for Black.

14... h6
15 Ne3 Qc5

Already Black is in strategic difficulties since White's coming **Nd5** cannot be prevented. Nonetheless, slightly better was **15...Qf8** and on **16 Nd5, Ne8.** Taking the e-pawn with **15...Nxe4** allows **16 Nh4!--e.g. 16...f5 17 Nhxf5, gxf5 18 Nxf5** or **16...Bd3 17 Nxg6.**

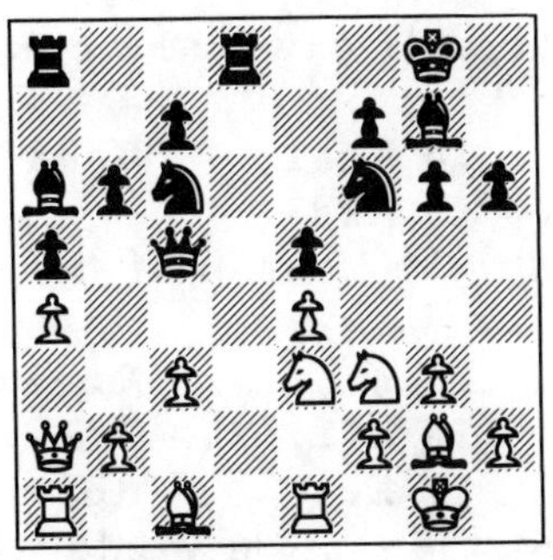

16 Nh4!

Threatening **17 Nxg6** and unlimbering the **Bg2** for more pressure on **d5.**

16... Bd3

The alternative, **16...Kf8** is clearly unpleasant.

17 Nxg6

Now, with the g-pawn gone, both **f5** and **e4** will fall into White's hands.

17... Bxe4
18 Bxe4 Nxe4
19 Nh4

Aiming at **f5.**

19... Ng5
20 Qc4!

Practically forcing a favorable endgame since if Black retreats his Queen, then the White Queen proceeds to the weakened King's flank.

20... Qxc4

21 Nxc4 Rd3

22 Bxg5!

Exchanging off Black's active Knight and leaving Black ever closer to a "good" Knight versus "bad" Bishop ending.

22... hxg

23 Nf5

Now White's strategy on the white squares has clearly triumphed.

23... f6

White threatened to win the e-pawn with **24 Nxg7** and **25 Nxe5.**

24 Rad1 Rad8

25 Rxd3

Soon even Black's control of the d-file will be neutralized.

25... Rxd3

26 Kf1 Bf8

27 Ke2 Rd8

After **27...e4**, the e-pawn would soon fall.

28 Rh1!

Another White trump: the passed h-pawn.

28... Kf7

29 h4 Kg6

30 Nce3 gh

31 gh Ne7

32 h5ch!

Now the advanced h-pawn will help tie down the Black forces.

32... Kh7

33 Rd1!

Simplifying down into an easily won ending since **33...Rc8** allows the crushing reply **34 Rd7.**

33... Rxd1

34 Kxd1 c6

Trying to build a barrier on the white squares (otherwise the White King penetrates via c4-b5-c6).

35 Nxe7 **Bxe7**
36 Nf5 **Bf8**
37 Ke2

The King returns to action.

37... **Bc5**
38 f3

Freeing the King from the defense of the f-pawn.

38... **Kg8**
39 Kd3 **Kf7**
40 Ke4 **Bf2**
41 Nd6ch **Kg7**

On **41...Ke6 42 h6!** wins.

42 Kf5

Now on **42...Bh4 43 Ne8ch, Kf7 44 h6!** wins since **44...Kxe8** allows **45 h7.**

Black Resigns.

ILLUSTRATIVE GAME #21

BAKU 1972
White: Vasiukov Black: Alburt

1 Nf3 d5
2 g3 g6
3 Bg2 Bg7
4 0-0 e5

See VIId for analysis of this line of play.

5 d3 Ne7

5...c5 would be covered in III.

6 Nbd2 0-0
7 c3

White is hoping to sneak in **b2-b4** before playing the usual **e2-e4.**

7... a5

But Black is alert to the strategic threat.

8 a4

Preventing the cramping **8...a4.**

8... b6

Black plays to "hyper-fianchettoe" his QB on **a6.**

9 e4 Nbc6

Weak is **9...c5 10 ed!, Nxd5 11 Nc4** with a big plus for White.

10 ed

Also good is **10 Re1**, but White prefers to open the long diagonal immediately.

10... Nxd5

10...Qxd5? would only expose the Queen to tactical threats.

11 Re1

Pressuring the center, in particular the e-pawn.

11... Re8
12 Nc4

Now White might follow up with **13 d4.**

12... Ba6

Which Black promptly prevents.

13 Ng5!?

White begins a very interesting tactical attack based on the **d5** and **f7** squares.

13... Qd7

Black calmly completes his development.

14 Qf3

This looks artificial, but this is a hidden point.

14... Rad8

15 Nd6!

A problem like theme. Now **15...cxd6 16 Qxd5** is much in White's favor.

15... Qxd6

Overlooking a cute point. Necessary was **15...Rf8 16 Qxd5, Ne7** though White is still better.

16 Qxf7ch Kh8

17 Qxe8ch! Rxe8

18 Nf7ch

The point. Now White wins the Exchange with an easily won game.

18... Kg8

19 Nxd6

Winning "everything" after **19...cxd6 20 Bxd5ch** and **21 Bxc6**, or **19...Rd8 20 Bxd5ch**.

Black Resigns

ILLUSTRATIVE GAME #22

SOCHI 1966
White: Lein Black: Polugaevsky

1 Nf3	**Nf6**
2 g3	**d5**
3 Bg2	**c6**
4 0-0	**Bf5**

The London System--see Chapter 1.

5 d3	**h6**

Black wants a convenient retreat for his QB on **h7** in the event of **Nh4** or **e4**.

6 b3

The fianchetto of the QB is very popular here, though there is the standard alternative **6 Nbd2** followed by **Qe1** and **e4**.

6...	**e6**
7 Bb2	**Be7**
8 Nbd2	**0-0**
9 Ne5	

Preparing **e2-e4**; more usual is **9 Qe1** or **9 Re1.**

9...	**a5**

Threatening **a4-a3** (or a4xb3) with counterplay.

10 a3!

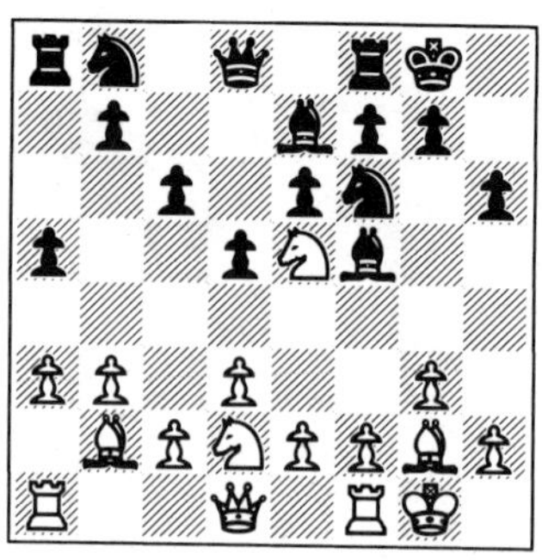

Now **10...a4** is answered by simply **11 b4.**

10...	**Na6**

A little better was **10...Nbd7** to challenge White's **Ne5** and simplify.

11 e3

White prefers a restrained approach; **11 e4** was, of course, quite sound.

11... Bh7
12 Qe2 Qb6
13 Rab1 Rfd8

Hoping to use the d-file in the event of **e3-e4, d5xe4.**

14 Kh1

A typical precaution, getting the King off the potentially dangerous **a1-a7** diagonal.

14... a4

Black tries to stir up play on the Queenside, but White meets this plan cleverly.

15 b4 c5

Otherwise White plays **c4** with fine play.

16 b5!

Closing up the Queenside, after which White can turn his full attention to the rest of the board.

16... Nb8

A sorry retreat, but **16...Qxb5** runs into **17 Nxf7!, Kxf7 18 Bxf6.**

17 e4 Nbd7
18 Nxd7 Rxd7

Of course, **18...Nxd7** drops the d-pawn.

19 ed!

Opening the center advantageously as now **19...ed** allows **20 Bh3!, Rc7 21 Be5, Bd6** (forced) **22 Bxf6** and Black's Kingside pawns are shattered.

19... Nxd5
20 Nc4 Qd8

Not **20...Qxb5** because of **21 Bxg7.**

21 Ne5 Rc7
22 c4!

Driving away Black's centralized Knight--the **d3** pawn is easily protected.

22... Nb6
23 Rbd1

With thoughts of **d3-d4.**

23... **Nd7**

24 Ng4!

Another fine move which avoids simplifying exchanges.

24... **h5**

Driving off the dangerous Knight, but now the h-pawn is weak.

25 Ne3

Again avoiding exchanges (25 Ne5, Nxe5).

25... **Nf6**

26 f4!

Preparing to open up an attack on the Kingside.

26... **Rd7**

27 f5

A timely interception of Black's threat to **d3.**

27... **Qb6**

28 Bh3

Pressuring **e6** and threatening to isolate Black's e-pawn.

28... **Rad8**

29 fe **fe**

30 Bxf6!

Weakening the Black Kingside defense.

30... **gxf6**

31 Ng2!

Preparing to jump back into the attack via **f4.**

31... **f5**

32 Nf4 **Rd6**

33 Rde1 **Bf6**

34 Qxh5

Now a pawn up with a powerful attack, White wins quickly.

34... **Kg7**

35 g4!

With the opening of the g-file the attack soon overwhelms Black's defenseless Kingside.

35... **Rh8**

36 gf **Bxf5**

37 Rg1ch **Kf8**

38 Ng6ch Bxg6
39 Qxg6 e5

After **39...Rxh3 40 Qxf6ch, Ke8 41 Rg8ch, Kd7 42 Qf7** is mate.

40 Ref1 Rxh3
41 Qg8ch Ke7
42 Rg7ch!

Now Black must concede as **42...Bxg7** allows **43 Rf7ch, Ke6 44 Qe8** mate.

ILLUSTRATIVE GAME #23

BRD 1987
White: Kindermann Black: N. Short

1 e4

The e-pawn route to the K.I.A.

1...	**e6**
2 d3	**c5**
3 Nf3	**Nc6**
4 g3	**d5**
5 Nbd2	**g6**

Choosing the "modern" fianchetto over the classical placement of the KB on **e7** or **d6**.

6 Bg2	**Bg7**
7 0-0	**Nge7**
8 Re1	**b6**
9 h4	

Probing Kingside dark squares.

9...	**h6**
10 e5	

Establishing the "standard" K.I.A. pawn outpost on **e5**.

10...	**Bb7**

Worthy of consideration was **10...Qc7** and on **11 Qe2, g5!?** (to undermine the e5 pawn) **12 hg, hg 13 Nxg5, Qxe5 14 Qxe5** and now **14...Nxe5?!** allows **15 Nc4!?**, but **14...Bxe5** is unclear.

11 Nf1	**Qc7**
12 Bf4	**d4?!**

Weakening **e4** and **c4**. Better was **12...0-0-0** with a sharp game and only a tiny edge for White.

13 Qe2	**0-0-0**
14 N(1)h2	**Kb8**
15 Ng4	

Note the aesthetically pleasing "overprotection" of the vital **e5**.

(See diagram on following page)

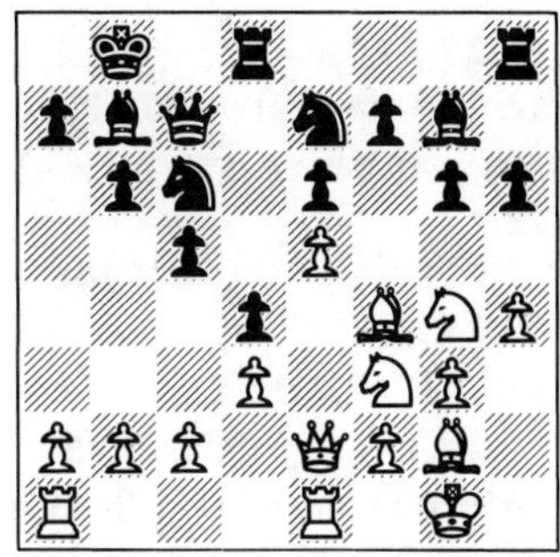

15...	**Nd5**
16 Bd2	**Rde8**
17 a3	

Preparing to play **b2-b4** with an attack on Black's King position.

17...	**Re7**
18 Rab1	**h5?!**

Black wants to bring his KR into play, but the pawn on **h6** ties him down, and now **g5** is weakened.

19 Ngh2	**Rc8**
20 Nf1	**Rd7**

Black masses his forces to try to stave off White's pressure.

21 Bg5

Clearing **d2** for Knight maneuvers.

21...	**Ka8**
22 N(1)d2	**Bf8**
23 Nc4	

A consequence of **12...d4?!**.

23...	**Ba6**

After **23...b5** White plays **24 Ncd2** followed by **Ra1** and **a4!** or even **Rbc1** and **c2-c4**.

24 a4

Preventing **b6-b5** for good.

24...	**Ncb4**
25 Rbc1	

Protecting the c-pawn in order to maneuver **Nfd2-e4.**

25...	**Bb7**
26 Nfd2	**Nc6**

27 Qd1

Avoiding the immediate **27 Ne4** since then Black could try to obtain counterplay via **27...Nxe5!? 28 Nf6, Nxc4 29 Nxd7, Nxb2.**

27... Rb8

28 Ne4

Again a result of **12...d4?!.**

28... Na5

Trying to trade off one of White's mighty horses.

29 Ned6

Happily invading on **d6** since now **29...Nxc4** fails to **30 dxc4!.**

29... Bc6

30 Nxa5

Now the **a5** pawn will be weak, but there was little choice for Black anyway.

30... bxa5

31 Nc4 Be7

Black has absolutely no counterplay since White has a positionally won game (weak pawns at a5, c5 and f7 plus the exposed Black King).

32 Bd2 Bxa4

Black has no good line of defense so he wants to mix it up coffee-house style.

33 Ra1 Bb5

34 Rxa5

Now the a-file will be a threatening avenue of attack.

34... Bc6

35 Qa1

With the idea of tripling on the a-file (Qa3 and Rea1).

35... Nb4

36 Bxb4 Bxg2

37 Kxg2

But not **37 Bxc5?** because of **37...Bxc5 38 Kxg2, Bb4** winning the Exchange.

37... Rxb4

38 Qd1 Qc6ch

39 Kg1 Bd8

40 Ra2 **Bc7**
41 Qe2

In order to play **42 Rea1** followed by **Ra6.**

41... **Ra4**

Black must try to exchange off some of the attackers.

42 Rxa4 **Qxa4**
43 Qf3ch

Seizing the important long diagonal.

43... **Kb8**
44 b3 **Qa6**
45 Re4!

Again that square (12...d4?!). Now the threat of **Rf4** is very strong.

45... **Qc6**
46 Qf6 **Bd8**
47 Qh8

Not **47 Qg7??** allowing **47...f5!.**

47... **Qc8**
48 Nd6 **Qc7**
49 Rf4

Now White threatens **Qg8** followed by the capture of the f-pawn.

49... **f6**
50 ef **e5**
51 f7

Black Resigns.

ILLUSTRATIVE GAME #24

NEW YORK OPEN 1987
White: Damljanovic Black: C. Hansen

1 g3

Still another route to our standard King's Indian Attack patterns.

1... d5
2 Nf3 Nf6
3 Bg2 c6

Black tries to limit the activity of White's fianchettoed KB by erecting a pawn barricade on the **h1-a8** diagonal.

4 0-0 Bg4
5 d3 Nbd7
6 Nbd2

Another method is **6 Qe1** and on **6...e5 7 e4, de 8 de, Be7 9 Nbd2, 0-0 10 h3!, Bh5 11 Nc4, Qc7 12 a4, Rfe8** White retains a slight plus (Gutman-Smejkal).

6... e5

Also possible is the more restricted **6...e6.**

7 h3 Bh5
8 e4 de
9 de Bc5

Another way is **9...Be7.**

10 Qe1

Unpinning and envisioning **11 Nh4-f5.**

10... Bxf3

Black hopes to reduce White's prospects by simplifying.

11 Bxf3 0-0
12 a4

Maneuvering for Queenside space.

12... Qe7
13 Qe2

The attempt to cramp Black's Queenside with **13 a5** is met by **13...b5!.**

13... a5

14 Nc4 Ne8

This is dubious. The proper course was **14...Nb6 15 Ne3, g6** (Nf5 must be stopped) **16 h4** with only the slightest pull for White.

15 Bd2 b6

16 Bg4

White, in typical positional fashion, gradually maneuvers his pieces into more active positions.

16... Nc7

17 Kg2 Ne6

18 c3

Sealing off **d4** from Black's pieces while reserving the possibility of a pawn break with **b2-b4.**

18... g6

Necessary to prevent **Ne3-f5**, but now White has a target for opening the h-file with **h4-h5**.

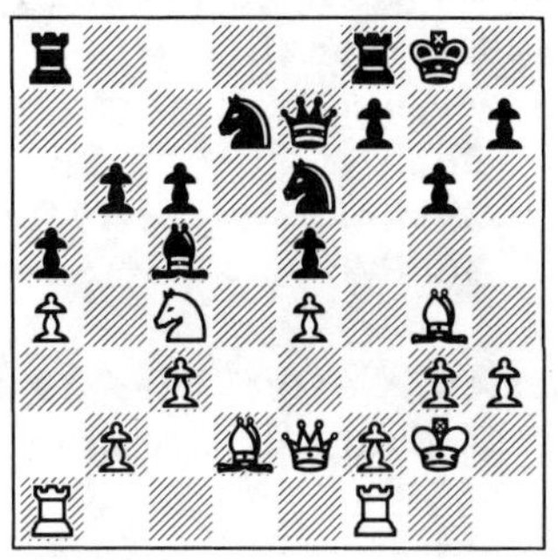

19 Bh6 Rfe8

20 h4 f6

21 Rad1 Ndf8

22 h5 Rad8

23 Bc1

Clearing the h-file for possible heavy piece penetration.

23... Rxd1

Black hopes to simplify enough to hold off White's pressure.

24 Rxd1 Rd8

25 Rh1!

Of course White refuses to trade further since his Rook has fine scope for attack on the h-file.

25... Qd7

Hurrying to invade on the d-file in order to provoke a Queen trade.

26 Qf3 Qd3

Avoiding the trap **26...Qf7 27 hg, hg 28 Nxe5!, fxe5 29 Rh8ch** and the Queen is lost (29...Kg7 30 Bh6ch).

27 Qxd3 Rxd3
28 Kf1

Stronger was **28 Bd1!** followed by **Bb3** with strong pressure on the **a2-g8** diagonal.

28... Rd8
29 Ke2 Kf7
30 f3?!

Another misstep. Correct was **30 Be3** with pressure on **b6** or **30 f4** to gain Kingside pressure.

30... Ng7
31 h6!

White's pressure in this ending is considerable (b6 is a potential target, plus White's Bishop pair).

31... Ne8
32 Be3

Working on **b6.**

32... Bxe3
33 Kxe3 Nd6

Again Black hopes to simplify his way to salvation.

34 Nxd6ch

But not **34 Nxb6?** because of **34...Rb8!.**

34...	**Rxd6**
35 b4!	

Opening another front for invasion.

35...	**ab**
36 cb	**Rd4**
37 Rb1	**Ke7**
38 a5!	

Decisive since the passed a-pawn is very strong.

38...	**b5**

After **38...ba 39 ba** White's Rook invades down the b-file.

39 f4

White, in severe time pressure, misses the more incisive **39 a6.**

39...	**Nd7**
40 Rb3	**Nb8**

To blockade the dangerous a-pawn and hoping to pressure **b4**.

41 Bc8	**Kd8**
42 Be6	**Na6**
43 Bg8	

Revealing the weakness of **h7** (a consequence of 31 h6!). A mistake would be **43 Rd3, c5!** (44 bc?, Rxd3ch 45 Kxd3, Nxc5ch and 46...Nxe6).

43...	**Nxb4**
44 Bxh7	**Nc2ch**
45 Kf2	**Rd2ch**
46 Kg1	**Rd1ch**
47 Kg2	**Rd2ch**
48 Kh3	**Kc7**

After **48...Rd1** White has **49 Rb2, Rh1ch 50 Kg2, Rxh6 51 Rxc2** with an easily won Rook and Pawn ending.

49 fe	**fe**
50 Rb2	**Rd7**
51 Bg8	

Threatening **52 h7** and **53 h8.**

51...	**Nd4**
52 h7	**Rxh7**

More "accurate" was Resigns.

53 Bxh7	**c5**
54 Bxg6	**c4**
55 Bf7	**c3**
56 Rb1	**Kb7**

57 g4
Black Resigns.

ILLUSTRATIVE GAME #25

MINSK 1986
White: Psakis Black: D. Pavnovic

1 e4

Once more an example of our King's Indian Attack pattern being reached by way of the e-pawn opening move.

1...	**c5**
2 Nf3	**e6**
3 d3	

Now Black's anticipated Sicilian struggle has been abruptly forced into our positional channels.

3...	**Nc6**
4 g3	**d5**
5 Nbd2	**Nf6**

Note that we now have a formation which could arise from a French Defense, e.g., **1 e4, e6 2 d3, d5 3 Nd2, Nf6 4 Ngf3, c5 5 g3, Nc6.**

6 Bg2	**b6**

More usual is **6...Be7 7 0-0, 0-0 8 Re1, b5.**

7 0-0	**Bb7**
8 Re1	

White avoids the immediate **8 e5** because after **8...Nd7 9 Re1, Qc7 10 Qe2, g5!** and White's **e5** spearhead is in danger.

8...	**Be7**
9 a3	

Preparing Queenside expansion with a further **c3** and **b4.**

9...	**Qc7**
10 c3	**0-0**

Alternatives are the sharp **10...0-0-0** and **10...a5** (restraining b2-b4).

11 e5

The leitmotif of this type of K.I.A. position. The advanced **e5** pawn forms the basis for a Kingside attack.

11...	**Nd7**
12 d4	

The more usual procedure to protect the e-pawn is **12 Qe2** followed by **Nf1** and **Bf4**. In this case White protects **e5** with a pawn to free his pieces for duty elsewhere.

12...	**cd**

Hoping for Queenside counterplay on the c-file.

13 cd	**Na5**
14 Nf1	

Also of interest is the peculiar-looking strategic retreat **14 Nb1!?** with the idea of blocking Black's pressure down the c-file after **14...Rac8 15 Nc3.**

14...	**Rfc8**

Threatening to invade on **c2.**

15 b4

The attempt to guard **c2** via **15 Ne3** fails after **15...Nc4 16 Ng4, h5!? 17 Ne3, Nxe3** followed by **Qc2.**

15... Nc4
16 h4

White begins Kingside pressure.

16... b5

Hoping to open more Queenside lines with **17...a5**. The immediate **16...a5** doesn't work because of **17 b5!**.

17 Ng5

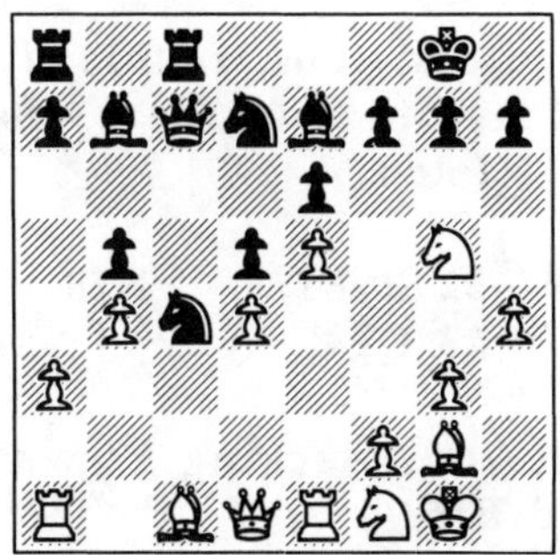

The first attacker approaches the King's residence. White hopes to force a serious weakening of Black's Kingside. For example, if now **17...h6** then **18 Nh3** followed by **Qg4** and **Nf4** (and possibly Nh5) is promising. Even sharper would be **17...h6 18 Nxf7!?, Kxf7 19 Qh5ch** with the possibility of a sac on h6 (Bxh6), though this line is rather murky.

17... a5?!

Black should have tried **17...h6** since now White has a strong retort.

18 Qh5!

Forcing Black to give up his vital dark-squared Bishop (which is even more serious because White will retain his QB to press on the weakened dark squares) since both **f7** and **h7** are attacked.

18...	**Bxg5**
19 Bxg5	**ab**
20 ab	**Ra4**
21 Nh2!	

A fine maneuver--the Knight heads for **g4** with intensified threats against the weakened dark squares.

21...	**Rca8**

Black runs into serious trouble if he snatches the b-pawn: **21...Rxb4 22 Ng4** threatening **23 Be7** followed by the powerful sacrifice **Nf6!ch.**

22 Rab1	**Nf8**
23 Qg4!	

With the idea of attacking **g7** with **h5** (to block the defensive Ng6) and **Bf6**.

23...	**Qc8**

Or **23...Kh8 24 h5, h6 25 Bf6!, gxf6 26 ef** with a winning attack.

24 h5	**Nd7**
25 h6!	

Forcing his way in on the dark squares.

25...	**g6**
26 Qh4	

With the idea of **27 Ng4** followed by **Be7** (to prevent the King from fleeing via f8) and **Nf6ch** with decisive threats.

26...	**Qe8**
27 Be7	**Bc8**
28 Ng4	

Threatening **29 Nf6ch, Nxf6 30 Qxf6** and mate follows.

28...	**f5**

The best try was **28...Kh8!?** though White's attack would still be too strong anyway.

29 ef e.p	**Qf7**
30 f4	**Nb8**
31 f5!	

Forcing open more lines of attack.

31...	**gf**

On **31...ef** White plays **32 Nh2!** followed by **33 Nf3-g5** with crushing threats.

32 Bxd5!!

A beautiful sacrificial motif. Now on **32...fxg4**, White has **33 Rxe6!, Bxe6 34 Qg5ch, Kh8 35 Qg7ch, Qxg7 36 h(or f)xg7ch, Kg8 37 Bxe6** mate.

32...	**exd5**
33 Qg5ch	**Qg6**
34 Qxg6ch	**hxg6**
35 f7ch!	

Now White's remaining pieces swarm in for the kill.

35...	**Kxf7**
36 h7	**Kg7**

Otherwise the h-pawn Queens.

37 Bf6ch	**Kxh7**
38 Re7ch	**Kg8**
39 Nh6ch	**Kf8**
40 Rf7ch	

Now it's over since **40...Ke8** is followed by **41 Re1ch, Be6 42 Rxe6** mate.

Black Resigns.

L-577 THE 1986 WORLD CHESS CHAMPIONSHIP: KASPAROV-KARPOV-British Chess Magazine. The story, the color and all the games annotated. Paperback. **$4.00.**

J-41 IMAGINATION IN THE ENDGAME-Brieger. The purpose of this book is to teach you some of the tactics of the endgame, encourage you to use your imagination, and thus improve your playing ability. Our sales have been extremely brisk on this book ever since it hit the chess playing public. Paper. **$3.95**

J-54 QUEEN AND PAWN ENDINGS-Averbakh. The book is divided into many parts covering every conceivable aspect of the common Queen endings. Here are 268 diagramed examples with excellent notes and analysis that are unsurpassed. Clothbound. List $21.00, ours **$10.00**

A COMPLETE CHESS COURSE: "The following books, if taken together, make a complete course that every player should have studied. I am talking about rating jumps of 100 to 200 points in the pupils I have worked with. They cover ideas, basics, the C to A players, and material for the Expert aiming for Mastership".-Ken Smith (FIDE 2363).

B-11 THE PSYCHOLOGY OF CHESS-Hartston-Watsen. Thought process, winning & losing, talent & motivation. Clothbound. **$9.95**

B-46 THE BATTLE OF CHESS IDEAS-Saidy. Evolution of chess thought. Ideas and the best games of the greatest players that ever lived. Clothbound. **$16.95**

E-41 THINK LIKE A GRANDMASTER-Kotov. Includes: Analysis of Variations, Positional Judgement, Planning, The Ending, Player's Knowledge. Paperback. **$14.35**

E-76 PLAY LIKE A GRANDMASTER-Kotov. A virtual textbook on the higher principles of play. Includes: Combinational Vision, Calculation and Practical Play. Clothbound. **$14.35**

E-88 TRAIN LIKE A GRANDMASTER-Kotov. Includes: How the Opening is Studied, Objectivity in the Ending, Studying the Middlegame. Paperback. **$12.95**

E-47 *TEST YOUR TACTICAL ABILITY* Neishtadt. It is one of the most important and/or best books or combinations ever attempted or published for stronger players. Paperback. $11.95.

D-20 A CONTEMPORARY APPROACH TO THE MIDDLEGAME-Suetin. Foundations of strategy, Chess Tactics, Linking Strategy & Tactics, Style, Dynamic Standpoint, Relate the Middlegame to the Opening. Clo
thbound. **$18.75**

J-105 ESSENTIAL CHESS ENDINGS EXPLAINED MOVE BY MOVE-Jeremy Silman (1988). Our newest International Master gives a commentary on every move. Paperback. $11.95.

ORDER FROM: CHESS DIGEST, INC.
P.O. BOX 741088
DALLAS, TEXAS 75374-1088

Add Handling & Postage Fees: $0 to $9.99 add $2.05; $10 to $24.99 add $2.85; $25 to $49.99 add $3.55; $50 to $74.99 add $3.95.

NOTES

NOTES

NOTES

NOTES

NOTES